Rupert Morgan wa
Scottish parents. He c
two daughters, on a b
There Be Lite, is also a

'Really brilliant . . . he is obviously a major talent'
Prunella Scales

'Outstanding . . . it's fast-moving and hilarious . . . Kurt
Vonnegut and Douglas Adams will be spitting feathers'
Esquire

'Taking pot-shots at a wide variety of modern ills – fast
food, tabloid media, downsizing, soap-opera politics . . .
One of Morgan's nicer inventions is a computer program
that boils down complex texts to their essentials. Its treatment of the Old Testament renders it down to: "Because
I say so, that's why"'
Independent

'Bittersweet, laugh-out-loud funny, and all too true'
Fay Weldon

'This is a first novel by someone who has perfected his
craft. The interweaving of plot and character is skilfully
executed. But above all it is so good to be made to laugh
– really laugh' *Oxford Times*

'Amusing and inventive' Peter Ackroyd

Also by Rupert Morgan

LET THERE BE LITE

and published by Bantam Books

SOMETHING SACRED

Rupert Morgan

BANTAM BOOKS
LONDON · NEW YORK · TORONTO · SYDNEY · AUCKLAND

SOMETHING SACRED
A BANTAM BOOK : 0 553 81361 7

Originally published in Great Britain by Bantam Press,
a division of Transworld Publishers

PRINTING HISTORY
Bantam Press edition published 2001
Bantam edition published 2002

1 3 5 7 9 10 8 6 4 2

Set in 10/12pt Sabon by
Phoenix Typesetting, Ilkley, West Yorkshire.

Bantam Books are published by Transworld Publishers,
61–63 Uxbridge Road, London W5 5SA,
a division of The Random House Group Ltd,
in Australia by Random House Australia (Pty) Ltd,
20 Alfred Street, Milsons Point, Sydney, NSW 2061, Australia,
in New Zealand by Random House New Zealand Ltd,
18 Poland Road, Glenfield, Auckland 10, New Zealand
and in South Africa by Random House (Pty) Ltd,
Endulini, 5a Jubilee Road, Parktown 2193, South Africa.

Printed and bound in Great Britain by
Clays Ltd, St Ives plc.

For Karin,
with all my love

CELL,
ENTROPOLIS PENITENTIARY,
FIVE A.M.

'Showtime!' Bergman announces a second after turning on the light.

I lie blinking on the bed, a silent groan in my head. Five a.m. I must have finally drifted off a little under an hour ago, dreaming that I was still lying there with my eyes open. It's a familiar sensation these days, but mostly the other way around – I can't stop hoping it's a dream when I'm awake.

The three or four phantom Bergmans I momentarily see slide on top of each other and become solid. He's standing military-style, feet slightly apart, hands behind his back. A big, blunt instrument of a man. I think he actually was in the army once – he's the kind of guy whose role in life is dictated by his body. None too smart, destined from birth to be a soldier, or a cop, or a prison guard . . . something in a uniform, given a mission. But I like Bergman – he's always been kind to me. He has a gentleness in his eyes, a melancholy air, that belies that great hammer of a face. I'm pretty sure he's gay, but it's possible that he's never put it into practice. He may not even know. Probably just thinks every guy cries at old war movies. Like I say – reliable, holds the road well, but he ain't first off at the lights.

'Hmmm . . .' I manage by way of acknowledgement, sliding my feet off the bed to touch the concrete. In a moment I will sit up. Shuffle to the showers. Shave and gel my hair. Put on the suit chosen by my lawyer. Blue for innocence.

What a fucking joke.

It's showtime all right.

Here's the funny thing: all my life I wanted to be remembered, and now I can't for the life of me remember why. If I could I would scrub myself from memory, let my name and my deeds swirl down the drain of the shower until I was left naked and anonymous.

My wish will be granted eventually, of course – probably well within my own lifetime. Almost everyone will forget Nick Carraway. The name, so familiar now, so easily tripping off their tongues, will become harder to find. It will ring fewer and fewer bells, softer and softer, until it finally shimmers into the past. Hell, we hear so many names, don't we? Every day the cast is changing, only the show goes on, unending. We have to forget the old if we are to make room for the new. After a few months we can't even remember the storyline. Where was that war? Who was fighting who, and why did we get involved?

Another funny thing – I'm nauseous with tension about the trial, but at the same time I can't take it seriously. I keep laughing when I talk about it. Part of me is ready to go down on my knees and promise anything if they'll let me go, and the other part wants to just spit on their feet. The part of me that's wise to what is going on here.

Wise to justice and law. Wise to Atlantis, this fine country founded on fancy words and a certain amount of genocide. Wise to Entropolis, and all the other places that pretend to be its equal. Wise to the soft sell. Wise to the loopholes. Wise to facts and statistics and the latest research. Wise to camera angles and editing. Wise to beauty. Wise to love. Wise to God. Wise to everything but the small part of me that wants to cry, the part of me that is innocent.

I never show that side, not even to my lawyer. I can't, because that would mean I have lost. He says I've got to come across as humble, and I know he's right. But it makes me gag. And I know the prosecutor's going to make me out as arrogant – oh yes, and amoral, cynical, godless . . . a terrible example of the younger generation's nihilism, ladies and gentlemen of the jury, for which we must blame ourselves while having the strength to punish when punishment is needed . . .

What a hypocrite. What a cynical fuck.

My generation? I don't know what that is supposed to mean, like people were cars on a production line or something, but if we're going to box ourselves into generations, then I think I came up with a defence for mine as I lay there last night:

At least we're not faking it. Espousing some kind of bumper-sticker morality.

Actually, no – I'm not talking for others any more. But, speaking for myself, at least I can tell a digital sunset from a real one, and a soundbite from a statement. And that matters, because the only issue I can see before me – all around me, touching every domain of my life and feeding into my very dreams – is knowing truth from artifice. And maybe it comes across as cynicism, but all I've done is try to make sense of life, same as anyone else in any other generation. Only there's more bullshit to cut through,

9

simply because more is being said. And maybe it's not surprising if some of us seem to take pride in our inability to be shocked, in our readiness to accept whatever new absurdity or obscenity society produces, to joke about horror and laugh about injustice, because a sense of reality and a sense of morality have become one and the same thing in our heads.

How could we have been otherwise when the generation before us so utterly reneged upon the ideals of the ones before, and didn't even have the courage to admit it? Where was *their* sense of decency, what did *they* believe in beyond satisfying their whims? A generation that reduced morality to a thing you buy in a shop.

Hallelujah, no bleach in the packaging! Let us join hands, brothers and sisters, that we may live in harmony and none may have a hand free to light up a cigarette. Let us kneel before the Lord that He may fulfil His contractual obligation to forgive us our sins in this window of opportunity we offer Him now, before the golf begins.

How can you not be a cynic? Growing up these days is like being a child in some Third World civil war, waving a machine gun around and laughing as the illusion of authority crumbles wherever you turn.

What would they have had me be? Where was the place of innocence where we were supposed to play? There was a fucking advertisement everywhere we looked from the day we were born.

If you cannot be innocent, you try to be impregnable.

Well, that didn't work out too well either, of course, so now I'm trying something new. Now I'm trying to be honest. I can afford to be that, at least, because I've nothing left to lose but the truth.

'They were talking about you on the radio this morning,' Bergman says beside me as I pad to the showers, towel

10

around my waist. He's keeping his voice down – either so as not to wake the other prisoners, or so that he doesn't compromise me by sounding too matey if any of them are listening in. Either way it's a nice gesture, even if he doesn't think to soften the stomp of his boots on the steel grids. 'Bet your picture will be on the front page of all the papers tomorrow. Even the *Post*.'

I believe he thinks this may be a comfort to me, so I smile tightly and nod as if to say that'll be nice.

'You read the *Post*, don't you?' I suggest in the same conspiratorial tone as Bergman.

'Yeah, I do!' he answers, raising his eyebrows. 'How'd you know that?'

'Wild guess.'

He eyes me, unsure whether I'm making fun of him, so I add, 'It's the best paper.'

Which is true, even if not so true as it once was.

One of my regrets – a minor one nowadays, obviously – is that I wasn't born long enough ago to have worked for the *Entropolis Daily Post* when it was still in its old building on Garrick Avenue. We used to pass it whenever my parents let me come to the TV studios for a recording of *Meet My Wife*, and I'd stand looking through the tinted glass of the limo, waiting for the *Post* building to appear.

Not a particularly attractive building in itself, granted, but it had those vast windows on the ground floor through which you could see the printing press – this enormous machine that snaked around the forged iron columns on which the building rested. The most exciting thing was if we came back that way late in the evening, once the next day's paper was being printed. I'd beg them to tell the driver to stop so we could get out and look at the pages racing around the maze of belts and wheels, the whole beast at work with dozens of overalled men tending to it on gantries and platforms, some of them so high above the ground that I had to crick my neck right back to see them. It seemed to be a living creature, that machine – something like a dragon to my awed little eyes. A handsome, fearsome dragon armoured with gleaming black plates and rumbling with the spin of a thousand well-oiled cogs. It even had teeth that bit the rolls of paper into pages, constantly chomping away and folding and swallowing the sheets down its long neck. More than that, in the darkness of the evening, the factory blazing with hundreds of bell-shaped lights that hung by their wires in row upon row of bright eyes, it seemed like the very heart of the city, pumping incessantly. You could feel the vibration of it through the sidewalk. My mother, tired as she was in more ways than one from playing Marcia Hudson, the perfect Atlantian housewife, usually stayed in the limo while my father indulged me by tracing the flow of the creature's digestion from the giant rolls of blank paper to the bound stacks trundling through the back wall of the building on a conveyor belt.

For me, the whole building was enchanted and alive because of that machine, and I'd gaze back at the offices on the upper floors as we drove away – all the lights lit long after the surrounding buildings were still and dark – and wonder what kind of people worked there. When did they sleep? When did they eat? Didn't they ever stop? It was easy to imagine them as being like sorcerer's apprentices, always busy weaving the spells that kept that creature breathing.

By the time I myself became an employee of the *Post*, the creature had died and the building was dark and empty. The offices had moved to new premises, occupying the twentieth to twenty-fourth floors of the Brady Tower, and the new, fully automated presses were somewhere else, far away. I don't even know where.

Romance is the first casualty of progress, I guess. To be honest, I never felt I matched up to the older guys who worked on the *Post*, the ones left over from the Garrick Avenue years, who'd seen their coffee tremble as the machine started up below their feet. I always sensed that they did not consider us lot to be true pressmen, that they had the ink in their blood whereas we were just media tarts for whom the paper was a job, not a vocation. Lightweights who had missed the glory days when the *Post* was staffed by heroically eccentric characters – foul-mouthed men fuelled by alcohol and with lives as bizarre and disastrous as their work was brilliant.

Not that I ever acknowledged anything of the sort, of course. I was on the side of the winners, whereas they were all hanging on by a thread – their experience not worth a damn if they couldn't keep pace with us. We were lightweights, for sure – leaner, faster on our feet, quicker to duck the blame or seize an opportunity. And just as good at our jobs as any of them – except the job had changed. That's what they must have hated most – to have worked hard all their lives, only to find all the attention being lavished on arrogant young jerks whose great trick was to do the very things they had trained themselves not to do. To write subjectively, placing ourselves in the stories, sharing our emotions – using *ourselves* as arbiters of truth. So in love with the sound of our own voices, considering it our right to see our photos on the page when they had fought for years just to get a byline.

Poor bastards. No matter that they knew what we did was easy, they could not match our casual confidence. They were taught to doubt their opinions, whereas we'd never accepted *anyone's* right to question us. Never. Our parents felt too guilty to cross us, and we knew it. Our teachers were afraid to contradict us, and we knew

13

it. We could see it all for what it was, all the old illusions destroyed.

We knew everything except what the hell to put in their place.

'I used to write for the *Post*,' I explain, smiling as his eyes light up, then regretting it almost immediately. Things have got pretty sad if I need to use a guy like Bergman to boost my self-esteem.

He turns on the shower lights and opens the door, saying, 'Is that right? I knew you were some kind of journalist, but you wrote for the actual *Post*? Like I would have read your stuff?'

'I guess. Probably.'

He's standing in the doorway as I take my towel off, absent-mindedly watching me like you might gaze at a couple in a diner when you're eating alone – not meaning to intrude, but drawn to their warmth. Basically, I don't think he realizes he's staring at my dick.

'It was before McQueen,' I say, in the interest of making conversation as I step towards the wall.

'Who?'

'The guy who owns the *Post* now,' I shout over the splash of the water. 'Bought it three years ago.'

'Kicked you out, huh?' Bergman sympathizes loudly. 'Always the same. It's a shitty way things work now.'

I turn to correct him, then let it drop. What's the point? Besides, he's being nice, and even if I didn't get the chop when McQueen came in, it's not as though there weren't plenty of other guys who did. The *Post* went from four floors of the Brady Tower down to three, the spare becoming the base for McQueen's new Internet company. Basically a quarter of the staff gone – a phone call on a Saturday, not there on Sunday. Fast and radical, like liposuction.

So Bergman's right anyway.

14

*   *   *

I only ever met McQueen twice.

The first time was when he was given a guided tour of the office by Kevin O'Neil, our editor. We'd only found out about the paper being sold the day before, Kevin giving us all the full sales pitch to bring us over to the idea. It was great news, he said, a good thing for us all – McQueen was going to invest heavily in modernizing the operation, and we were all going to get state-of-the-art computers, mobile phones and new office furniture. Potted plants. Big leather armchairs. He knew how to talk it up to us all right.

A lot of people tidied up their desks the day McQueen came in, but I made it a stupid point of honour not to straighten out one single paper amid the bedlam around my computer.

It's not as though I intended to quit, like some people. I wasn't any hotter on becoming part of InfoCorps than they were, but I never bought the line that McQueen is evil incarnate. His papers sell. He gives people what they want, as he's always saying.

Besides, where do you go from the *Post*?

The *Post* is Entropolis. This is still a newspaper town, even with all the 24-hour-news channels, weather channels, cop channels, business channels, court channels and celebrity-garbage-can channels. And it always will be, I think. Not because Entropolitans are more sophisticated than the inhabitants of other cities – although we are – but because of the architecture.

Entropolis reaches up into the sky and it digs roots deep into the ground. It's a pedestrian city, not a sprawl of freeways connecting boroughs. You can't cover Entropolis with a helicopter, and a TV van just gets stuck in the traffic. People commute by train. They take the subway. They use the sidewalks. They cannot avoid

15

passing newspaper vendors, and nor would they want to because the architecture dictates that paper – not TV, or radio, or a computer – is the city's most effective medium. I think it's better that way. TV towns have no soul. No sense of community.

Not that a sense of community is an entirely good thing, as I'm learning.

'Actually, I quit,' I inform Bergman, drying myself. 'I didn't get fired.'

'Oh . . . OK . . .' he replies, looking confused. 'Sorry, I didn't mean to . . . I dunno . . . it's not like I thought you—'

'Don't worry, I didn't take it that way. Really. But I did quit.'

It took time before I realized how different things really were after we became part of InfoCorps. There was no single, cataclysmic overhaul of the paper's direction or how we went about filling its pages, but in a hundred memos relaying directives that in themselves were questions of micromanagement McQueen gradually swept away the last vestiges of the *Post* from those famous 'glory days'. The old guys were all gone now, and so were all the things that had enabled them to exist. You practically had to go to court to get your expenses paid. There were time sheets and every number you dialled was computer-checked to catch people having private chats on company time. A representative of the advertising department sat in on the editorial meeting every morning. Gradually, it all seemed to be less and less about the stories and more to do with demographics, target readers, ad sales and promotional offers. I mean, who gave a fuck?

Oh, and we never saw the damned potted plants and armchairs, either. I think Kevin just made that up.

16

I stuck it out as long as I could, not feeling depressed so much as mildly deflated. Sluggish, like an under-pumped tyre. Something was missing, but I was a little slow realizing what. I eventually had my moment of epiphany – sitting on the toilet, as a matter of fact, gazing vacantly between my legs, when the horrific realization hit me.

It was so obvious I didn't know how I could have missed it.

I stormed straight from there to see Kevin O'Neil, slamming the door of his office behind me and shouting, '*Where are they, Kevin? Give them back right now!*'

Kevin tilted comfortably back in his chair in surprise, raising his hands in surrender.

'Nick! Calm down!' he said. 'What are you *talking* about?'

'You know *damn* well what I'm talking about, O'Neil!' I seethed, and ripped down my pants to show him.

'Oh . . . that,' he answered, looking a little embarrassed. 'Didn't you get the memo?'

'*Memo?*' I screamed. '*What fucking memo?*'

'That's corporate policy, Nick. No testicles. You didn't get the memo?'

'I don't know!' I exploded, pulling my pants back up. 'I never *read* memos! *Where are my balls?*'

'In a safe place, Nick. Stop *shouting*!' he ordered, getting irritated in turn. 'If you'd read the memo like everyone else, you'd know that this is standard InfoCorps procedure with all its subsidiaries. Anyway, it was implemented months ago, for heaven's sake, and you've only just *noticed*?'

'I've been *busy*!' I thundered. 'It's McQueen, isn't it? He's got my balls!'

'Mr McQueen has *everyone's* testicles, Nick, not just yours,' he sighed. 'Look – this is the reality of a global company. You cannot run an operation the size of InfoCorps if everyone has their *own* balls. It would be chaos! One man has to have *all* the balls. Have you never heard of the economies of scale? Anyway – you still have a penis, don't you?'

'Oh . . . great! What can it do, Kevin? It can pee and, in a state of high excitement, it can . . . what . . . *puff*? *I want my balls back!*'

O'Neil shook his head ruefully. I knew it wasn't his fault this had happened – he probably didn't like being part of InfoCorps any more than I did, but he was the editor and it was his head on the block. In fact, it was rare for a man in his position to keep his job following a takeover by McQueen. I can see now that he was in a difficult position. He was a good editor, Kevin, and I think he felt he owed it to the paper and all of us who worked there not to give up on what truly mattered to him over a question of testicles.

'Look, Nick . . .' he returned softly, 'I do understand your feelings. I'd hate to lose you, because you're a good journalist, but if you feel that strongly, then . . . obviously you can have your balls back and go to work for someone else. But can I give you some friendly advice? The world is changing, Nick. Pretty soon it won't be possible for any paper to survive without an InfoCorps behind it – and they're all the same. That's the way it is now! We've got to adapt. You have a good career ahead of you, believe me . . . but you have to decide whether you want that career, or complete control of your genitalia. Because it's one or the other, Nick – the days of the lone guy with the big *cojones* swinging between his legs are over. Everyone is restructuring, downsizing, consolidating . . . the future belongs to eunuchs.'

So that's how it happened. I knew he was being sincere, and meant well, but I quit. I cleared my desk, collected my testicles in a cryogenically frozen case marked 'Carraway N., Journalist', and just walked away. Allowing for poetic licence, that's pretty much how it was.

After the story had been told a few times.

PROCESSING ROOM,
ENTROPOLIS PENITENTIARY,
SIX A.M.

'Nick! Big day! Looking good!' Wolsheim exclaims, checking me over as Bergman closes the door behind us. He must have got here early because there's paperwork all over the table. All over, like his attaché case threw up. I've been ready for over twenty minutes now, but the release papers say six a.m., so Bergman and I have been gazing at the floor of my cell, conversation dry. My fault. He tried.

'The man in the blue suit,' I introduce myself.

'The blue suit!' Wolsheim enthuses, clapping once with satisfaction. 'That's the look, Nick – you're perfect, believe me!'

'I still don't much like blue.'

'I know, but listen – it's proven, OK? Statistically. Juries go for blue. You can't argue with a fact.'

This from a lawyer of all people.

If I know one thing, it's that there are no facts. Only circumstantial evidence. All of it. Hell, not even one plus one is two is a *fact*. Mathematics is a language, an assumption – so one-plus-one is just the starting point for a system to define our way of perceiving things, that's all. Seriously, I doubt that little green men buy their groceries that way. Nor, for that matter, are we ever going to succeed in explaining the universe as if it were like taking a stock check in a Piggly-Wiggly superstore.

So if those facts, the very basics, are just rules for the game as we've decided to play it, how much less faith can you have in the kinds of facts you read in the papers or hear in a court of law?

Victims and villains, good guys and bad guys? Give me a break.

I'm beginning to suspect that all that differentiates the people I've been living with these last months from the rest of society is luck. Doesn't matter how many people you lock up – some guilty as charged, some innocent – you'll have pretty much the same proportion of crooked and honest people walking down the street at any time of day. The ones in here are unlucky. The whole justice system is a sinkhole for bad luck, for losers.

From top to bottom, society is riddled with people breaking the laws, fucking over their fellow men, running scams, cooking the books, cheating, conning, stealing, lying, and killing. But so long as their luck holds out, so long as they don't *lose*, that's OK. So don't tell me the laws of man elevate him above the laws of nature. They're the same damn laws, and the winner takes all, every-where, and always has. The difference is just a trick of the light, a question of the angle of perception.

And I know something about angles. I am the master of angles. Give me a newspaper, any newspaper on any day, and I will find you a little story tucked away some-where that could have made the front page if only the guy behind it had taken a better angle. Most journalists are pretty mediocre at their jobs, same as any other profession.

At least, whatever happens today, I won't have been mediocre.

Why, I'm so good that I have become the front page myself.

Wolsheim has stopped talking in exclamation marks and high fives, adopting his other voice as we sit down – soft and rapid. He still freaks me with the way he switches like that – it's practically schizophrenic, except neither of them is really him, of course. Somewhere, far behind the eyes, there's a person who never shows his face. But I've no idea what that person is like. If I try to picture him at home with his family, I draw a blank.

Can a person be so good at their role, I wonder, that they cease to exist?

I suppose that's a question for my mother, may she rest in peace.

'You sleep any?' Wolsheim asks quietly, eyes flicking to Bergman and the other guard. I don't know the other one, but he's got a look I've come to know well these last months – there's a kind of guard who blames you for the fact that he's wound up working in a prison, like it's your fault he's not a brain surgeon. They have this simmering resentment in their eyes – just *dying* for you to give them an excuse to lash out. The instant I see it, I cut him out of my field of vision, but I feel his gaze stuck on me like chewing gum on my shoe.

'Not a whole lot,' I answer.

He nods, gathering papers from the table and placing them in an orderly fashion in his attaché case.

'That's only to be expected. It doesn't matter – you don't have to do anything today but stand up and say "Not guilty", right?' he says, looking up with a smile.

'The rest of the time, just try not to yawn. The jury will think it's a nervous reaction, makes you look guilty. If you have to yawn, then cover your face with your hands like it's all getting on top of you. Know what I mean? That's an innocent reaction. Emotional. And you'll sleep better tonight. Generally speaking, people are too exhausted after a day in court to keep thinking about it.'

He glances at his watch – slim, rectangular, and discreetly expensive.

'OK, we've got about an hour before we need to hit the road,' he announces. 'Do you want some coffee?'

'I don't think Room Service is available.'

Wolsheim grins and reaches under the table to produce a thermos from the leather briefcase on the floor.

'Always be prepared!' he chuckles. '*Latte* OK? I even have fresh-baked blueberry muffins, but you're probably not hungry.'

Blueberry muffins. Fuck me, there's a world out there where people can buy fresh-baked blueberry muffins an hour before dawn. After a few months in state custody, stuff like that starts to seem surreal.

He pours me a *grande latte* into a styrofoam cup bearing the logo of the chain where he got his thermos filled, gives me a couple of their paper sugar bags and a plastic spoon. I practically want to cry it's so heartbreakingly familiar. So safe. Almost like being home, like catching a smell from my childhood.

'No. I'll have a muffin.'

Wolsheim tilts his head slightly, impressed that a man about to face trial for murder could stomach blueberry sponge. He reaches down again and places a paper bag of muffins on the table, opening it towards me.

'Good news, incidentally,' he confides as he waits for me to serve myself before reaching in with his own hand. 'They're definitely going to do as I said. Bosch is going to be their first and principal witness. Their big gun.'

I nod, sipping the warm, milky taste of freedom. I would give my right arm – the very arm holding the coffee cup – to be in the coffee house it came from right now. Truly. For none of this to exist, my arm not existing would be a fair price to pay. I could live with that, no problem. On the other hand, I would hate, just now, to lose the arm with which one gives people the finger.

So I'm kind of torn.

I bite the muffin, accidentally looking up as I do so and catching the anonymous guard's gaze. It's funny – his face is blank, expressionless, and yet I can see the sneer there. I know that shouldn't be possible, but it is. His aura is sneering. Somehow, in his mind, I have just majorly upped my scum quotient by being prepared to eat a muffin on the morning of my trial. Hate is just like love, really – it catches hold of the strangest things.

'Way overconfident, like I said.' Wolsheim smiles. 'So we're relaxed, Nick. We let them do it, and then we fuck them. Ambush the detective, and the rest of their case falls like dominoes.'

'You don't think they know?'

'Can't do. If they knew, they'd never put him on the stand. Certainly not first out, anyway. So he hasn't told them anything, which is hardly surprising under the circumstances, and the DA's office is filled with arrogant, ambitious little shits who are so certain that you've already been tried and condemned in everyone's mind that they think the trial is just a formality. They're too cocksure to see that everything they have is circumstantial.'

There's a glint in his eyes as he says it, a bloodlust. An adolescent impatience that takes twenty years off his face. He can hardly wait.

'Glad to see you're looking forward to it, at least.'

24

There's a note of disapproval in my voice that I didn't really intend, and Wolsheim pauses with his cup on the edge of his lips, putting it down slowly.

'Nick . . .' he sighs. 'Relax. You're in good hands.'

That, I know. Nobody becomes as widely despised as Meyer Wolsheim without being very good at what they do. I'm lucky to have him. And it's not as though I have any right to quibble with his style, considering he's doing this for free.

'I know. I didn't mean to suggest otherwise.'

'If a case is believed to be a foregone conclusion, Nick, then the defence has a huge tactical advantage,' he explains softly. 'We *want* a jury that is against us. We *want* the media to have already condemned you. Because then the *only* way left for the argument to move is from certainty to doubt. And a doubt is all we require.'

I shrug, gulping down the muffin. Wolsheim frowns, disappointed that he's not getting more from me, and he leans across the table.

'It's all about *drama*, Nick,' he whispers. 'A courtroom is a theatre – the greatest theatre in the world! My job is not to argue the facts, but to direct the play in the jury's head. Make them *want* to believe a certain story, and all the evidence in the world won't stop them choosing to do so. Believe me – it's more exciting for them if the villain turns out to be someone unexpected.'

He stares hard at me, driving home his point, and then picks up his coffee cup again, raising it in an imaginary toast.

'Thank you, Detective Frank Bosch,' he grins.

I first heard Frank Bosch's name a little over three years ago now. If I remember correctly, he was first invoked as 'that fucking cunt motherfucker Bosch'.

Every day people ring up newspapers because they

think they have a story to sell. They don't know who they want to speak to, so the switchboard just puts them through to someone in the newsroom at random.

'You want some dirt on the police?' this one began tearfully when I picked up the phone. 'The truth about those fucking bastards?'

Most of these people are time-wasters. A lot of wild rumours presented as hot tips, a lot of crazies peddling non-stories that basically boil down to an excuse to vent their unhappiness and hatred of their own lives, but you have to hear them out because some of them turn out to be offering you good stuff.

Initially, I had Jordan Baker down for a time-waster. She was emotionally overwrought and broke down in tears before I'd had a chance to figure out what she was talking about.

'They took my girls!' she was sobbing. 'I paid them off but they still took them! Fucking bust the door and dragged them away!'

She sounded around forty years old, her voice deep like a heavy smoker even through the hysteria. I pictured her fat and pig-nosed. Some drunk, single mother on welfare who'd had her children taken into custody and was too moronic to even consider the possibility that she was unfit to be a parent. There was a lot of noise in the background, and everything was coming out in a confused jumble, but it sounded like that was what had happened. What can you do with these people? I was thinking. Walking, talking contradictions, both wailing their victimhood and damned sure that they're smarter than anyone – the kind of schizoid idiots responsible for dragging society's problems from one generation to the next, yea unto the end of time itself.

I guess you could say I lacked empathy in those days.

But the thing that I couldn't figure out was this 'pay-off' she kept talking about. Was it some kind of rent problem? She'd said something about the 'house being closed down', about her being arrested, so maybe she was being evicted *and* her children put into care?

'I'm going to *fuck* them, though!' she seethed, her anger suddenly calming her down. 'I've got it all on video!'

'What?' I frowned, massaging my forehead. '*What* have you got on video?'

'A pay-off! To that fucking cunt motherfucker Bosch and his partner! Thirty fucking per cent of what the girls made! I have them on video, taking the cash! They're *fucked*!'

Suddenly, the light came on and I sat up straight. The house was a brothel. The girls were prostitutes. The cops had been demanding pay-offs, but had ended up raiding the place anyway. She'd been arrested.

That was the story. A usable one, too. Why on earth she was offering us the video rather than using it to bargain her way out of the rap, I had no idea. If I knew anything about the Entropolis PD – especially Gossom precinct, which is where these cops were from – she didn't have a problem. She had them over a barrel. Apparently she was more concerned about getting revenge than looking after her own interests, though, because she didn't even seem to want to *sell* the story – she just wanted to see them exposed, their faces splashed all over the paper.

Luckily for me, this happened a couple of months before McQueen bought the *Post* and we all still had a large degree of autonomy in our working methods, so I didn't even bother to explain to anyone where I was going that afternoon.

Jordan Baker insisted on meeting in the bar at Central Station. Rather melodramatic, but she was the kind of person who lived the movies.

She said she'd be wearing dark glasses and a fur coat, for god's sake.

Central Station Bar, there's another place I'd like to be right now. I love that bar.

I love the way that it's situated above the station concourse and has that whole long wall of arched windows so that you can watch the trains arriving and departing below. The muffled drum of the diesel engines, the distant screech of whistles and the slamming of carriage doors. And always, sounding like a waterfall somewhere out of sight, the low rumble of thousands of feet.

I love its vaulted ceiling, the chandeliers and frescoes of destinations the lines run to, painted back when they seemed exotic. The tables in booths that echo the compartments on old-fashioned trains, with their polished oak benches and brass luggage racks. The long bar and the waiters' immaculate uniforms.

The place is redolent of antique glamour, of the first thrill of long-distance travel. Impregnated with a melancholy air from all those millions of partings and reunions. Life rolling through year after year.

Presuming I can have my arm back, I'd offer a year off my life to spend just one evening there now, with a cold beer trickling moisture onto a mat, a pack of cigarettes, and a table by the window.

Jordan Baker was neither fat nor pig-nosed. She was a surprisingly good-looking young blonde. About twenty-five. I did a double take, looking around for someone else in a fur coat and dark glasses because I'd had her down as so much older.

She had a finely etched face, the kind that suited sadness, and the bar was a perfect setting – the sweet sorrow of a big train station, a fragile beauty with a glass of wine.

She didn't take her glasses off when I sat down, but I could tell she had a black eye, even with the make-up. Her smile attracted me on the instant – forlorn and yet hopeful, thinking I was the answer to her problems. Her fur coat – a fake, of course – was wrapped tight around her, even though the place was pretty warm, and she was nervously smoking, tapping ash between every puff. She seemed fairly middle-class. Educated. Frankly nothing like the prostitutes I'd met through my work in the past.

Men have this fantasy about a beautiful, warm-hearted prostitute who's like a bird with a broken wing, waiting to be saved by them. It's total bullshit – in my experience they're irrevocably fucked up, self-destructive and bitter. And anyway, let's face it – most men can't even put up a shelf straight, let alone mend a broken wing. But Jordan Baker actually seemed like that mythical whore.

She was a lot calmer than when we spoke on the phone, her tears dried and an exaggerated air of dignity in the way she sat. She held out her hand as she thanked me for coming, but palm down, like she expected me to kiss it. Wasting no time, she asked if I had a recorder on me so she could recount her story more coherently.

I sat listening as she went back over it, giving all the names and dates and figures I could possibly need to build an article, and I found myself wondering more and more what could have fucked up so badly in this girl's life that she had ended up here. She came from a small town near Dumona. She was humorous and intelligent. She didn't appear to be hooked on anything worse than tobacco. There was no clear reason why she shouldn't be living a normal life, doing a normal job. I just didn't get it.

Apparently she'd surreptitiously filmed one of the pay-offs to the two detectives because they were becoming greedier and more threatening as the months went by, and she figured that she might soon need some kind of bargaining chip on her side.

'But you're not using it,' I interrupted, now more than ever thinking that she shouldn't waste her tape on what would, frankly, only be a second-string story for the *Post*. 'You could trade it now.'

She paused for a long time, looking slightly away.

'I don't want to trade with those fuckers,' she announced. 'I don't trust them. Even if they dropped the charges, there's a lot they can do without arresting you. I want it this way.'

'They'll only come down harder on you.'

'Ah-ha!' she countered cheerfully, brushing my warning aside with a knowingly theatrical air. 'I shall slip through their fingers and vanish into the night.'

I raised my eyebrows, dryly commenting, 'It's not so easy disappearing these days. How much can you do in life without needing to use a card or ID?'

'I'll be somewhere where they can't touch me,' she insisted.

'*Where?*' I asked, leaning forward. 'Those places don't exist any more. No matter where you go, sooner or later someone or something will betray you. All they have to do is wait. And then you're in worse trouble than when you started. If you won't make a deal, you'd be better off just doing a little time. You're not a serious criminal, so the way the law works you'll probably be sent somewhere that isn't too bad. Some of the female penitentiaries are OK.'

'They won't be sending *me* to any female penitentiary,' she announced firmly.

Jordan reached into her coat and produced the cassette, pushing it across the table to me. I looked at her – searching for some sign of doubt – and then gave up, placing my hand on the tape.

'Thank you, Mr Carraway,' she said, getting up from the table. She offered me her hand again, palm down, saying in the sweetest convent-girl tone, 'Promise me you'll fuck them?'

'So you're taking a train out of here right now?' I asked, shaking on it.

'Right out of here,' she smiled, her slim fingers clasping mine with surprising force. 'You won't follow me, will you? A girl must have her secrets.'

I nodded and watched her leaving, knowing the promise was as good as broken already. Of course I wouldn't reveal where she went, but my own curiosity was too strong not to see which train she boarded. It was pretty easy following her from a distance, that fur coat allowing me to keep track of her in the crowd like the one dancer in a chorus line who's out of synch with the others.

She checked the arrivals and departures board, looking at her watch, and then made her way swiftly towards the platforms. There was a train going through Dumona leaving from Platform 10, and she began walking along it. I hung back by the gate, my curiosity satisfied but still needing the closure of seeing the train actually pull out before I left.

Passengers were hurrying on board as the whistle blew, but she strode on, ignoring the nearer carriages and heading towards the front car, her fur coat wrapped tight around her in the wind.

The whistle blew again. She stopped by the furthest carriage, placing her foot on the step, her neck bowed . . .

The guard shouted something to her, and she shook her head, her foot sliding back to the concrete. The guard shrugged and began to walk away, blowing his whistle for the last time.

I didn't understand what had made her change her

31

mind about going home, but she didn't seem too sure about it – she stood there on the far end of the platform, watching her train recede along the tracks until it disappeared into a tunnel. I took a few steps backwards, placing myself beside an advertising panel that I would be able to slip behind when she came back to the concourse.

But she didn't. She just stood there, looking down the tracks.

I heard the announcement about the train arriving at Platform 9, but didn't give it any thought until I saw the headlights coming into view in the tunnel. Beginning to sense what might be on her mind, I started to walk cautiously onto the platform – my walk turning to a run as I saw her move across to the other side, her gaze fixed on the incoming train. I realized that I would never reach her in time when I was only halfway down the platform.

She let her fur coat drop open, and stepped up to the edge. I shouted her name, sprinting now, and that was when time seemed to stop.

Her head turned slowly my way, that sad smile still on her face, and she let the fur coat slide off her shoulders to the ground. She was naked underneath, her slim white body and small breasts standing out against the concrete like a single flower on a coffin. The train was just seconds away from her as she turned her back to the rails.

Suddenly I stopped dead in my tracks, understanding, and stood there in shock, watching as Jordan Baker raised his arms high above his head, falling gracefully backwards onto the rails before the desperately braking train.

They weren't sending him to any female penitentiary.

Courtyard,
Entropolis Penitentiary,
Seven a.m.

Everything by the clock, by the rules, by the numbers. Again I don't know the guard in front of me, the one who opens the outer door, but he's been expecting me. No curiosity registers on his face as Bergman hands him the release papers to sign, and date, and hour.

Bergman is being especially nice today, even by his standards. He was very gentle when he put the cuffs on me. Almost apologetic for the humiliation he was inflicting. I don't know what I've done to deserve such special treatment – either he's impressed by the high profile my case has in the media, or he's grateful for the fact that thanks to me he's getting a day out.

'Told you it was going to be a beautiful day, Nick,' Wolsheim says beside me as we squint in the morning sun.

I haven't smelled morning in months. Yard time is four in the afternoon, rain or shine, when the day is already stale. I guess they think that we need to let off some energy before bedtime, like children, but the truth is that you're so fucking lethargic from being cooped up all day

33

with nothing to do that you generally just sit out there for an hour.

I don't want to smile, but it's hard not to. The cuffs and the stone expression of the guard are nothing compared to a taste of fresh air bearing the scent of warming dew.

Wolsheim smiles in the crisp sunlight too, as though he has unseen chains and guards of his own, and I wonder what kind of world this would be if days didn't grow old, if the air was always as fresh as now and the sun never became oppressive. I wonder if anyone has ever compared human behaviour to the atmospheric conditions, and found a temperature and ion level at which people start to get aggressive. I wonder if a guy like Wolsheim could use that as a courtroom defence.

I was lying listlessly on the couch when Frank Bosch called that day. It was around five in the afternoon, summertime, and the air in the apartment was heavy, pinning me to the cushions. To add to my irritability, the afternoon's interview with Tom Harris – the politician, not the movie star – had been cancelled at the last minute despite being set up three weeks before. Part of me was glad not to have to work, but the day felt like it had been wasted and I seemed to be determined to compound the waste by staring at the ceiling rather than accomplishing any of the dozen other tasks that I knew needed to be done.

If the phone hadn't been on the table just behind my head, I would have been tempted just to let the machine take it.

'Hi, Cunt, it's me,' Frank began, as he always did.

I could hear a siren in the background, and knew he was on his way to the scene of some incident.

'Uh-huh?' I replied, already half-decided that I was not

34

in the mood to follow up whatever lead he was about to put my way today.

'There's been a shooting on the subway,' he continued. He was on a mobile, his voice echoing and metallic over the hiss as it bounced up into space and back down to me. 'I'm on my way to Gossom Fields station.'

'What's the story?' I asked, raising myself on an elbow as my interest caught. 'What happened?'

'What do I know? I'm in my fucking car.'

'Didn't they tell you anything?' I persisted. 'Don't you know how many victims there are, at least?'

'Twenty-three.'

'*Twenty-three?*' I squawked, sitting up now.

'No, I'm just jerking you off, you morbid fuck. I have no idea. At least one dead, I think. Do you know what it means when I say that I'm *in my car*?'

'Can you get me into the station?'

The arrangement I had with Detective Frank Bosch was simple. He knew what kind of stories I would be interested in and, from time to time, he gave me a head start on the competition. Ever since the cops stopped using open radio bands it's become the best way of keeping pace with events. Frank was by no means the only Entropolis cop leaking tips to the media, of course, but he was a particularly well-placed one.

That's the real reason why I quit the *Post* – because with a source like Bosch, I figured I'd make a better living freelance.

'Is that the agreement?' he sighed irritably. 'I don't think it fucking is, is it?'

'I'll be discreet.'

'Yeah, right. A discreet journalist. That's like, what – a pacifist soldier?'

'I can't do anything on the outside.'

'Always pushing your luck, aren't you?' he growled

35

over the phone's crackle. 'Every fucking time.'

Four months had passed after Jordan Baker's death before I contacted Frank Bosch. I took care to find out everything I could about him and the second detective, Phil Wagner, eventually deciding Frank was the safer one to approach. Wagner was a family man. He scared me more because I would not just be threatening him personally, but those he loved as well. Plus he was bigger – they called him Big Phil at the precinct to differentiate him from Little Phil, another detective, but he was big in comparison to Phils everywhere – and known to have a temper.

Frank Bosch, on the other hand, was like me – he had no attachments outside his job, and a fairly loose notion of fidelity within it. Not quite loose enough to agree with my definition of our relationship as 'a gentleman's agreement', but close. He preferred to refer to it as 'a cunt's agreement'. That's Frank all over – total bastard, but if you asked him for a spade, at least he wouldn't hand you a shovel.

On the other hand, neither of us ever used the correct word.

That would have been 'blackmail', of course.

So, I'm trying to be honest now, am I? Well, if that is truly the case then I have to face one thing above all else.

I'm a coward.

I *hate* that, but it's the simple truth. And I know what I'm talking about here because, like all cowards, I'm very adept at spinning myself more complex versions of the truth. Even then it's often not easy convincing yourself that you haven't done a shitty thing. There's this insistent little voice in your head saying, 'Come off it, Nick, the *simple* way of looking at this is to say—'

'Yes, but can I just interrupt you there?' you answer yourself. 'Surely it's vital that we *don't* fall into the trap of being simplistic about this?'

'But I didn't say simplistic, I said simple. It's not quite the same thing. The *simple* approach is—'

'Absolutely, yes – always the best! I agree! But only if the issue is clear-cut, which this one clearly isn't, as you said yourself.'

'What? When did I say that?'

'Well, you pointed out – quite correctly – that simplistic and simple are not quite the same thing, which is why we have to be wary of *both* until we're sure *which* one we're dealing with. I think we're basically arguing the same point here, aren't we?'

'Which is?'

'That this isn't a clear-cut issue.'

'How can you say that? I haven't managed to say what the issue even *is* yet!'

'Exactly! So if we can't manage to define what the issue even *is*, as you so rightly pointed out, then the conclusion is very simple, isn't it? Clearly it means we're dealing with a very complex question here, where there *are* no simple answers.'

'Sorry? What question – the issue or the approach?'

'You see what I mean?'

And so on until you tire the little voice out, basically. That's how a coward lives with himself, day after day, twisting his conscience up in knots. It's why we're so well suited to careers in politics, I suppose. Or the media, in my case. And lawyers, of course . . .

Hell, come to think of it – we run the world.

Seriously, there may be some truth in this. It figures – all the people with moral backbone either argue them-selves out of the job or crash and burn. That only leaves us cowards. It's not like we even intended it, really, we just got there by default. Like the man said: The Meek shall inherit the Earth.

Well, I don't know exactly who The Meek are, but they sound like a pretty yellow-bellied bunch to me.

None of which, however, excuses the fact that I fucked over Jordan Baker.

Sure, I told myself it wasn't betrayal. The way I rationalized it was to say that two cops on the take hardly constituted a big story in Entropolis, but that if I *used* the tape to make them feed me stories then I was basically doing to them what they had done to her.

Him.

Herm.

Whatever.

So I was avenging Jordan Baker.

A well-sculpted piece of bullshit, I must say. Why, it looks so like a rose you almost want to stick your nose in it. But I could have had the decency, at least, not to walk away that day.

For a moment, I had found myself staring at the horrified train driver after he brought the train to a screeched halt just yards from me, his eyes wide with panic as he looked imploringly at me through the glass. He was a hefty guy, a barbecue and ball-game male, but he was begging me to confirm with a sympathetic look that he couldn't have known, that it hadn't been his fault. My own mouth still hung open with shock, and my first thought, as our eyes stayed locked on each other, was that I had to get away from there. I could not get involved. I could not answer questions about what I had been doing there and what I knew about the person under those wheels. How was it possible, after all, that I had been sitting talking to this person in the bar just moments before they threw themself onto the tracks, and yet claim to have no real connection to the event? I wasn't about to tell the police, of all people, about what I had on the video.

I raised my hands helplessly as we stared at one another, denying any connection to what had happened, and turned away. I walked briskly back down the platform, aware of the first curious regards from passers-by on the concourse, their attention caught by the train's sudden, screaming halt. I resisted the temptation to run, seeing their eyes look away again as their thoughts returned to their own journeys, and prayed that I would be able to lose myself in that busy crowd before a guard came to see what the problem was with the incoming locomotive. There was a shout far behind me, but I ignored it. I marched towards that concourse – fast and busy, like any other person in Central Station – and breathed a sigh of relief as I melted into the mass.

The little voice and I did a lot of talking after that.

The bus is black, beetle-brilliant in the morning sun. The back doors are open towards us, and a guard stands waiting. I don't know who makes them – there's no manufacturer marked anywhere, front or back – but you can see that it's basically a customized school bus, with bars on the windows and a steel mesh to isolate the driver. Bergman walks us towards it.

Wolsheim shakes his head, placing both his cases in one hand to free the other for pulling himself up the step, grunting, 'I do hate public transport.'

People can say what they like about lawyers such as him – he's an opportunist, certainly, and only interested in my case because it has a high media profile – but that doesn't change anything from my perspective. Which is that most lawyers, even those being paid, would have contented themselves with meeting me at the other end.

Frank Bosch knew I had the tape. In a safe place, of course. But we never mentioned it.

Our meetings were always friendly, despite the fact that he always called me Cunt. But then he would have called himself that, too. Frank had never deluded himself that he was on any kind of moral crusade – his job, as he saw it, was simply to manage crime in Gossom. To contain it, give it some kind of structure and stability, and keep the statistics generally positive. So long as they could maintain control over the figures, everyone was happy. His superiors needed certain statistics to advance their careers, and by helping to supply them he could advance his in turn. The politicians needed those statistics to be able to tell the voters that they were doing a good job, and the voters needed them to feel safe in their beds at night.

So Frank managed the situation. He concentrated his efforts on crimes that could produce a conviction, and ignored the rest. He arrested people for things he could arrest them for, and didn't waste too much time looking for some nameless, faceless culprit to hang an unsolved crime on. You could call him a cynic, or you could say that he was simply trying to do what he believed was best for society. They are not contradictory points of view.

I don't know what the young man who first joined the police was like, what ideals and ambitions he may have had, but by the time I came to know Frank Bosch he was quite able to accept being blackmailed by a journalist. I don't think it cost him any sleep.

'You can do it,' I encouraged him lightly. 'I know you can.'

There was a hissing pause over the line in which I listened to his car's siren wailing as he thought it over.

'If you're outside Gossom Fields in fifteen minutes, I'll get you in,' he announced. 'Be late, and fuck you.'

I had a small motorbike that I used to get around town – as much because I hated taking the subway as out of a need to travel fast in situations like these. A subway train is basically a huge hypodermic injecting viruses into the city's veins.

There was an irate crowd milling outside Gossom Fields station by the time I pulled up. The gates had been closed just far enough across the entrance to leave a passage for one person at a time, and a young cop stood guarding that, looking increasingly rattled as the crowd's frustration grew more vocal.

'Move along, please!' he was shouting. 'There's nothing to see.'

'What do you think we're *trying* to do, son?' a balding guy in a suit yelled back, a large knot on his forehead pulsing red. 'This is the *subway*. We come here to move along the *tunnel*!'

'The subway is shut, sir,' the rookie answered. 'Now, *please* – move along!'

'*Where*, for god's sake?' came the reply. 'Are you suggesting we move in the *wrong direction*? *Why* is the subway shut?'

'There has been an incident.'

'What *kind* of incident?'

'Just an incident, OK?'

I don't know why the cops always do that. Why not just say 'Sorry, sir, but there's been a shoot-out on a train, and there's blood and brains *everywhere*!'?

People would understand.

They wouldn't get angry about finding their travel plans disrupted. Seriously, it would *make* their day rather than ruining it.

Frank was waiting in his car a few yards away, and I

waved as he jumped impatiently out, scowling at me as I took off my helmet.

'I'm not a fucking tour organizer,' he muttered as he strode past, pulling out his badge.

He cut a way through to the front of the crowd, flashing his credentials at people like Moses parting the waters, and waved me through ahead of himself once we reached the uniformed cop. The rookie didn't even look at me – for all he knew, I was a specialist in Public Transport Psychopaths or something.

A three-man TV crew was pushing through the crowd not far behind us – apparently equipped with their own inside source at the precinct – but as we disappeared inside I heard the cop on the gate shout, 'Sorry. No media.'

I enjoyed what I did for a living, I truly did. I miss it.

Inside, the station was unnaturally still. Once past the cop on the entrance, there was nobody on the concourse but Frank and me. He pointed me over to a corridor heading to some other closed exit, down which he could be sure none of his colleagues would arrive.

'You stay here, out of sight, for ten minutes, do you understand?' he ordered irritably. 'When you come down, you do not know me. You do not approach me, or acknowledge me. Are we clear?'

'Thank you, Frank.' I smiled. 'You're an angel.'

'Are we *clear*?' he insisted.

'Totally.' I nodded. 'I do not know you.'

'Fuck, if only,' he sighed, stepping back. 'One of these days I swear I'll . . .'

He finished his sentence with a frustrated wave of his hand, and jumped the turnstile in one fluid motion. It was impressive for a man of his age. And, ridiculous as it sounds, if he hadn't done it I don't think I would be in prison today.

'Mind your head,' Bergman mutters as I climb into the back of the armoured van. It's hard getting up the step with my hands locked behind my back, and I stumble, feeling his fingers tighten around my arms, catching me in mid-fall.

I curse under my breath, more from humiliation than anything else. Rapidly placing my feet again, I straighten up, shaking Bergman's hands off a little more roughly than I intended. It's not his fault – were it his call I'm sure he'd be confident enough to dispense with the cuffs, at least for now. I'm not a difficult prisoner, and where the hell am I going to escape to anyway? The bus is sitting in the damned courtyard, with steel doors, thirty feet of wall and a guntower between me and freedom.

But it's not about security. Like half of the way everything is done in prison, it's about stopping you from imagining, even for one instant, that you are still a full human being. It's about chaining your mind, turning you into someone who doesn't answer back or resist an order. A bullock to be herded.

Only we're not cattle, and it doesn't work – most prisoners are either too dumb or too smart to be tamed like that. All it does is make you hug your resentment closer, treasuring the warmth of your hatred, until your silence becomes total and your eyes speak for you. And by then your animosity is so pure and hard that there's nothing and no-one who can breach it, not even one of the good men, like Bergman. They're the ones who get hurt most.

I'm not there yet, which is why he likes me.

But I can see that it will come, and one day, if I stay here, I'll drop the man who catches me now.

If Bosch hadn't jumped the turnstile, I wouldn't have tried to jump the turnstile. If I hadn't tried to jump the turnstile, I wouldn't have broken the lens on my camera. If I hadn't broken the lens on my camera, none of this would have happened.

That's how it goes.

My left foot caught on the barrier – I landed palm first, the rest of my anatomical features apparently barging past each other in the race to slam into the concrete next, and somewhere amongst the whole undignified bruise-fest I distinctly heard the camera crack, even through its bag. It was another couple of minutes before my pains had subsided enough for me to check what had happened. Superficially, it looked OK. Then I tried to focus it.

I took it to the camera shop a few weeks later, and they told me it would be cheaper to buy a new one than to repair it. Well, of course it would be nowadays – new ones are made by some poor sap the other side of the world who gets paid in rice or something, whereas fixing it once you've bought it over here means paying for a whole Atlantian. So it goes in the garbage. More and more that's the way it works these days – not so long ago a disposable razor seemed an extravagant idea, now we chuck whole appliances. There's something pretty weird happening, if you think about it – things themselves are losing their intrinsic value, and that's being replaced with a world where the only factor is the relative price of different human beings. Almost like *we* are the things being traded now.

A guy could get a little riled if he thought about it too much. Kind of makes you want to start lining management consultants up against a wall.

But I guess they're safe enough from us, so long as we stay the expensive ones.

The first person I came across after getting down the escalator was Duncan Hayes, the victim. I was striding along the long, white-tiled corridor to the platform where the train stood immobilized when a team of medics came running towards me, trundling a stretcher between them. One of them was leaning down over their patient as they ran, muttering encouragement.

It would have made a good shot.

As they came alongside me, I saw that the patient was conscious but losing blood from somewhere around his abdomen. He looked up at me with bemused, faraway eyes as I began trotting alongside, back towards the escalator.

'Can you tell me what happened?' I asked, proffering my tape recorder.

The medics glared scornfully at me, but their patient was genuinely keen to speak, lifting his pale head from the stretcher and urgently whispering into my recorder.

'Sorry, what was that?' I asked, leaning down to catch the precious words.

'*Sh . . . sh . . .*'

He winced with pain, his hand clutching his abdomen, and groaned.

We reached the bottom of the escalator.

'You're in the way,' one of the medics announced, placing a hand on my chest to bar my advance.

Hayes's hand reached out and grabbed my arm, pulling me down towards him as the medics moved onto the escalator.

'*Shanug?*' he gasped in my ear before letting go of my arm and collapsing back onto the stretcher.

I didn't really have an answer to that.

The platform where the train stood immobilized was hot and an atmosphere of simmering fury charged the crowd as it waited vainly for something to happen. I wrinkled my nose at the overwhelming smell of the melting pot.

The subway staff had closed off the station to new passengers well before the cops arrived, but there were already two or three trainloads of people waiting by then and, despite tannoy announcements asking them to seek alternative modes of transport, a majority seemed to have remained, either out of curiosity or because they refused to give up hope when there was a train actually sitting there right in front of them.

The crowd was just loose enough for me to be able to shuffle my way along the platform towards the space the cops had cleared around the carriage containing The Incident, as the euphemism would have it. As I got closer I started having to flash my press card to get through, until I found myself standing on the perimeter with a party of Kandonese tourists. They, at least, seemed to be enjoying themselves. Forget the sights, forget the shops, this was real-life Atlantian violence and mayhem. I suspected, from their excited chatter, that they would be dining out on it for years to come.

From there, I could see a blood-splashed window. The carriage doors were open and there were plenty of cops inside, but no sign of Bosch. A few passengers still sat in there, most of them clearly in a state of shock. Some were being comforted by medics, others were talking to the police, giving statements. The actual Incident was somewhere out of sight. The Kandonese tourists kept shuffling about, swapping their cameras around so that everyone would have a few shots of themselves smiling against a genuine backdrop of urban insanity. I needed to get nearer the train to see what was going on behind the red glass, so I barged my way through their apertures, smiling apologetically as the flashes continued around me. At last I made it to a spot where I could see through the middle doors of the carriage.

* * *

'Mummy?' I asked cautiously, opening the door a crack.

My mother was very protective of her time in the bathroom. It was something sacred. Some days she would be in there for ages, from time to time adding more hot water to the bath, and I was under strict orders not to disturb her. She needed time on her own, she said, to remember who she was.

She had come back from the studio alone that day, my father having more work to do on the show, and she'd retreated into her sanctum while I had been out back playing in the garden.

Now, however, it was bedtime, and Theresa said it would be OK for me to go up for my goodnight kiss, which was also sacred. I saw my mother's reflection in the bathroom mirror, asleep. I opened the door a little wider and stepped in, looking at her unsurely as I wondered if I was allowed to wake her. She got very tired sometimes, what with the show and all the public appearances – sometimes she was so tired that I could tell she wasn't really hearing me when I told her things, her eyes glazed and distant behind her smile.

It was so quiet in there that I could hear the bath bubbles popping.

'Mummy?' I whispered as I moved closer, not wanting to startle her.

Still she did not wake up, and I stood for a while longer, asking myself if I should go without my kiss that night. I frowned, unsure which of the two rituals took precedence, and finally stepped right up to the bath, thinking that maybe she'd wake up if I was beside her.

But she didn't. She just lay there blissfully, head cocked to one side, her chin forming a dent in the bubbles.

I thought that she'd wake up with a start if I touched her, so instead I put my fingers in the warm water and stirred it gently, hoping the waves would tickle her into

47

consciousness. The water made a lapping noise under the bubbles, which fizzed softly from the disturbance, but my mother carried on sleeping, oblivious.

'*Mummee!*' I whispered more urgently, frustrated by the situation, but to no effect.

I took my hand back out of the water, not knowing what to do. If my father had been home I could have asked him to wake her up, but there was just Theresa and she wasn't allowed into the bathroom under any circumstances apart from when cleaning it.

Eventually, feeling at once sad and very grown up, I decided that I should let her sleep, because she got so tired. I wiped my hand dry on the towel and stood for a little longer, kissing her goodnight in my mind.

I was just turning to go when something caught my eye.

For some reason, the brilliantly white towel now had a red smudge on it.

The diesel engine clatters into life, making the whole bus throb. Through the steel grille I see the driver signal to the guard in the booth by the main doors, who lazily raises his hand in acknowledgement. The doors jerk once, electrical pulleys snapping taut, and begin to open, pulling slowly apart on their rollers.

As the breach widens in the high concrete wall, sunlight pouring through, I can make out silhouettes of men waiting for us on the other side. There are about a dozen of them. The press photographers stand alone, probing with their lenses to see which side of the bus I am sitting on; the others are paired off. The pairs are the TV crews, comprising a journalist and a cameraman, videocam on shoulder. The journalists are standing with their backs to us, already talking to the camera.

'Ready to face the world?' Wolsheim asks beside me, needlessly running a hand over the bald patch on his crown.

I sit up a little straighter in my seat, fixing my gaze dead ahead.

Everything from now on will be on camera.

Showtime.

The sight of death doesn't bother me now. I have seen eleven corpses, mostly through covering crime in Entropolis with my job, and there is really nothing to be bothered about. Sometimes a dead body can even be quite beautiful, frozen peacefully in time, like a dried flower. The person is gone, and while their *story* may be tragic, their body ceases to matter.

That said, my neck tingled as I made out the top half of the man's body – his head resting in a large, dark pool spreading across the carriage floor. His eyes were wide open, staring at the ceiling, but there was clearly no more life behind them than in a waxwork dummy – even from there I could see they were still and dry. What made my skin quiver was that the back of his skull was too flat against the floor to contain a viable amount of brain.

I saw Frank Bosch nearby – he was squatting on his haunches, talking earnestly to a blonde who was kneeling in the pool of blood, softly shaking her head. Her shoulders twitched with tears and although the forward swoop of her hair veiled her face, I felt sure she was pretty.

I can close my eyes and picture the scene now precisely as it was – Bosch, the blonde, the blood, and the body. There was something poetic about the tableau they formed, some kind of majesty – the blonde at once a tragic and hopeful figure. A horrific and beautiful scene, but that is life. Life *is* horrifically beautiful. And this was the perfect shot of it.

But I had just broken my camera.

Even now, with all that has happened since, it guts me

to think of that. Not because of the price I could have got for that shot, but because it so warranted preservation. My whole career has been about disposable information, about reporting events whose interest will only last for a day or two at most, but this was a moment that transcended time, a sight that would fascinate and move people of any age. It was a work of art. There was no need to know who these individuals were or what had happened, they captured everything that is most terrible and everything that is most fabulous about life in one moment.

To add to my agony, there was this Kandonese guy right next to me, snapping away with just about the biggest fucking camera I had ever seen. This thing had a lens so long you could practically do portraits of bacteria. And he was pointing it right at my shot.

I briefly considered offering to buy the camera off him and decided it was pointless. Even if he spoke the language in the first place, the guy was on holiday. He obviously wasn't short of money, and he wanted to take pictures – why would he sell his camera?

But then I had a stroke of luck – he came to the end of his film.

I realized what I had to do before the whirring of his automatic rewind had even finished. His camera bag was on the floor, it had fresh films in it, and I figured him for a guy who would never go anywhere without film in that ridiculous apparatus of his. So he had to take the old film out.

I practically held my breath as he opened the camera and knelt down to replace the roll, leaning across and watching from the corner of my eye to see where he put the used film. He finished the changeover and got hurriedly back up to carry on snapping.

Honesty was not an option. Maybe if he'd been an

Atlantian we could have come to some arrangement, but I couldn't risk refusal. I took a few shots of pure fuzz with my own crippled equipment, pretended to come to the end of the film and knelt down to replace it. A few seconds later, his roll was in my pocket.

I was proud of myself in a funny way. Those pictures had a higher calling than sitting in some photo album in Onawa. They belonged with me. And besides, he was already snapping away again, ordering his companions about in an excited jabber. He'd have so many shots by the time he got home that he probably wouldn't even realize there was a film missing.

But then, just as I was congratulating myself for having salvaged the situation, the blonde did something that would have made an even greater shot. Two cops had arrived with a black body bag, laying it out just beyond the pool of blood before taking up positions at either end of the corpse. Suddenly, still replying to some question of Frank's, she rose partially on her knees to lean across the corpse with an outstretched arm. She hooked one side of her hair behind an ear, affording a brief glimpse of her face before the hair fell forward again, and gently closed its eyes. And then sat back down.

I can't express how powerfully that struck me. Perhaps it wasn't so very extraordinary – just a normal, humane gesture. But it suggested incredible strength that she could act with such soft grace, touching that shattered head without a trace of fear or revulsion. Suddenly the roll of film in my pocket was a poor consolation for all that I was missing – I wanted it all, I wanted to have caught her every movement on film.

I wanted to capture the way she brushed the moisture from her cheeks as the cops half-lifted and half-dragged the body across to the bag, the way she crossed her arms over her chest, shivering as if from a sudden draught. She

51

was the most perfect thing I had ever seen, her every movement enough to take my breath away, and that was without even getting a proper look at her face. Whatever she looked like close up, she had to be beautiful. Her face would fit her nature.

Bosch said something and offered her his hand, but she refused with a small smile, flexing her thighs and rising to her feet with the effortlessly smooth control of a dancer. Suddenly I was very jealous of Frank. I would have loved to be in his place, to be the voice of sanity this woman was hearing amid the horror. And my jealousy of him, this corrupt cop who was supposed to be in my pocket, only grew as he took her by the arm and led her away, infuriatingly heading towards the exit at the far end of the carriage from me, so that I still didn't get to see her face.

I felt at once exhilarated and cheated, like an adolescent who had teetered on the edge of a first kiss, only to miss the moment and see it slip away.

Perhaps I am wrong to blame so much on that camera. Perhaps my hunger would not have been satisfied just by capturing her on film and seeing her take the front page of the *Post* the next day. But I can't help feeling that things would have taken a different course if I had.

I can't help feeling that she would still be alive, and I would not be standing trial for her murder.

ON CAMERA,
SEVEN FIVE A.M.

The bus rolls slowly out, its motor throbbing low, and I can hear the rapid *chkk-chkk-chkk* of cameras through the glass. Even in the bright morning sun, the interior of the vehicle shimmers with the light from their flashes. I do not turn to look at them, I will not acknowledge them.

Television trucks are parked along the street either side of us, their satellite dishes beaming us up into space and back down across the nation, live and direct. The TV journalists are talking smoothly to camera, positioning themselves with the slowly moving bus as a backdrop. I cannot hear what they are saying, but they are very good at what they do – talking fluently in the few seconds they have to get the shot, their one chance to get it right, yet also paying close attention to their positions so that none of them encroach on the others' apertures. It's a whole other profession to the one I followed, and probably not one I would have done well.

I hate TV cameras.

I grew up with them watching over me like hawkish maiden aunts, seemingly there whenever my mother took me anywhere. They are there in my earliest memories, dazzling me with their lights. Sometimes they came right into the house, trailing their cables down corridors and into the living room. They went upstairs to my playroom, looking through my toys, and they came out into the garden to watch me open my birthday presents and play with my friends. They were there at my mother's burial, watching me as I stood before my father. And then they went away at last.

Until now. Now they are back, returning for more.

Only nowadays I understand what it is they want, and they will not get it. I will not look one of them in the eye, will not acknowledge their existence or let them steal a single one of my thoughts or emotions. I smiled for them as a child, as my mother wanted me to, and they took her from me. I kept still as strange, overdressed women leaned down to caress my cheek and say 'Aren't you just *adorable*?' before turning to my mother for confirmation, smiling, 'Isn't he just adorable?' And my mother would smile back beside me on the couch, sitting creaseless and beautiful, and agree that yes indeed, I was adorable and she was so lucky, and a little glint in the corner of her eye as she looked at me told me not to squirm or ask who the person was.

I was well versed in the art of being polite, and, because I wanted to please my mother, I knew better than to ask questions or make demands until she told me it was all right. I just smiled for them and hoped they would go away soon. But at the time I didn't understand why they were there or what they wanted.

I didn't even know what a doorable was.

I didn't understand why my father, when he took me on

his knee, told me we had to say that my mother had fallen down the stairs. But he explained that that was what she would have wanted, and so I never said otherwise to anyone, screaming furiously at Theresa one time when she tried to talk to me about the bath. I did not find her in the bath. I did not break the rule about disturbing her. It was not my fault she died.

She fell down the stairs.

And I thought that at least, if I did that, the cameras would leave my mother alone and I would be left with her things to comfort me – her dressing room, the hairbrush with her hair still in it, the bottle of perfume containing her smell, her rings and brooches. Her memory would be mine to treasure. But, of course, it was not to be, because the cameras had taken her with them and she was still there on TV, playing for them. There were repeats of the show, and special gala tributes at Christmas time, which I was expected to attend, and tragic archive footage of happier days, of me opening my birthday presents. It was like she was theirs, not mine.

Gradually, of course, they lost interest in her. Once the ratings fell and the advertisers moved on to more fertile ground, I suppose. I don't know how long that took – it seemed like my whole childhood, but I daresay it wasn't. People had short attention spans even then.

It was only years later, amazingly late in the day now that I think back on it, that I realized my father had been anything other than a victim like myself, obliged to play along. It didn't even occur to me at the time that *he* was responsible for the tribute shows and repeats, still playing the producer. Not that he didn't try to move on – there were numerous attempts to start new shows, to find a new formula to replace what he had lost, but none of them worked. So I guess he needed my mother to earn a living, even after she was gone.

He was in show business, after all. And the show must go on.

But it's not going to this time. Not with me.

I decided that last night.

Kevin O'Neil

Kevin O'Neil found out that he had a tumour in his head about a year after I left the *Post*. He kept it quiet for as long as he could, but there came a point when secrecy was no longer an option because the treatment had cost him his hair.

They say McQueen offered to let him take a gentler, overseeing role on the paper while he fought the illness, leaving the day-to-day editing to his deputy, Dan Woo. Kevin refused, for obvious reasons. Even if McQueen's offer was sincere, the chances of the arrangement remaining temporary were minimal. Woo wouldn't have been up to the job – he was efficient and an able organizer, but he didn't have big enough balls to make a good *Post* editor. So, sooner or later, McQueen would have decided to fire him and bring somebody else in from the outside. Kevin knew that, even if his boss didn't. And the new person would never have accepted simply to keep Kevin's seat warm for him until he returned.

Instead, once the truth of his tumour was out, Kevin realized that he could turn it to his advantage. So long as the illness didn't affect his work, McQueen couldn't possibly fire him – to do so would have left the *Post* wide open to an unfair dismissal suit, entailing massive damage payments given the cruelty of the situation. Instead, the cancer became Kevin's favourite weapon.

'What the *fuck* is this?' he'd scream at any journalist who handed in weak copy, ripping off his baseball cap to display his bald crown. 'Have you got a *brain tumour*? Are they giving *you* mind-warping chemicals?'

I'd heard that he was working harder than ever, and expecting everyone else to match him hour for hour. He was getting involved in aspects of the paper that he'd previously been happy to delegate, stalking the newsroom like some kind of wounded tiger, twice as aggressive in the light of his weakness. Kevin always was the sharpest editor in town, but the fact that everyone knew the Reaper walked by his side gave him a whole new edge. He had lost about three stone in weight, and his skin was sallow and sagging, but he buzzed with a kind of mad energy that had them all scared shitless. He kept a bucket beside his desk in readiness for the sudden need to vomit, and had been known to use it in mid-editorial meeting. Often, it seems, when he didn't like what he was hearing. He would apologize for the interruption, of course, but it did make it hard for whoever had been talking to finish their point.

At the time I couldn't understand why he kept going. It seemed to me that if you were staring death in the face, your priorities would change. What would your career matter any more? Kevin had children – or access to them, at least – and surely any normal person would want to spend some QT with them while it was still possible?

Not Kevin O'Neil.

It sounds an appalling thing to say, but I suspect he was having the time of his life. The *Post*, after all, was selling better than ever, and that, finally, is what he cared about most. He was a newspaperman through and through.

58

There was a story, which seemed less likely to be apocryphal the better you knew the man, that he found out his wife was suing him for divorce in the diary section of the *Entropolis News*. Imagine how that must have felt. His own family, for fuck's sake. And the competition had the story.

She knew how to hurt him, all right.

It was no problem me getting in to see my old boss that afternoon, especially when I let it be known that I had pictures to sell. The shooting was common knowledge by then, of course – already the lead bulletin on the city's radio stations – but I was pretty damn sure that whoever the *Post* had working on the story wouldn't have been down on the platform, as I had. So I had a front page to sell – eyewitness report, with pictures.

The jackpot.

Kevin received me in his office, coffee brought to my chair as I explained what I had to sell. He was wearing the faded Entropolis Eagles cap that had become a permanent fixture of his wardrobe these days, slowly taking it off and laying it on the desk before him when I named my price. I knew he had the budget for it, but even so he made a great show of being shocked – blowing out his cheeks and running his palms over his hairless head.

'That's reasonable,' I added as he regarded me with his sunken, burning eyes.

He whistled softly and spun his chair around to face the back wall of his office, looking over the framed front pages there.

It was a good moment. There I was – back at the *Post*, facing my old boss, or at least his chair, and knowing that I finally had the upper hand. Sure, I'd sold him plenty of stories since leaving, but nothing of this magnitude – this time I wasn't skirting around the fringes of the news, placing small pieces on the inside pages. This time my old colleagues in the newsroom couldn't give me those superior smiles, so sure that they were at the top of the tree.

Today I owned tomorrow.

There was no doubt he was prepared to pay what I asked – I just had to stand my ground and not let him beat me down on the price. Even as we prepared to negotiate they were rushing my film through the lab, dropping everything else to get those precious pictures developed.

I heard a large sigh emanate from the other side of the big swivel chair and told myself to stay calm. I would need my feet planted square on the ground once he started haggling. Kevin had a way of destabilizing people, able to blow hot and cold at will, switching from laughter to anger in the space between two sentences, and rattling you into accepting whatever words he chose to put into your mouth. I'd seen him do it often enough – he'd beat down a price like a lawyer ripping apart the testimony of a witness, talking them into a corner and twisting their own arguments against them.

I braced myself, determined to remain focused. My story was worth any of those framed front pages he was looking at right now. They weren't the biggest stories the *Post* had covered in Kevin's time – certainly not in terms of their importance to society – but they were the ones that gave him the most pleasure: the confessions of political mistresses, inside stories on celebrity meltdowns, and disaster-victim eyewitness accounts. They were compelling tales, the kind that drew the eye inexorably down like the ribs of a corset. I knew he was reading them right now. He liked to mull over them when he was thinking, letting their headlines trip mantra-like off his tongue: *Sex Shop Shock Rocks Top Cop* and *Mayor 'Bays At Moon' – Official*. Great stuff. Small moments of perfection in a chaotic world, smooth balls of language that calmed him in times of stress.

Doom Looms For Poll-Flop Pols.

Kevin once told me that he considered them to be poetry. Life captured in Technicolor language. He genuinely believed that one day some of these pages would hang in a gallery. I smiled as I reread the one that he once revealed to be his all-time favourite – *Pill-Pop Star Totals Car, Kills Tot* – and told myself that I was ready for whatever he had to throw at me.

He swung the chair back round.

'There's a big fucking problem with your story, Nick,' he announced as his opening gambit.

That was when his pager went off. He raised a hand to stop me replying, snatching it off his belt to check the message.

'*Yes!*' He grinned. 'I knew it!'

He jumped up from his chair with an energy that belied his condition, and bolted round the desk to throw open the office door.

'*Feeding time!*' he yelled out over the newsroom floor.

Through the glass walls of his office, I watched in bewilderment as everyone leaped to attention. There was a flurry of action as people gathered around the computer nearest to them, and Kevin bolted back behind his desk, grabbing the mouse and clicking on an icon that meant nothing to me.

'I knew it, I knew it, I knew it!' he repeated excitedly as a window popped open on the screen, showing a field of long grass. 'It's been five days, right? I *know* these bastards!'

He looked my way, grinning manically – all thought of our negotiation apparently gone. I guess my bemusement must have been written large on my face, because he tilted his head to one side and pointed at the field of grass.

'You don't know about this, Nick?'

I examined the screen before answering. It wasn't a field, I now realized, but some kind of savannah. The picture jumped to show the same place from a different angle, a high shot from a camera that was manifestly up a tree. I saw movement in the grass.

'You've got me.' I shrugged.

'Shit, Nick!' He frowned. 'You're out of touch. You haven't heard of *freshkill.com*?'

I hate it when people do that to you. Like your whole life is just a waste of time if you're not up on the latest place, fad, or revival. Like you're an idiot if you happen to still think whatever they thought a month back about some corny old singer whose songs have since been declared *cool* corn. So maybe you get into him too, but by then they say he's passé because too many people have jumped on the bandwagon. Or maybe you liked him all along, and then you suddenly find they've appropriated him for themselves and claim to have a finer understanding of his appeal than you do.

The only thing that hasn't changed is the guy's songs.

You know, they say there's no accounting for taste, but I say there's a whole damned industry of taste accountancy out there – taste accountants forever rejigging the sums so that somehow you're never in credit.

So, no, I had not yet heard of *freshkill.com* – it's hard to imagine a world without it nowadays, I know, but somehow we did manage, didn't we?

The screen jumped again to show a shot of some kind of watering hole. It was morning, and there were gazelle and antelope drinking at the water's edge.

'Live,' Kevin announced in an awed hush. 'Direct from the savannah. Solar-powered webcams cover the watering hole from every angle. There's a guy somewhere in Entropolis who juggles the shots. It's fucking addictive.'

'You must have to wait a while before anything happens,' I snorted.

'The fuck you do!' he retorted, flicking me an urgent, sincere regard before returning avidly to the screen. 'There's *always* something happening! Always some little critter snooping about the place. They take it in turns – different animals at different times of day. Dawn and dusk are the busiest, but you can tune in any time of the day or night and be sure that something's going down. Some people prefer the infrared cams because they think it adds to the tension. Personally, I like to look at the pretty animals, you know?'

He turned to me with a lurid *hyuck* of a chuckle, adding, 'And watch them get eaten!'

I leaned in closer as I made out the low profile of a she-lion creeping softly through the long grass, almost invisible as her golden hide blended in with the high seed stalks. I had to admit that it became instantly compulsive when one knew it was live.

Kevin chuckled again and held up his pager, lowering his voice to a whisper as if not to alert the lion on our screen.

'The beauty of it is that if you subscribe to *Pagekill*, you never have to miss a hunt! They page you whenever blood is in the air. That's how they make their money. Great idea.' He slapped the desk for emphasis. 'Fucking *great* idea!'

The guy who was channelling the camera angles knew his job. I couldn't tell how many cams he had to choose from, but he was obviously familiar with the terrain and the location of each and every lens – he was juggling them in a way that gave the viewing a narrative drive, switching from shots of the lions closing slowly in to shots of antelope and gazelle at the water's edge, calmly drinking.

'Stupid fuckers!' Kevin cursed them, 'I *knew* this was

63

going to happen! It's been five days since the pride last killed – they were bound to be on the hunt this morning!'

His hand reached out and touched my arm as we were treated to a perfect high shot of a lioness as she skirted a tree, and he knowingly confided, 'That's Mama. She's just had her litter. Four of the *cutest* little fluffballs that I ever—'

He cut himself short as Mama's head suddenly whipped towards the camera. The shot changed to show the animals by the pool looking round in panic. We returned to the tree shot, but Mama was gone.

'*Fuck!*' Kevin shouted, rising from his chair. 'Must have been something up the tree!'

There was a brief flurry of changing angles as the operator searched for the lions, and I found myself rising from my own chair.

'*There! There!*' I yelped as a wide-angle shot towards the water showed three of them bounding through the grass as the antelope broke and scattered ahead.

'Don't . . . lose . . . them . . .' Kevin muttered tensely, leaning in closer to the screen. The picture stayed on the same shot until the lions dived to the right, choosing their target, and immediately switched to a closer camera, showing a group of animals pelting through the grass, the lions in hot pursuit.

'Don't . . . lose . . . them . . .' he repeated, gripping the edge of his desk.

The lions flew underneath in a broad arrow formation and the shot changed to face the other way. The lead female was just a couple of strides behind the slowest antelope.

'*Break, damn it! Break!*' Kevin screamed, slamming his palm on the desk.

The antelope dived right, but the outside lion had

64

already anticipated the move and was cutting across to intercept.

'No-no-NO!' I found myself hollering as their paths closed inexorably. The antelope tried a second break, turning sharply away, but the manoeuvre cost it a fraction of a second, enough to bring the lead female just an arm's reach from her rear. The cat's legs were a blur of muscle in the grass, and then suddenly she was flying, rising up through the air, her front paws stretched to catch the antelope's behind.

She connected. The antelope was knocked over, rolled and scrambled to its feet, but too late – the third lion caught up with a straight, open-jawed dive for its neck.

'YES!' Kevin cried. The entire floor of the newsroom exploded into cheers, arms punching up as the poor victim disappeared beneath a billowing carpet of golden fur, all three lions pouncing upon it at once.

A single quivering hoof could be seen underneath the deadly mound of muscle . . . it briefly spasmed, and stilled.

I dropped back into my chair in shock and exhaustion, gazing blankly at the screen as the operator finished the tale with a broad shot of the rest of the herd scattering over the savannah. I was numb with adrenalin.

'Fuck that guy's good!' Kevin announced as he sat back down in his broad editor's chair.

He grinned at me, his gaze focusing on my hands. I looked down and saw they were trembling.

'Gets you, doesn't it?' he chuckled, his eyes glistening bright with excitement as he gestured to the silently writhing pile of golden fur. 'That's *now*, Nick! Can you believe that? The blood is still hot!'

Through the glass walls I could see the groups breaking up around the computers, flushed-faced journalists slapping each other's palms as they returned to their tasks.

'I got everyone hooked up to it,' Kevin commented, acknowledging their grins with a wave. 'It's good for team spirit. Morale. All that management shit . . .'

He removed his cap and wiped his forehead with his sleeve, breathing out with a smiling whoop of excitement. I was still too stunned to respond, my mind several thousand miles away as I watched the antelope being torn apart.

'So, anyway . . .' Kevin continued, closing the *freshkill* window with a click of his mouse, 'your story's a piece of shit, Nick.'

Under the circumstances, it took me a moment to realize what he was talking about. My concentration was so completely lost that I had not only forgotten all my arguments for justifying the price I had named, I had even forgotten that was why I was there in the first place. Kevin could not have chosen a better moment to strike.

'What?' I frowned. 'What do you . . . ? No, it's not.'

There was a look that Kevin O'Neil got in moments of extreme editorial distress, not unlike a man bracing himself to push out an oversized turd. It was an expression that struck instant fear into the minds of those who worked for him – his eyes and mouth scrunched in towards his nose, his whole face clenching into a fist – signifying as it did that he was about to explode. He stared at me through slit eyelids, and then threw himself back in his chair, exclaiming, 'What are you on, Nick? What . . . what . . . *what drug are you taking?*'

'I don't understand,' I answered, totally off-balanced.

'What *happened* to you? You were a pretty good reporter before you got delusions of grandeur.' He leaned forward. 'I only ask because I'm on some pretty fucking heavy medication myself, and I'd hate for the same thing to happen to me.'

I didn't get what he could be talking about. Words

totally failed to connect in my mouth and I just sat there, stammering incoherently like a man scrabbling up a sand-bank, sliding backwards faster than he climbed. Kevin shook his head in despair, rising from the desk to throw open the office door.

'*Macauley!* Kurt!' he shouted. 'Come in here!'

The men, both erstwhile colleagues of mine, dropped what they were doing and walked over at a pace that was just a gust of wind short of trotting. They nodded hello as they saw me.

'Our former reporter here wishes to sell us a story,' Kevin explained, reseating himself. 'He says that there was a shooting on the subway this afternoon over a woman – a damsel in distress caught between competing lovers. Apparently, one lover killed the other out of jealousy and then, remorse taking hold, he shot himself.'

Macauley Connor and Kurt Paz looked from him to me and back again in bewilderment.

'Now, why don't you have this story?' he demanded, slapping the table.

There was a pause as they turned to each other in confusion.

'Because it's bullshit!' Connor answered finally. 'It's just . . . just . . . *bollocks*!'

Connor was slurring slightly. He'd always been a drinker, but I'd heard it had been getting worse lately. Apparently his marriage was breaking up.

'It didn't happen like that, Kevin!' Paz added, obviously unsure whose story the editor believed. 'The argument was over something completely different, for a start. This Hayes guy was haranguing the passengers and begging for money, and then this Randall Walcott guy shot him when he threatened to pull the emergency cord if they didn't cough up. Then Walcott was going to start emptying his clip into the rest of them, but the *woman* wrestled the gun

67

off him and shot him at point-blank range. *That's* what happened!'

'Uh-huh? And how do you know this?'

'We've got *four* eyewitnesses!' Connor announced, regarding me disdainfully. 'They all told the same story, give or take a little. The cops aren't revealing her identity yet, but there's no fucking way we are wrong about it!'

I suddenly began to worry, with a sick feeling in my stomach, that I had talked to the wrong guy. I'd got my story from one of the cops there – it had been clear to me at the time that he was none too bright, but I'd figured he was at least a reliable source.

'You're so full of shit, Nick!' Connor accused me, sneering.

Not so long before, Connor would have treated me with respect. He was always ambitious, but he knew I was at least his equal. Now that he was the star of the newsroom, though, his arrogance was all too clear. I have to say that I was extremely pleased when, a few months after this, he got fired for physically attacking a female Senator he was interviewing. I hear he's working for the *Public Investigator* now, which is about as low as a journalist can fall, frankly.

Not counting those of us in prison, of course.

Kevin looked at them blankly, nodding softly.

'Do you know . . . I think you're right,' he announced at last.

He swivelled his seat to face me and leaned forward across the desk, an eyebrow raised.

'I think my boys are right, Nick,' he whispered, his voice rising with irritation as he continued. 'I think you've got the fucking story wrong. I think you're trying to sell me a bullshit story that would turn me into the laughing stock of the whole fucking city if I printed it. What do *you* think?'

I was silent, horribly aware of the blood beginning to flush my cheeks. Connor and Paz broke into smiles, knowing their boss was moving in for the kill and relishing the fact that they were not the targets this time. I saw them glance at one another, both looking forward to the mauling they were about to witness.

'How much is he asking for the story, Kev?' Connor asked from behind his boss, grinning at me as he drew a finger across his neck and pointed my way.

Kevin named my price and the two of them widened their eyes in amazement before bursting into laughter.

'OK . . .' I seethed. 'So I'll take my photos to the *News*, then. I assume you guys got photos, right?'

'Photos of *what*, Nick?' Connor asked, still laughing. 'Presuming you took the lens cap off, of course . . .'

'Randall Walcott lying in a pool of his own blood with a certain beautiful blonde kneeling beside him,' I announced coolly.

The laughter stopped.

I think Kevin himself had forgotten that side of the bargain – he tipped his seat back and looked at the ceiling, suddenly breaking off the attack. A thrill of victory flowed through my veins, erasing the humiliation of their mockery. Thank god for the photos, I thought, thank god for Kandonese tourists with huge fucking cameras and a strange idea of holiday snaps.

'How the hell did you get that?' Connor demanded. 'They locked down the entire station right after the shooting happened.'

I simply shrugged. Under the circumstances it was infinitely more pleasurable to let them stew, keeping my secrets to myself. It was a moral victory, even if I had got the details of the story wrong – the fact was that I had been there, on the scene, while they had followed it all from a distance.

'I assume you still want to buy them?' I asked Kevin.

Kevin narrowed his gaze, picking up his phone and dialling down to the lab.

'O'Neil here,' he announced curtly. 'Where's that film I sent down?'

He flicked a glance at me as the voice on the other end quacked softly.

'Uh-huh,' he grunted. 'So why am I still waiting to see them?'

The atmosphere in his office was uncomfortable as we waited for the pictures to arrive. Connor and Paz were unhappy with the thought that I had scooped them on their own story, of course, especially since I had screwed up so badly on the facts. I knew how they felt – it's infuriating, when you put in long hours for a pretty moderate salary, to see some guy waltz in and pocket a big cheque for a few minutes' work. Kevin kept the conversation going, talking about the hunt on *freshkill.com* and trying to get the three of us to act like old buddies. I was happy to play along, but I knew that he was only being sweet until he began to play hardball over the price again.

The prints arrived at last, a nervous-looking technician advancing only so far into the office as was necessary for him to hand them over to Kevin, leaning at full stretch before scooting back out. Kevin shuffled through the pictures, frowning with concentration.

'How come you took prints instead of trannies, Nick?' he muttered, not looking up from his analysis of the shots.

'I . . . yeah, I was caught a little unprepared,' I admitted, realizing that I hadn't even thought to check what kind of film it was that I'd stolen.

'These are pretty interesting,' he admitted, nodding softly. 'Unusual shots.'

'Well, you know I'm not a photographer, Kevin,' I bluffed. 'But I do my best.'

Kevin came to the end of the pile, and stared hard at me. I braced myself for the negotiation.

'One question,' he sighed, bending the pictures between his fingers like a deck of cards.

One by one he released them, sending each photo flicking onto the desk for us all to see. A silent scream began to build inside me as I stared in horror at the images spinning across the tabletop.

There was the carriage all right, and Walcott's body, and the bowed head of the nameless blonde, just as I had promised. But as they rained down, and the true nature of the film was revealed, my entire professional life seemed to collapse before me like a house of cards.

'Do tell me, Nick . . .' Kevin asked in a strange, sweet voice, 'why did you choose to place a smiling Oriental in the foreground of every fucking shot?'

ENTROPOLIS BELTWAY, SEVEN TWENTY A.M.

I hear the helicopter swing by above us yet again and I know for sure now that it's a TV chopper, relaying our progress live to the nation. All they'll be getting is footage of us stuck in this traffic jam, which pleases me immensely – despite my vow to ignore everything said about me in the media, I'd actually quite like to hear what the bastards are finding to say right now.

'Thanks, Ayesha. We're going to leave the studio now to rejoin Mike Archer live in the helicopter. Mike, what can you see from your end?'

'Well, Steve, I can see . . . the bus . . . below us right now. From here it looks so ordinary, so much like any other bus, and then you remember that this is not just a large vehicle stuck in traffic, but an intense drama wheeling its way towards the final act. The Beltway seems a sombre place this morning, the cars moving along at a funereal pace . . . maybe averaging about ten miles an hour . . . and surely that must mirror Carraway's own feelings right now – the sensation of being caged . . . trapped on a bus that will be stopping off at Judgement Day. Who knows what thoughts are going through his

mind at the moment, what hopes briefly spark alight, just as the circulation sometimes loosens – who knows why? – only to jam itself up all over again. A while ago it seemed like things were starting to move, and the driver – who is armed – actually changed lanes, but now we're looking at some very dense, serious traffic below us. The bus . . . as I look down on it now . . . is profoundly stationary.'

'I was going to say it looked like Carraway had switched out a lane. I don't know if that was such a good idea, do you, Mike? From here it seems as though there's more movement on the *inside* lane . . .'

'Yes, I can confirm that, Steve – the inside lane does have movement just now. However, we took a sweep up ahead a minute ago and I think our viewers will be seeing some acceleration in Carraway's lane pretty soon as well. OK, we're directly over them now and you can see that the bus is stuck behind a . . . green saloon car . . . it might be a Sumera, I think.'

'Well, Ayesha and me were just discussing that, Mike – we reckon it's a Meridian.'

'Yes, that's certainly possible, Steve . . . it could be a Meridian. Both are, after all, family saloon cars. Both no doubt . . . available in green. We'll try to swing closer and get a visual confirmation on—'

'Welcome back. I have to apologize for interrupting Mike Archer reporting live from the helicopter there, but some fresh information has just come in. It appears that Carraway had a *muffin* before leaving prison this morning – can you give us more detail on that, Ayesha?'

'Yes, Steve. I should mention that this is exclusive to *Justice Live* – a source *inside* the prison has informed us that Carraway *did* eat a *blueberry* muffin a little over an hour ago.'

'Well, perhaps we should turn to our studio guests here.

Judge Warner, what do you think the muffin reveals about Carraway's state of mind this morning?'

How could they have found out about the muffin? My bet would be the guard with the killer stare – he could probably get a few hundred bucks for muffin information this morning. It's possible – after all, everything else I have said or done these last months has found its way into the media. Hell, even Wolsheim has been at it – for his own tactical reasons, of course.

I understand what he's doing, the double game he's been playing. All along he has been vociferous in his condemnation of my treatment in the media, of the way I've been portrayed as the villain long before my day in court, and yet he's stopped short of demanding the trial be held elsewhere. He's clever. *He* has kept my story in the news whenever it seemed to be fading for lack of new developments, giving press conferences damning the press, issuing libel writs and publicly accusing the state prosecution of leaking information to the media. He's played his hand subtly and courageously, skirting the limits of being in danger of prosecution himself, and all the time slowly turning my apparent disadvantage into a weapon, getting ready to play on people's innate sympathy for an underdog.

I understand all of that, but I can't play his game. I don't want to give the media anything, not one damn thing, even if it is only a decoy. That's all you can do, because fighting them is impossible – trying to battle against the way you are portrayed in the media is like waging war on shadows. You cannot make your blows connect because they control the way the light falls.

I suppose they became my enemy that day at the *Post*, the day Kevin O'Neil humiliated me in front of my former colleagues. I suppose my life changed from the moment I found myself standing on the street outside the Brady

Tower, my skin burning and the din of the avenue deafened by the rush of thoughts in my head. Even now, almost two years later, the memory of it makes me blush. I can still see the disdain in their eyes, still recall with perfect clarity the horror as they called others into Kevin's office to check out my photographs. I can return, any time I want, to that moment and still be as utterly helpless to halt my humiliation as the pictures were handed around a hooting pack of journalists, their hilarity growing as each new take on the scene down in the subway featured yet another smiling Kandonese tourist in its foreground.

I knew they were no doubt *still* laughing as I stood there on the sidewalk, passing the photos around the newsroom and putting ever more outrageous twists on my version of the story.

As if they didn't make mistakes. As if every newspaper, every day of the week, is not riddled with inaccuracies. It is inevitable – the faster we communicate, the more verbiage we produce, the more we get the facts wrong. And then the mistakes become accepted truth, get used in other people's arguments, bandied around dinner tables and bars until you can no longer correct them. Huge swathes of what we think we know are just plain wrong.

But they weren't honest enough to admit that. They wanted to humiliate me because I had dared to think I could get by without them, and so they behaved like my garbled version of the facts was something unheard of rather than an everyday occurrence. But above all it was those photos . . .

What could I have told them? That I stole the film from a tourist's camera bag? That I hadn't seen precisely how he was framing his shots? They would only have laughed louder.

If I ever *did* want to murder somebody, that was the

moment. And everything else that happened, the un-stoppable determination with which I pursued the story afterwards, even to my own destruction, was caused by that laughter.

And it is still echoing now. The sound of the chopper overhead is the sound of laughter.

I could not sleep that night. You know how it is, when you put out the light and your head hits the pillow, but your thoughts are still clanging about your head like a bottling plant? I wanted so badly to make those fuckers pay for laughing at me. My anger swelled in the darkness of the bedroom, mushrooming into a fury that was blind and so bereft of any sense of proportion. I wanted to punish them far beyond the scale of their crime. I scripted whole conversations we would have as I exacted some terrible vengeance, visions of myself towering over them like a wrathful god, making them beg for mercy.

I think that's only human. We've all felt that way before – in the schoolyard, at least. But there's a difference between feeling it in the schoolyard and being made to feel it as a grown man. When you're a kid, it hurts just as much, but you can tell yourself that one day you will be a grown-up and you will show them all. You can't do that when you're an adult. There's no more way to grow. You are you by then, and nobody should laugh at that. These were my peers, the people who were supposed to respect me, the ones I wanted to be better than. This was the way I had chosen to make my little mark on the world. It wouldn't have mattered what it was about or what profession we were in – there are murderous passions in cheerleading squads, in flower shows, in bake-offs . . .

Of course I lacked a sense of perspective, an ability to laugh at myself. If I'm honest with myself, I still do. I'm not so stupid that I can't see that. But only losers have a sense of perspective, and I still haven't lost, not yet.

It's all about pride. That's our real weakness. The problem with this world is not so much that humans are hateful, or greedy, or violent . . . everything comes down to pride in the end. That's the real killer. Nine out of ten guns get fired because of pride. Pride is our number one health problem, behind most of the ulcers, high tension, heart attacks, cancers, and mental implosions. Pride is responsible for our divorce statistics, pride is the wife-beater's reason and, so shoot me down, the beaten wife's reason for staying.

It is the last thing that remains, the bitter brew in the bottom of the coffee pot.

That's why I had to find out who the woman in the subway carriage had been. It was, I realized after finally getting out of bed, the only way to get my revenge. I had to find that woman before they did, get an exclusive on her, and then make them beg me for a little piece of the action. Kevin O'Neil himself would eat shit to get back on my sweet side. Sure, they would track her down eventually even if the cops were keeping her name confidential, but I didn't need to do it the hard way.

I had Frank Bosch. And Frank knew.

FRESHKILL

There is a social hierarchy in death just as there is in life. The four lead items on the news the night of the subway shooting all concerned deaths, for instance, but the late Randall Walcott – despite being a maniac with a gun, which normally would have assured him top billing – had to be contented with fourth place.

I remember the ordering precisely, because it was so indicative of the way news is handled. The top spot was still, for the second night running, being held onto by the collapse of an apartment block in New Toulouse. That was an obvious choice because the death toll was not only high, but not yet finally established. The cautious estimates were now putting it at around twenty, but they had managed to find someone who was prepared to go as high as sixty. His argument was that many of the apartments had been let out to illegal immigrants, and who the hell knew how many relatives had snuck over the border? So in a way there was a serious political angle here, too.

So the story had a body-count issue, politics, plus the extraordinary manner in which the explosion had come about to assure it of top billing. The night before, the suggestion had been that it was a gas leak – a theory that had taken some knocking by the following morning once the print journalists established that the building wasn't actually *connected* to the city gas system.

But then someone had come forward with a radical new suggestion.

It was gas, they said.

The hypothesis – still unproven, but looking more probable all the time – was that the building had a serious design fault in the way it was hooked into the sewage system. 'Gaseous natural wastage emissions', as the experts were choosing to describe them, had been building up in a pocket below it for years now. There was no way of knowing what sparked it off – a rat chewing an electric cable, maybe, or two particularly hard turds striking one another – but the resultant explosion had ripped straight up through the building's core drainage column, collapsing it from the inside.

Probably the only warning anyone had had of something unusual was when their toilet detonated.

The cherry on the cake was that there were other blocks that had been built to the exact same specifications, all over the country. So we waited agog to hear if we too were in danger: who and how many of us were sitting on lethal fart-bombs even as we watched the TV?

Second came the death of a visitor to one of the nation's main theme parks, ejected from his seat on the showcase Big Bang rollercoaster after apparently dislocating both his shoulders coming out of the triple corkscrew.

Clearly this was a major public interest story – a death in an amusement park.

It could have been any of us.

Finally, the Entropolis subway story had been pipped to fourth place by the passing away from natural causes, at forty-five years of age, of Jojo, familiar to generations of children as Booba in the *Jungle Jess* films. True, he was just a chimpanzee, but he was a *famous* chimp. That counts for more than a lunatic on a train. Plus it was a perfect story for TV – a chance to run a montage of classic Booba moments from the movies and to dig out some ageing film stars to reminisce about the little fella. Only then did we get the maniac story.

Poor Randall Walcott, humiliated even in the final, catastrophic meltdown of his life. Beaten by a monkey. One which, I should add, was apparently a vicious little shit which bit everyone but his trainer. They didn't say that on the news, because it would have spoiled the poignancy of the story – Booba's death as a reflection of our own lost innocence, yadda-yadda – but the truth is this was one dislikeable simian prima donna. Had to have fresh-picked bananas in his trailer every day – still on the bunch, flown in direct from the tropics, or he wouldn't touch them. Huge talent, of course, but hell to work with. Apparently all the other animals hated his guts.

But I knew the real story was the woman on the train. She was what the papers would go with in the morning because they, unlike the TV journalists, didn't need pictures.

In a way it was even better that nobody knew who she was because it added mystery to the cocktail of violence and courage that made her such a perfect heroine. Obviously she was going to get bigger – journalists can't let a story like her alone just because the person in question is publicity-shy. It goes against our nature. The first thing Kevin O'Neil would bring up at tomorrow morning's editorial meeting was how to follow up on the story, how to get an exclusive on that woman. Only I would already have cut them off at the pass. The frustrating thing was that I had to wait until morning to get hold of Bosch. Despite the closeness of our relationship, he'd never deigned to give me his home number and, like all Gossom cops, he was ex-directory.

I was too tense to sleep and, after spending an hour or so making my way through the TV channels before I decided that there was nothing I could decently watch without being paid, I had the idea of logging onto *freshkill.com*.

It was early evening at the watering hole and the main action was provided by a herd of elephants bathing themselves. That calmed me down almost immediately, but not in a way that helped me sleep because I got far too engrossed in watching them. I told myself that I'd just watch until they finished their ablutions, but they weren't in any hurry and by the time they eventually started mooching lazily out of the water, the attention had switched to a pair of gazelle or impala – those deer-like creatures with long, crescent horns, at any rate – who were working themselves up to a fight. They must have spent at least half an hour aggressively strutting and circling around each other before any contact was made. I figured the fight was over a woman – an entire harem of women, no doubt – and pegged the paler of the two as the challenger. There was something cheeky about him, a certain flashiness that the darker one didn't seem to find necessary. He just stood his ground, taking the odd run at his opponent whenever he got a little too cocky.

By now my eyelids were getting heavy – it must have been around half three in the morning – but I had to stick with the creatures until they got down to the rough stuff. All the preliminaries were getting frustrating – I was half-convinced that the pale one was going to bottle out, anyway – but the fact that I knew it was live, that this was happening right now, far across the world, made it almost impossible to switch off until there was a natural break in the story.

So with over sixty TV channels at my disposal – *sixty* channels of comedy, drama and action – the only thing that actually held my attention was a web site on my computer featuring a bunch of animals doing mundane animal shit. So much for human creativity.

When they did at last fight it was very short-lived. I didn't catch what changed the tone of the stand-off, but suddenly they charged, locking horns and rising up on their hind legs to lash out at each other with their front hoofs. There was a violent thrash of legs, lasting maybe twenty seconds, and then the pale challenger broke off, trotting away to a safe distance.

That was it.

You'd think it would have been an anticlimax after all the foreplay, but not at all. It was economical, yet cathartic – the issue had been resolved to their satisfaction and mine, and I logged off before I found myself getting dragged into the next story. An hour and a half had passed since I opened the site – time enough for a whole movie – and although nothing much had happened, I have to say that I was more satisfied than I generally am walking out of the cinema.

They were definitely onto something, these guys.

I only got about three hours' sleep before I was up again, my impatience to speak to Bosch driving me out of bed even though I knew he wouldn't reach the precinct until around nine. I killed the time by drinking too much coffee. I bought all the papers and spread them out on the living-room floor. Just as I had thought, the Entropolis papers had all led with Randall Walcott. They were about evenly split between those who stuck to the straight Terror Train story and those who focused on the Unknown Heroine angle. That was good – a sign that the story was starting to move exactly in the direction I

82

had predicted. The *Post* got around the picture problem on its front page by featuring the lithe silhouette of a woman with a huge white question mark on her body. It wasn't exactly journalism, but it caught your attention better than the others. Tumour or no tumour, Kevin was still the best in the business.

I couldn't have hoped for more – having built the woman up as some kind of mystery *femme fatale*. Kevin would be desperate to track her down for real. And everyone else would be following his lead. I counted the minutes until I could phone my contact.

'Thanks for yesterday, Frank,' I opened cheerfully when he finally picked up.

There was a pause, and then he sighed, 'Cunt. What a nice surprise first thing in the morning.'

'So why don't you tell me about her?'

'You'd be talking about the gorgeous mystery blonde?' The detective laughed. His tone made it clear that he was finding this morning's fevered interest in his case fairly hilarious.

'Naturally,' I answered, trying to sound relaxed.

'Can't do it, Cunt.' He yawned. 'She's off limits.'

'Come on, Frank,' I insisted. 'Tell me *something*! Is she a looker? She looked like a looker from what I saw.'

Frank hummed to himself, thinking it over. I guess that he'd been too involved in the incident as a crime to think about her in those terms until that moment.

'Sure,' he replied. 'Now you mention it. Didn't you see her? I got you in there, for fuck's sake.'

'Too much hair,' I admitted. 'But she's a babe, right?'

He laughed again. He was in a good mood today, no doubt about it. Revelling in his position like a high-school stud acting cool about his latest conquest.

'Not bimbo-babe,' he corrected me. 'Not model material, but sexy, I guess. She's . . . interesting. You

know I can't tell you more – she's asked to remain anonymous.'

'So?' I insisted. 'Give me a description, at least.'

Frank hummed again, picturing her in his mind.

'Caucasian female, aged between twenty and twenty-
five years old, green-blue eyes—'

'No, *describe her*!' I cut in. 'Don't give me a fucking
autopsy – I want to know what you thought of her!'

The detective cackled, thoroughly enjoying himself. For
once he was at liberty to be as unhelpful as he wished
in the interest of protecting the subject's right to
anonymity, and I reckon he was milking it for all it was
worth.

'Sorry. Force of habit,' he apologized insincerely.

He hummed again, thinking it over.

'She's the kind of girl you wouldn't dare try a line on,'
he announced eventually. 'The kind who wouldn't have
time for a little shit like you, anyway. Looks a mite bad-
tempered, maybe even arrogant, but she's not really . . .
not at all. I liked her. Not my type, but I did like her.'

'What do you mean she's not your type?' I asked, frustrated by the vagueness of his answers.

'She's too . . .' he mused, searching for words. 'Don't
reckon I could handle her, to be honest.'

He paused for reflection before adding, 'But probably a
great lay.'

I knew he was teasing me, but it worked.

'Single?' I asked, not out of personal interest but in view
of her increased story value.

'Certainly not married, but beyond that I didn't ask,'
the detective answered. 'At a guess, I'd probably say
so. She didn't phone anyone. I can't quite picture the
kind of guy she'd be with, anyway. Probably the wrong
kind. Maybe she *would* go for you, now I come to think
of it.'

'Who is she?' I demanded bluntly, my patience giving way.

'You know I can't tell you that. I have to respect her wish for privacy.'

'Come on, Frank,' I pushed, a little too hard and a little too soon. 'People will find out. It's just a matter of time. She can't hide in the city – somebody is going to tip the media off.'

'Maybe, but not me,' he answered, his tone hardening. 'I give you leads, but this is different. It's a question of right and wrong.'

'Don't talk to me about right and wrong, Frank,' I murmured softly. 'It's a little inappropriate coming from you, isn't it?'

That was it.

There was an invisible line in our relationship that I had just barged across: we never alluded to what I had on him, never mentioned Jordan Baker or the video. That was like blasphemy. So long as we never talked about it, he got to preserve his dignity and I didn't have to face the fact that I was blackmailing him.

There was a long silence down the line.

'Be very careful,' he whispered finally.

Something in his tone was curious. It was bristling, the aggression clearly there, and yet at the same time he almost sounded concerned on my account, warning me not to wreck everything. It was a delicate thing, our relationship – founded on coercion, but dependent on trust – and Frank was trying to stop me making the small, impetuous gesture that was all it would take to break it.

Unfortunately, that was a low priority for me at that moment. I was obsessed and deaf to advice from anyone, most of all Detective Frank Bosch.

'I just want her name.'

I heard a soft, almost inaudible curse. Our voices

seemed to be softening the more our stances hardened.

'I should stop this right here, Nick. For both our sakes,' he warned me unhappily. 'You're asking too much. Think about it.'

I had thought about it. I'd thought about it all night, insomuch as any decision taken in the maelstrom of my feelings could be said to have been thought about. My determination was such that I didn't even notice at the time that he'd just done me the courtesy of using my name.

'I'm not really asking,' I informed him.

'*Why the fuck are you doing this?*' he burst out angrily. 'She doesn't *want* publicity and she has rights! You're way out of line! This is *not* the deal!'

'There *is* no deal! The only deal is that I have the video of you and your partner extorting money.'

'I don't believe you'd do it. Not over this.'

'Don't be so sure.'

He must have heard the determination in my voice because he went silent again, weighing up his options. To be honest, I didn't know where I was going with this – in the version of events that I had pictured for myself last night, Frank had not put up this kind of resistance. Sure, I knew I would be pushing the boundaries of our relationship, but I hadn't expected to go to the wire like this.

'For fuck's sake,' he persisted. 'Why is it so *important* who she is? She's just a girl. Why are you making such a big deal out of finding her?'

'Why are *you* making such a big deal out of hiding her?'

'I like her. She deserves to be treated with respect – it's not like it's in the public *interest* she be named, is it? Fuck, she's not even a big story!'

'I think she's a very big story.'

'Big enough that you'd fuck everything up for it?'

86

'Whatever it takes,' I announced flatly. 'Please . . . *don't* imagine I'm bluffing.'

I can see now that I gave too much away. Frank could hear my desperation and, even though I was supposed to be calling the shots, he started to realize that he had a little room to manoeuvre. His distaste for betraying her anonymity seemed entirely genuine, but if I wasn't giving him a choice then it made sense for him to cut the best deal he could. It called for a cool head and an ability to play brinkmanship, but the advantage he had was that I quite clearly did *not* have a cool head.

'OK . . . you're not bluffing,' he answered slowly. 'But this is not our agreement. You're putting me over the line, so you have to make concessions.'

'Such as?'

'You want her name. I want the tape.'

An alarm bell went off in my head, all right, but I was too pumped up to play the game by the rules.

'Forget it!' I scoffed.

'Glad to,' he sighed coolly.

And he put the phone down.

'What the fuck are you doing?' I snapped when I got back through to him about thirty seconds later.

'You're asking *me*?' he cut back. 'You come to me, expecting something we never agreed on, but not offering anything in return. That's not business. Fuck you – go ahead and publish. There's no *margin* in me giving in to you on this because if you do it once you'll do it another time. And another. I can't live with that. So publish. I'm not going to let you fuck with me.'

And he put the phone down again.

I admire the bastard's balls, thinking back. He took it all the way. Maybe he sensed that I was desperate enough to give him what he wanted, but he couldn't have *known* that.

As it was, I phoned back.

We agreed to meet at the usual place. I suggested we do so in an hour's time, but he insisted on my being there in thirty minutes. Any later, he said, and he'd be gone. He didn't explain, but I know why.

He didn't want to leave me time to make a copy of the video.

ENTROPOLIS BELTWAY,
SEVEN THIRTY A.M.

'Relax, Nick.'

My head snaps round to see Wolsheim smiling beside me. I don't know how long he has been watching me while I have been gazing at the jam of cars. My thoughts were blessedly far away, observing the harried executives alone in their company vehicles, jabbering on the phone, picking their noses, drumming the steering wheel in frustration. I had a wonderful impression of calm, but now I notice that I've been jiggling my leg manically.

'Just put your trust in Papa Meyer, OK?' he suggests softly. 'You don't have to do anything today but enter your plea and let me handle the rest. You sit calmly. I don't want you jiggling your knee like that while I'm talking, Nick – makes you look guilty as hell.'

'I'm sorry.'

'Don't apologize – of *course* you're nervous. But you need to focus on the final equation here. The bottom line is that you are innocent, and the burden is on them to prove the opposite. Which they can't. They can place you at the scene, that's all, and it's not enough – even if you were breaking the law by being there, that does not make you a murderer. There is no weapon. There is no clear evidence of foul play. Her death was an accident, pure and simple. It's a fucking joke, Nick, you know that! The entire case rests on circumstance and the presumption of a motive. Believe me – it takes a hell of a lot more than that to make Meyer Wolsheim sweat!'

I nod. He's right, of course. Wolsheim stares at me, frowning.

'The leg, Nick,' he says.

I look down. It's started again, the nervous jig. I force it to stop and rub my hand along the thigh to massage out the tension, laughing, 'Sorry – mind of its own, apparently!'

'That's OK. Just keep an eye on it, yeah?'

'Uh-huh. Sure. It's just . . . you end up *feeling* guilty, you know?'

'Of course you do!' he agrees. 'This is a *witch-hunt*! What could be worse than having the whole damn *world* think you were responsible for someone's death, for god's sake? Someone they idolized! They *want* you to be guilty because they can't bring themselves to accept that this person whom they adored, this beautiful young woman they couldn't get enough of, died as a result of a *stupid* accident! You're a scapegoat for their frustrated appetite for her! A victim of mass hysteria, of overemotional people whipping each other up into a frenzy and howling for blood! Which is, make no mistake about it . . . *absolutely terrifying*! They all want a sacrificial victim! But once we go into court, Nick, none of that matters any more. It doesn't *matter* what the media are saying, or what the man in the street thinks. It's just me and the other guy. It's a controlled environment. And you have to believe me when I say that there's nothing to worry about – this is what I do, and I do it very well, and they have no idea how ridiculous their case is going to look by the time

I get through with them! They don't have *any* cold facts, any forensics, and their so-called witnesses aren't worth shit!'

He smiles and reaches down into his briefcase, pulling out the video.

'Defence Exhibit Number One!' He laughs. '*Boom!* Exit Detective Frank Bosch! Great start for them – the prosecution's star witness turns out to be a corrupt cop who forces hookers to pay him thirty per cent of their takings! Looks good, doesn't it? But that is *nothing*, Nick, compared to the real killer fact here – that you *knew* this, and Bosch knew that you knew long before he arrested you! Case . . . closed.'

'Except I don't come out of that very admirably either, do I?'

'You come out looking unscrupulous. Sure,' he admits, shrugging. 'But there is a long haul to make from unscrupulous to murderous, my friend. And they come out of it with a far bigger credibility problem than we do. Who has the motive for wanting to see someone out of the picture now – you or Bosch? I still can't understand why the man has let himself get into this situation. Does he seriously think it's not going to come out?'

'He doesn't think there's a copy of the tape,' I answer. 'He assumes I would have used it long ago to try and bargain my way out of the trouble when it first started. Which I would have done, had my first lawyer not told me to wait. The one good bit of counsel he gave me, as it happens.'

Wolsheim laughs, genuinely relishing the situation.

'And therein lies the moral of the story,' he chuckles. 'Life is chaotic, insane and brutal, and the sole, unique wise thing a man can do in the face of it all is to take legal advice.'

FRANK BOSCH

Runyon's is a pleasantly shabby café in a side street not far from the precinct. It had been a popular hang-out for Gossom cops until Runyon made the mistake of filing a complaint with Internal Affairs because so many of them had run up tabs that they apparently had little intention of paying. The upshot was that he recuperated some of the money but his café was nowadays boycotted by everyone on the force – which made it an ideal place for Frank and me to hold our occasional meetings.

I got there five minutes early, the video stuffed in the inside pocket of my jacket. Frank was already there, sitting stone-faced at his favourite table – the one furthest from the windows – nursing a large cup of coffee. He marginally raised an eyebrow in greeting as I approached.

'You really want to do this,' he announced once I'd sat down. 'I hoped you'd change your mind.'

'Cheer up, Frank.' I smiled, unzipping my jacket to show him the tape. 'You're getting a good deal.'

'I'd rather it had been some other way,' he shrugged. 'I don't have to like it just because it means I'll be free of you.'

'What *is* the big deal here, Frank?' I asked. 'Someone

will trace her sooner or later – you're not changing anything by giving me her name.'

He looked flat at me, sipping his coffee.

'I made a promise,' he informed me, keeping those dull eyes fixed on mine. 'You're making me break that promise. I don't appreciate that. At all.'

I felt a little twitch of apprehension at the veiled threat in his tone. The eyes made it hard to judge just how angry Frank ever was – still as a windless pond, his emotions making no more ripple than tiny insects landing upon the water. But this, I suspected, was a mood I'd never seen him in, a darker one even than the first time we'd met, when I laid the situation out before him.

'A man of his word,' I commented glibly.

'Because you don't think that possible, from the little *you* know about me?' he snarled. 'You think I don't have principles, is that it?'

'I didn't say that.' I smiled, raising my hands in surrender before the exchange got any more antagonistic. 'I'm just surprised because, morally speaking, this seems like less of a big deal than putting the squeeze on someone, Frank!'

'We're not talking about a pimp here,' he rasped. 'This is a *good* person. It's different.'

'Jordan Baker was not a bad person,' I retorted. 'Just . . . fucked up.'

'I didn't say she was a bad person, and what happened to her was not my fault,' he snapped, alluding to the episode for the first time in our relationship. 'I had no idea the vice squad were going to raid her place. By the time I found out what had happened, it was too late, do you understand? Too . . . damned . . . late! I was sorry about the way it turned out, but she *was* fucked up, as you say, and through no fault of mine. *This* girl isn't. Yet.'

93

I sat back in the chair, smiling with amazement at the fact that he apparently didn't even know Jordan Baker had been a man.

'What?' he spat, not understanding why I looked shocked. 'You're not going to come over all lily-white with me and pretend that *you* have never fucked up someone else's life? Please.'

'All I'm going to *do*, Frank . . .' I explained '. . . is make her a heroine! What's so terrible about that?'

'She doesn't *want* it, OK? Why can't you just respect that?'

'How could anyone *not* want to be a hero?' I argued. 'Can you explain that to me? It doesn't make any sense.'

'Why should she have to make sense to *you*? Maybe she just values her privacy. You people are so sure that everyone's biggest wish is that *you* should talk about them! You're so full of it . . .'

'Full of what?'

'Your own bullshit.'

I put my fingers to my temples, somewhat riled by the barrage of criticism I was getting here.

'OK,' I said, 'I get your point. Can we drop it now?'

'Oh . . .' Frank smiled sarcastically '. . . so when *you* don't feel like talking about something, that's OK?'

'I guess,' I announced through clenched teeth. 'Kind of similar to when you feel like breaking the law, Frank.'

A silence settled between us, Frank's glazed eyes gazing at me as he took another sip of coffee. The odd thing was that I could understand it if Frank hated me because of what I had over him, but that didn't seem to be the issue here. In fact, it seemed pretty clear that he would rather things carried on as they were than end it all by handing over this one name.

'What's so special about this girl, Frank?' I asked in a more conciliatory tone. 'Why's she so important to you?'

Frank leaned forward across the table. He frowned, searching for the right words, before announcing in a tone that was less aggressive now that he'd spoken his mind, 'That's just what I'm asking myself about you. Thanks to me, you make a good living. Why would you blow that on her? What could make that worth your while? I don't get it.'

I couldn't tell him the truth, of course. He might have understood if I'd told him about my humiliation at the *Post*, but you can't tell a guy something like that.

'I have a feeling about her,' I shrugged. 'I think she may be something special. Look at you, after all – you say she's not your type, but you're not yourself today. Now, why is that? What's she got that a tough Gossom detective, after meeting her just one time, is suddenly coming over all protective? You can't tell me that I'm not right to be intrigued.'

He tilted his head, silently granting me the point, and sucked in his cheeks as he thought it over.

'I'm impressed, that's all,' he answered finally. 'You've never had a gun pointed at you, have you?'

'So it sounds as though she can take care of herself.' I smiled. 'What could be so scary about a few journalists after you've been through something like that? What's she got to hide?'

Frank whistled softly, shaking his head as he slumped back in his chair.

'There you go – straight off you assume she has something to hide. That's so typical – anyone who doesn't throw themselves in your arms is immediately suspect! What are you all so paranoid about?'

'If they've nothing to hide, why should anyone be scared of the truth?'

'You know what you sound like?' he sighed. 'The fucking Inquisition! What gives you the right to judge

95

people? All the people, all the time . . . God, when I think of some of the bullshit I see written about the Gossom PD . . . it's like you think we should be *perfect*! We're not allowed to fuck up. You're always finding someone to blame for every killer who isn't caught, every mistake we make, every problem that won't go away . . . I've seen good men put everything they have into a case only to get ripped apart, called incompetent, stupid . . . even dishonest! We're just trying to do our job – whose fucking side are you on?'

'The public's, of course. We're defending the public interest.'

'Why is it in the public's interest for them to be told the police are a bunch of incompetent jerks? We're not, but how are they supposed to know that when you don't *ever* praise us for getting it right? Are you surprised we're suspicious of you? We know you'll hammer us if we give you the chance, so we try to keep you off our backs and give ourselves a little time to work it out, but then you accuse us of having "a culture of secrecy", don't you? Suddenly we become the *bad guys*! Do you know what that feels like? We're dealing with some of the worst shit the world has to offer, and to cap it all there are these *cunts* sitting behind their computers, telling everyone that we're a bunch of assholes!'

'OK – point taken!' I frowned, hoping to stem the diatribe. 'Why are we talking about this, Frank? What has it got to do with the woman?'

'*Public interest!*' he seethed, slapping the table. 'She's not a politician, she's not even a civil servant – she's just an ordinary member of the public. I'm trying to make you think about *that* kind of "public interest"! I'm hoping you're going to *listen* for once in your life! You have *no* right to drag her across your newspapers.'

'It's also our job to tell people how the world really is

96

– that's what they read papers for, Frank.'

'How the world really is . . . Sure,' he drawled. 'So tell me, why do people think that there are murderers on every street, paedophiles in every playground, and rapists in every park? There aren't. Life is safer today than *ever* before! If people think that, it's because of *you* cunts! You don't tell people how the world *really* is, for god's sake! You tell them what will make them buy the damn papers, and don't you see how destructive you can be with that? You've got everyone so fucking scared that they're buying guns and bolting their doors, and *then* you say society is going down the tubes because everyone has a gun and nobody knows their neighbours any more! You're sending society crazy! But read the papers and it sounds like the *only* people who care about "the public interest" are the fucking journalists! *Everyone* else is an idiot or a scumbag – the cops, the politicians, the bureaucrats, the doctors, judges, teachers . . . basically anyone who tries to do something constructive. You know, if people were that bad and that stupid we wouldn't *have* a fucking society for you to bitch about – we'd all be gnawing on each other's bones by now! And *you* don't think you're scary? So what has this girl got to gain from talking to you? Don't you think she's smart enough to know that you'll end up prying into every aspect of her private life, digging up old boyfriends and publicizing every mistake she ever made? *Now* do you get it?'

He looked questioningly at me. Expectantly, like he hoped that maybe I was going to see the light now and realize that I worked in the worst profession in the world. I think he may have believed he was the first person to tell me any of this stuff.

'There's no point talking to you,' he announced wearily, seeing that I wasn't going to answer. 'There is no reality for you beyond what you cunts talk about, is there? You know, you bitch about politicians who spend their whole lives in politics, but what about *you*? You're just the same, for fuck's sake! You don't live in the real world – you treat it like a *show* for your personal amusement! You should try *doing* something once, try *making* something. You might find that it's not as simple as it looks from a distance, and it's not often a thankful task, but the reward when you manage to accomplish something is worth a hell of a lot more than your fucking *celebrity*!'

He looked away from me, a despondent curve in his lips.

'I give up,' he decided. 'You want to do this trade or not? I have better things to do than waste my time talking to you.'

'Shame.' I smiled, taking the video from my pocket. 'We've never really had a good discussion before.'

Frank turned back to me, laughing bitterly.

'I insult your whole way of life, and you call that "a good discussion"? An *argument* has to involve blood, does it?'

'I'm used to people not liking what I do,' I admitted. 'It comes with the job. A bit like yours, probably.'

'Don't fucking patronize me,' he growled. 'We're different. OK? Worlds apart.'

I shrugged, refusing to concede the point but not wanting to push it any further. I placed the video on the table, keeping my hand on it. 'Show me yours and I'll show you mine . . .'

He reached under the table and produced a brown envelope.

'I didn't give this to you,' he warned. 'So far as I'm concerned, this photocopy does not exist.'

'Sure,' I answered, opening it at once to glance at the contents. It was a statement, dated last night. As I proffered the tape in return, I remember being surprised by the firmness with which he took it, yanking it from me like I was a hoodlum to be disarmed. He slipped it into his jacket and announced, 'I hope you find she's worth it. A better businessman would never have let me have this.'

'Everything has to end some time.' I smiled, quite aware that he was right, but that so was I under the circumstances. 'It was good while it lasted.'

He stood up to go, shaking his head with a pitying expression. 'You don't take anything very seriously, do you?'

I was silent, not quite sure what he was saying. Nothing seemed further from the truth to me, obsessed as I was with avenging my humiliation at the *Post*. He saw the bemusement in my face and leaned down over the table, placing a hand on my shoulder and patting it in a slightly patronizing manner that was quite unlike him.

'Let's hope we don't come across each other again, Nick.'

'Frank . . .' I frowned. 'We're quits, aren't we? End of story.'

A tiny glint of something that might have been anger showed in his eyes and he squeezed my shoulder roughly.

'That's what you just don't get, isn't it?' he whispered. 'It's not a story.'

He released me but stayed leaning over the table, still staring down with that strange expression of pity.

'Every action has a reaction – ain't that the whole problem with life? The world is such a fucking mess because nothing is *ever* over. Hell, even death doesn't stop some people causing shit. Some of them are just getting started.'

I looked searchingly at him, unsure if he was making a general comment about life or talking about Jordan Baker

99

in particular. What hid behind those eyes – a sense of regret, or a threat?

'Well . . . can *we* call it quits?' I asked.

He straightened up and took a deep breath, his eyes half closing as he felt his lungs fill. After a long pause, he let the breath out and looked back down.

'I'll offer you one better,' he suggested in a compromising tone, smiling as he let his fingers touch the folded statement there on the table. 'Leave this girl alone, Nick, and we'll say we're friends. How about that?'

No sooner had he said it than the little voice piped up in the back of my head, urging me to accept. I didn't know why – I could see no reason why I should feel bad about following up this story like any other. But something about her had clearly touched Frank Bosch – enough that he was willing to wipe the slate clean between us on her behalf. Perhaps, I thought momentarily, I should just respect whatever it was, and walk away.

But then I remembered Kevin O'Neil and Macauley Connor laughing at me, and shook my head.

'Can't do it,' I sighed, spreading my hands. 'It's my job.'

The smile wilted on his face, and his fingers broke their contact with the statement.

'Have it your way,' he announced flatly. 'Then let me save you some trouble. You'll find her working in a Down, Boy! on 5th and Easterhouse.'

My head snapped up, and I began to grin – so that was it. That was why she didn't want the publicity. She worked in a Down, Boy! She was a stripper.

'Uh-huh . . .' Frank grunted. 'I thought so. Give you a great . . . *angle*, won't it?'

And then – very slowly, as though it pained him to do so – he unfolded the photocopy and pointed a finger at the box where the subject's name was written.

'That's her. Jamey Gatz. Now . . . I assured her that I

100

wouldn't tell anyone that, but I also assured her that if she was in any kind of trouble she could always call me. I won't break a second promise.'

'What do you think I'm going to do?' I laughed. 'Fucking *rape* her?'

'No . . . you're one of the good guys, aren't you?' he whispered coldly. 'But let me give you another angle on this, huh? *My* angle is that you are *stalking* her . . .'

'*What?* Come off it, Frank – don't you think that's a little bit of an exaggeration?'

'All depends how you tell the story, Nick . . .' He shrugged, turning to go. 'You should know that.'

ENTROPOLIS BELTWAY, SEVEN FORTY A.M.

Jamey Gatz.

Born Otterway, State of New Albion, twenty-six years ago.

Single, Caucasian, Female.

No distinguishing characteristics.

I have to smile when I think about that moment, seeing her name for the first time, the cold facts of her identity outlined on the top of the form. No distinguishing characteristics . . . except there's a helicopter buzzing around over us, probably a hundred or more journalists waiting for us at the other end, and an audience of who knows how many million waiting to see the trial of the man presumed to have killed her.

And I, that man, have one of the country's best-known lawyers sitting beside me, providing his services for free because he knows that if I walk out of that courtroom a free man, his reputation will be finally sealed, unassailable. Millions of people will have seen him get Nick Carraway off the hook. A miracle worker.

All this over a woman with no distinguishing characteristics.

I still don't know what it was about Jamey that made her so special. I may have been the first to see it, to sense that she had a quality that would make people want to get close to her, know her tastes and opinions and the details of her private life, but I still don't know what to call that quality. It was just there, screaming at me from the very first moment I glimpsed her kneeling in Walcott's blood. To say she was sexy is to put the cart before the horse, frankly – yes, of course, she was . . . but *why*? It's hard to recall now that her face is so familiar, so photographed and studied that she seems like the embodiment of some female ideal we've always aspired to attain – either to be it as women, or to merit it as men – but she was not obviously attractive. Were it not for that other thing, that quality I cannot define, she would not be considered beautiful. No-one would choose her to advertise their product, or adorn their TV show. No-one would go to a surgeon saying they wanted to look like that. And yet we could not get enough of her. Literally – there was not enough of her to satisfy public demand.

Every day she was there. Jamey Gatz on a magazine cover, staring frankly, with a slight defiance in her smile. A shot of Jamey Gatz arriving at a premiere, all the more beautiful because a glint in her eyes let you know she wasn't taking this too seriously. Jamey Gatz on the radio, instantly recognizable by the soft, quiet cunning of her hill-country twang. Jamey Gatz on some crass chat show like *Lola Colaco*, slowly raising an eyebrow at a stupid question and pausing with crushing emphasis before she replied, 'Well . . . what do *you* think, Miss Colaco?'

And then she'd break out that red-blooded laugh, letting her interviewer off the hook, and Lola – or Georgia, or Conrad, or whoever the hell it was that day – would bellow with TV-host hilarity, that extravagant whoop they all have that comes from nowhere, that sounds genuine and yet cannot possibly be real unless they have some kind of brain damage. And not even they, in their overweening arrogance and vanity, were foolish enough to think they could get the better of her. She put them back in their place, exactly where they were supposed to be, and everyone loved her for it.

She was fresh, like a wind from the hills blowing away the haze of the city and reminding us all how sharp everything can look on a clear day, how bright the colours can be even in Entropolis. She made the hardest things in life seem obvious, like the fact that happiness is just an attitude and there is really no mileage in or excuse for looking at the world any other way. Sometimes I would watch Jamey on TV when I was depressed, and she had the strange, almost unique ability to make me wake up and realize that there was nothing profound about the way I felt. That's why people liked her – not because she was sexy, or smart, but because she brought light.

But what was it and where did that light come from?

What does every single one of those pictures have?

Something.

Something . . . I do not think we have a word for, but it is the part of us that is almost divine.

The trouble is that you cannot dissect her. If you analyse her, element by element, the parts do not equal the sum of the whole. Only her eyes stand alone – absolutely feminine in their contours, almost lemon-shaped, and the irises a shade of green that would look quite wrong on a man. Soft eyes, yet proud and fiercely intelligent. They are beautiful in themselves, but the rest has nothing in common with the pneumatic, beach-babe beauty we are supposed to desire. The nose is too big. The set of the jaw almost masculine. The skin a little rough. But it's right, isn't it? Somehow she is perfect, thrilling.

Jamey Gatz was *entirely* distinguishing in her characteristics.

And it was an act by then, but it was not a lie. The person she was pretending to be was real enough – it was the person she had been before Randall Walcott. Before I came into her life. Before the facts of who she was and what she had done got so irretrievably distorted that even now most of these people buying the magazines and watching TV and hating me have got her all wrong. And she could never get back to who she had been because we were all watching. After I did the deal with McQueen and she became an InfoCorps client, there would never again be a normal day when she just did normal things and could truly be Jamey Gatz rather than the media personality who had that name, an object of adoration.

In that sense, Jamey Gatz died that day on the subway after all.

Duncan Hayes

Frank was right, of course. We are swimming in bullshit. Everything gets so distorted. There's some law of physics about how it's impossible to observe matter on its smallest levels because the very act of observation exerts an influence on it, but you don't need to get down to neutrons or whatever they are to see that happening – just by telling a damn story we change it. You take an angle. You draw a conclusion. You have to – that's what a story *is*.

And if, as so often happens, you get the basic facts wrong, then god help you if you ever want to set the record straight. You can't. By then the story has its own momentum, its own life, and you can't turn back time. So someone says a movie star is gay and that's it – the man can sleep with every woman in town and it won't change the fact that he is under suspicion of lying about his sexuality. Hell, he could be sleeping with all these women precisely *because* he's gay!

So Randall Walcott was a total psychopath. Duncan Hayes was an innocent bystander, a victim. Jamey Gatz was the heroine who fought the psycho for control of his gun and shot him.

Wrong, wrong, wrong.

By the time I heard what had really happened, from Jamey's own mouth, it was too late. I could not seriously expect to change the story, and I couldn't even see that there was any point in trying – Walcott and Hayes were both dead, so what did it matter? Jamey didn't like being called a heroine, but even she eventually accepted that it was too late to change anything. There came a point where, had she tried to set the record straight, people would have *blamed* her for not being the person they thought her to be, for letting the falsehood get started.

But it's all bullshit. It's a myth.

What really happened was far more extraordinary.

Duncan Hayes was not a victim.

Duncan Hayes was the cause of the whole damn thing, he and his good intentions. His *shanug* philosophy.

I have trouble taking people like that seriously. *Shanug* is all very well where it belongs, way up in the mountains around the other side of the world. The people of Kashtan are welcome to it, and I believe them to be entirely sincere and laudable for their beliefs, but it's pretty out of place in Atlantis. Not that it's hard to see why it's become a popular form of spirituality over here – it's vague and elastic, explains the universe, gives people a reason for all the shit that happens, and doesn't require you to actually *do* anything. Perfect.

What could be simpler – *shanug* is everything and everything is *shanug*. The birds are *shanug*, the bees are *shanug*, birth, life and death, *shanug, shanug, shanug*.

The Kashtans have the situation covered.

'*Shanug!*' they announce with a quiet smile when a child is born into the world.

Says it all. And if tragedy later strikes and the toddler charges off the edge of a chasm in those hard mountains they call home, the elders gaze philosophically over the precipice and softly reflect, 'Shanug . . . Shanug . . .'

One word to combine an expression of their sadness and a celebration of a short life ended, to acknowledge that this was in the way of things, to show a gesture of forgiveness towards the chasm itself, and even, I daresay, explain why fences are not the answer.

Basically, the Kashtans have developed a spiritual system that enables them to cope with living in one of the most desolate, unforgiving places on the planet. Good on them. And they are a gentle and wise people, I don't doubt it. If they can see what is *shanug* about even the worst things, like the fact that Sinosia invaded their country forty years ago, burned their monasteries, raped their women and ate their goats . . . well, I'm not going to tell them they're wrong.

But I do have a big problem with people like Duncan Hayes, lucky enough to be born to a life of peace and prosperity in the most advanced society the world has ever seen, telling us all we have it wrong and these peasants up a hilltop have all the answers. Sure, they are simple where we know only greed. Forgiving where we are driven by jealousy and revenge. Humble where we are proud. As pure as we are undoubtedly sick. One has little choice but to admire them, although it is kind of unfortunate their women are considered to be lower than yaks in spiritual terms.

The one thing I will say for Hayes is that at least he was into *shanug* before it became fashionable. These days, of course, there are people offering *shanug* management courses. You can eat *shanug* food, listen to *shanug* music, and even get a *shanug* interior designer – whatever the hell that is, because, so far as I understand Kashtan thought, the whole concept of interior design is a no-no in *shanug* terms. Not that it's an issue there, given that most of them live in hovels. But this is a free country, right? If you happen to consider that a lentil is basically always a lentil, and that just because some lentils are guaranteed on the label to be *shanug* lentils by a genuine exiled Kashtan monk it doesn't mean that all the other lentils are necessarily *faking* it, then that's just fine. No-one's forcing you to pay more for *shanug* lentils. So what's to get upset about?

I can imagine, though, that a guy like Hayes could have found it all a mite irritating. I can imagine that he'd have been a little pissed off to find movie stars turning up to anti-Sinosia demos when, a few years back, it was just people like him and nobody gave a shit. And I don't blame him for hating the way his belief had become a fashion accessory – hell, if following the *shanug* means attending charity Free Kashtan balls packed with millionaires and their surgically enhanced wives, then we might as well just fill all the fucking chasms in with cement and be done with it. I'm sure that was why he'd taken the philosophy further than most people and stopped using soap, why he felt obliged to abandon traditional Atlantian dress and ultimately, I guess, why he started haranguing strangers on the subway about their way of life, even though that isn't a particularly *shanug* piece of behaviour, either.

The irony, though, is that the more authentic Duncan Hayes tried to be in his beliefs, the further he was getting from the Kashtan ideal – he'd cut himself off from his fellow men and women rather than achieved harmony with them. He had become a threat to everyone he approached, a ripe-scented weirdo dressed in rags and furs who set alarm bells ringing in their heads the moment they saw him coming.

But I think his self-obsession was such that he could not even see it. He thought *they* were the problem. He imagined, each time he stepped into a subway carriage such as the one in question, that he was an open book – a walking invitation to his fellow citizens to share a moment of peace and love with him – but they refused to even look his way.

Yet he was not so easily ignored. And the more of an outcast you become, the easier it is to transgress the most basic laws of behaviour, such as the rule that one does not talk to strangers on the subway. And I guess he couldn't help himself by then – he looked around the sullen, rush-hour faces and probably felt the irritation surge over him. Didn't Atlantians realize what they were *wasting* by living this way? Here they were, a couple of hundred living beings of every breed and background, each with their own story to tell, their own hopes and desires, and their own love to give . . . but instead of recognizing that they were part of something fabulous and intense, they preferred to piss away the minutes with dead eyes and flat lips, like gently rocking corpses.

What could they possibly hope to get from a life lived like this? he must have thought to himself. How could they blame anyone or anything but themselves for their private sense of imprisonment?

The packed carriage rocked on through the tunnel, its occupants sharing nothing but bacteria, and Hayes gazed down at the honey blonde whose nose was swaying back and forth across the region of his armpit. A strong nose, both sensual and suggestive of a certain tomboyish energy locked within her urban cool. She was beautiful, he no doubt realized, poring over each subtle feature of her face and appreciating the melancholy charm of the first, faintly sketched suggestion of where laugh lines would one day be, only visible this close and in the harsh lighting of the carriage. She wore a white cotton shirt, knotted to reveal a small patch of flat belly above her black leggings,

110

and made it seem elegant as anything that ever sashayed down a catwalk. She had a relaxed beauty, the kind that could carry off anything from a cocktail dress to a boiler suit with the same easy grace, her face unadorned by make-up other than a touch of mascara to her lashes.

Sensing his regard, she glanced up his way.

'*Sam shanug*,' he smiled.

The woman frowned, her body tensing with alarm at finding herself being singled out by the carriage freak.

'It's Kashtan for "May you be one with happiness",' Hayes announced.

She offered him a polite but not encouraging smile – its curve going awry as a small muscle at the edge of her mouth flexed, all the tension of the city caught in that one involuntary twitch – and looked away again.

'You should reply "*Massudi Shanug*",' he continued. 'It means "May we be so together".'

The woman took a deep breath, holding it in her lower abdomen as she'd learned to do to calm her fright before going on stage, and glanced about herself for support. Those whose eyes had been drawn towards them looked swiftly away, refusing help, and she turned slowly back to meet Hayes's waiting, indulgent regard.

'And how do you say "May you back off, Mister"?' she warned, her normally soft, lilting accent coiled aggressively.

Hayes's smile broadened, unperturbed by the rebuff, and she turned to the side, hoping that they would soon arrive at the next stop and she would be able to move away from him as the carriage disgorged its share of passengers. She waited nervously, then felt her skin prickle as he leaned down and announced in a kindly fashion, 'The Kashtan have a saying: "He who does not lend his ear will find he has lost his voice".'

'Yuh. Pity that never happened to you,' she growled,

snatching a glance back at him and moving as far aside as the pack of the carriage would allow.

That was when the train ground to a sudden halt, pitching everyone forward. She lost her balance, but was caught by Hayes, whose other arm had a grip on the ceiling rail. The train jerked violently, hissing underneath, and she broke free, pushing his arm away and snapping, 'That's fine. Thank you! Keep your hands the hell off of me, please!'

In the confusion of the moment, it wasn't clear to others in the carriage that Hayes had intercepted her fall and their immediate conclusion was that his grab had been motivated by a quite different desire. The passengers backed away from him, his existence at last acknowledged by a corps of accusing, hateful regards.

'I was just trying to help!' he explained, laughing at their judgemental expressions.

They turned away, nobody wanting to find themselves trapped into any kind of exchange with him, even visual, but their faces remained as hard and sceptical as ever.

'Hey . . .' he continued, reaching out to touch the woman's arm. 'All I did was catch your fall, OK?'

'All *right*,' she answered, twitching her arm away. 'Thank you. Can you please leave me alone?'

If only the train hadn't remained at a halt, nothing would have come of it, probably. If it had got under way again and pulled into the next stop, the situation would have broken up as some got off and others replaced them. Hayes himself might well have got off. But the train did not move. The hydraulics hissed, and the judder of the engine petered away to nothing.

They were stuck, all of them, but especially Hayes. This might last seconds, or it might drag on for agonizing minutes, but either way he was cornered by the injustice of the situation. That random technical intervention –

perhaps just a red light only the driver could see, or perhaps some nightmarish grid failure – had turned it into a matter of principle.

'*Sam Shanug*, everybody!' he proclaimed with defiant cheerfulness, his smile a little too broad to be true.

'What's the reply?' he demanded, looking around the studiously averted faces. 'Anybody . . . ? Come on, you were all listening a second ago, don't pretend you weren't! Be one with happiness, I said – I'm wishing you something *nice*! Isn't *anyone* going to answer me?'

In the ensuing silence, the lights flickered briefly. The hydraulics hissed again and the carriage jerked once, violently. The passengers began to glance nervously at one another – they weren't mechanics, but the general prognosis seemed to be that it didn't look good.

'Can't you see how *stupid* this is?' he laughed, not appreciating that only maniacs laugh in public. 'We're all brothers! All children of the universe! Why is it so bad to talk?'

Those who had books or magazines were by now deeply immersed in them, though they found it almost impossible to make sense of the words before their eyes. Others regarded the floor, the advertisements for cheap holiday flights, or that odd spot a foot or two beyond their nose where the human gaze can erect its own imaginary wall.

That was not acceptable.

'*Leave us alone – we just want to get home!*' he mocked them in a whining, childish tone. 'Is that all you can think about? Don't you see how sad and . . . *cowardly* that is?'

Hayes gritted his teeth, his nostrils flaring as he breathed in. He no longer knew what he was doing, only that he was right. He gazed around the passengers, eyes ablaze, until his stare landed on the one individual who was looking back at him – a thin, bespectacled man sitting nearby, somewhere in his forties, his delicate hands clasping the soft leather briefcase that lay on his lap.

'You!' Hayes shot, quite losing his grip on the situation. '*Sam shanug!*'

The man regarded him with a curious intensity, as if he were mute but boiled with the desire to reply. Whatever it was he wanted to say, whatever thought was battling to overcome his ingrained reluctance to speak his mind in public, it made his body visibly shake.

'*Massudi Shanug?*' Hayes prompted him, his tone verging on ridicule.

Hayes frowned as the man's sullen expression began to quiver apart before his very eyes, his facial muscles tugging in conflicting directions as emotions collided – anger wrestling with fear, frustration with doubt. He had little chin to speak of, but what there was began to jut forward, trembling defiantly as he stared back at his aggressor and reached a hand into his briefcase.

What happened next must have seemed too absurd to be taken seriously, for Jamey told me that Duncan Hayes smiled in complete disbelief as the skinny little man stood up, letting the briefcase drop from his lap to reveal his hand gripping a small, rather pretty handgun.

Only, it was serious.

The gun was not just for show, despite its sleek designer barrel and polished bone handle. It was real, and was loaded with a dozen real, shiny little bullets. And it rose to point at Hayes across the narrow carriage, and fired one of them straight into his chest.

RANDALL WALCOTT

Randall Walcott, the story had it, was a quiet loner. Well, they always are. And a model employee – that's another classic. Somewhere, over the last few years, that description went from being an admission of bafflement to becoming a kind of psychological dress code for people whose lives end in a sudden explosion of violence, randomly killing their fellow citizens. We've become so accustomed to hearing it that it almost sounds like an explanation.

It sounds dark and full of hidden menace to our ears now: 'He was a quiet loner. A model employee . . .' We instantly imagine deep, violent undertows pulling under the placid surface of those words.

Well, most of us are quiet loners, frankly. Sure we have our friends, perhaps a family – but how much do they know of what goes on in our heads? Do we let it all out, cry on their shoulders or dance on tables? Are we out partying every night or, as the years go by, do we spend more and more of our evenings quietly at home? And when we close our front doors, do our homes buzz with conversation or are we finding that the silences are becoming longer than they used to be, the exchanges more practical, and our thoughts less easy to share?

And, I daresay, we are all model employees.

If we want to comprehend why some of us go into a psychological meltdown, why the Randall Walcotts happen, it is not by imagining them as islands that we will do so. We do that for our own benefit. We call them quiet loners simply so that we can set them apart from ourselves and move on. Until the next one comes along, of course.

I suspect Randall Walcott wasn't that different from a lot of us. I can't prove it, or claim to have any expertise, but I don't believe he thought of himself as a loner. Quite the opposite – almost every day of his life he felt himself to be right in there, struggling towards the same goals as the rest of us, beating his way against the tide alongside shoals of other people, trying to keep up. He walked in step with us along the corridors, stood between us on the escalators, thanked the person in front of him for holding the swing door and held it in turn for the person following behind. He was right in the thick of life – dealing with clients all day long at the insurance company, his ear hot from holding the telephone against it for hours on end, listening to the misery, the anger, the panic of people right in the thick of their lives. He sympathized, he tried to calm their distress, he offered help where the company guidelines allowed him to do so. And when he got home in the evening, he turned on the television so as to drown out the clamour of all those voices and lives.

Quietness and solitude was precisely what his life probably lacked.

That's my opinion, anyway. These days. But I don't claim to know any better than anyone else. This is just a theory, an alternative story that doesn't conflict with the facts.

Say he had bought the gun for his own protection. It seems probable that his anxiety about the dangers of Entropolis would have been exacerbated by his work, by every day dealing with tales of thefts and muggings and hospitalizations. And he was past his prime – not that he'd ever been a good physical specimen, but nowadays he felt the fragility of middle age setting in with a certain shortness of breath and reluctance to run for the train. It was a small gun, so he wasn't a freak getting his kicks from holding some fucking great weapon that could take a man's head off. It was just an insurance policy.

His particular model was a NightShield. It is popular with women – small and light enough to fit into a handbag, simple to use and, above all, beautifully designed. Precisely the sort of gun that could appeal to someone who does not especially want to own a gun. The manufacturers, looking for something radically different, hired an outside design agency to come up with it. The creative team decided, from the outset, not to refer to other pistols when they were developing the concept. It is actually based on a hairdryer – the barrel and butt flow smoothly into one another, the handle undulates softly with the imprint of fingers, the trigger is little more than a subtle protuberance. Supplied with a child safety lock and not much heavier than a can of soda, it is a profoundly satisfying object – it somehow invites you to touch it and feels good in your hand, like polished marble. A range of gorgeously produced black leather holsters come as accessories, allowing owners the option of carrying it under a jacket, strapped to their thigh under a skirt, or clipped to the inside of almost any bag. A lot of people apparently buy all three, like outfits to go with a doll.

Randall Walcott had carried his with him everywhere for two years now.

At first it had made him feel secure – able to eye worrying characters with the confidence of a man who knew he was secretly master of the situation. He found that even when there was no potential danger, when he was merely subject to the constant stresses and aggravations of daily life, it reassured him to know that he owned the gun. Feeling it soothed his insecurities and centred him – no matter how great the bedlam of the city, he had only to touch this symbol of calm assurance to feel its power flow from his palm, along his arm and over his body. His scalp tingled with satisfaction.

It brought him distance from the confusion.

And what happened, I think, is that the distance grew over time – so subtly over the months that it was imperceptible, until he and the gun were left alone. The relationship became ritualized, like that of an actual couple, with a special moment set aside in the evening for polishing the steel, a special place on his dresser for the pistol to sit, a particular point in the morning when he would clip it into his briefcase.

And then maybe one night, when he thought he heard a sound in the apartment on going to bed, it moved across to his night table. And maybe on another night, when he could not sleep, it moved under his pillow. And maybe there finally came a night, as he was touching himself, when his other hand slid across the sheets to close over the gun, and he began to caress himself with it.

And from that moment on, the relationship was different. If the gun had been a comforting friend, it turned out to be a callous lover. It began to taunt him, its seductive power mocking his ineffectuality. It had a clear purpose where he had only the meaningless cycle of working in a job to pay bills, bills that arose from living a life that consisted of little but the job. The gun simply was.

Very gradually, the balance of power began to tilt further and further towards the gun. In theory, he was the master, yet it was the gun that commanded respect. It stopped being his servant and began to own him. Being the man who carried the gun became his identity. It gave him a new purpose in life.

But the gun, a living entity in his head by now, wanted more. It wanted to know what it felt like to shoot something. And, the relationship having gone too far for Randall Walcott to break it off now, it simply became a matter of time before the gun got its way.

Whenever Randall Walcott was crossed by somebody, whenever he was jostled or beaten to a seat, whenever he was kept waiting in a queue or given a surly look by a cashier, the gun would be there in his head, saying 'Now! Do it now!'

None of the traumatized passengers on that subway train could explain what it was in Randall Walcott's eyes after he shot Hayes that made them so certain he would keep firing his gun into the packed carriage, letting the bullets find their targets at random, but perhaps it was simply that they were not looking into Randall Walcott's eyes by then.

Maybe he and the gun had traded identities.

Jamey Gatz

The sound of the pistol firing, like an oak beam snapping in two, brought an immediate response. The carriage began to scream even before Duncan Hayes had collapsed to the floor, passengers diving away from him, ruthlessly pushing others aside to put flesh between themselves and the gun. Only the woman whom Hayes had so disastrously tried to engage in conversation was left standing, too stunned by the proximity of the shot to react.

Jamey Gatz.

Her ears deafened by the shot, she saw Hayes fall backwards as if watching a series of still photographs strung together into a primitive film, her perception of time broken into jerks. She felt her head turning towards Randall Walcott, her body strangely still, and saw him lower the gun to point at the tangled body, and heard the oak snap two more times.

She didn't hear the screams, or sense the other passengers sucking away from her towards the extremities of the carriage. There was a stillness after the third shot, a moment that seemed stopped in time as Randall Walcott stared down at the body, and that was when she saw both the horror and the exhilaration in his expression. His face was lit in an almost orgasmic fashion – eyes flickering between enlightenment and confusion. And then slowly, in that same time-free instant, a dangerous calm settled onto his face and his head rose her way.

They looked at one another.

Jamey knew that he would keep on shooting now. There was an objectivity in the way he regarded her, a disconnection from events that told her it was not within his power to stop the gun from firing again. She realized she was alone, that there were no bodies packed about her any more, and if the gun were to spend its bullets he had no choice but to start with her.

It was not his decision.

Jamey told me that she had no memory of having thought about what she did next. She saw his arm begin to move, the gun rising inexorably towards her, and knew there was no conceivable escape, or cover, or hope of dodging her fate in the few heartbeats left before her. She felt herself to be incapable of movement, watching help-lessly as the gun levelled to her chest . . . and that was when she saw his expression change, losing something of its impregnable certainty, and realized he was no longer looking her in the eyes. She followed his gaze, and saw what it was that had given him pause.

Her hands were unbuttoning her shirt.

She watched her fingers undo the last button and pull apart the simple knot at the bottom of the shirt, exposing her bare chest to the gun, letting it see the smooth, pale skin that it would puncture. And then she looked back at Walcott.

There was doubt there, panic. It should not be like this. Where were the tears, the pleas for mercy and promises to do anything asked of her? That was what the gun wanted. Total humiliation. A reduction to something less than human. Something killable. The barrel flicked to one side of Jamey, then the other, searching for an easier target, but she was blocking his aim on other passengers with her shield of soft, defenceless skin.

The gun came back to face her, quivering dangerously.

Jamey knew that she had only a moment in which to step through the temporary breach in his madness. Even if he could not quite bring himself to shoot her just then, in that split second, he might be able to do so the second after, or he had only to turn to face the other way down the carriage to have an unobstructed aim at the passengers behind him.

She could not force the gun from him. He was not a big man, but no doubt stronger than her, and he had the force of his madness to make up for what he lacked in muscle. And yet, she told herself, he was not all mad. Something there was still capable of reason. Of desire.

'Let me choose for you,' she said gently, unsure where the words had come from.

She took a step forward, the barrel still pointing at her bare breast, and raised her hands, palm upwards, towards him.

She kept her eyes fixed on the eyes that once were Randall Walcott's, willing him to agree. She told herself that he was just a man, that he had once been a child, and somewhere under whatever misery had brought him to this moment still existed someone who wanted only a soft, feminine touch and a gentle voice. His eyes remained uncertain, panicked, and she stepped forward again.

As he hesitated, gun shaking, she raised her left arm and brushed his cheek with her fingertips before letting her hand glide down his grey sleeve to land upon his wrist – just barely touching the soft hairs so as not to alarm him. She paused with the barrel touching her breast, then slid to the side, her right arm travelling around his waist until her hand came to rest on the small of his back, almost as if they were about to dance.

Fearing the bow-like tension she felt in his back, she brought herself as close as she dared, letting her breasts brush softly against his chest and her crotch tremble a paper's breadth away from his own, still looking intently up into his eyes.

'Let me choose for you . . .' she whispered again, her heart pumping so furiously that it became hard to feel her own body or control its movements as carefully as she knew she must, not to break his eggshell-thin trust. Then, turning her gaze to look down his arm and along the barrel, she pulled herself tighter against him until they would both see the same target in its sighting line, and began, still so softly that she was barely touching his wrist, to guide his aim.

'Look carefully . . .' she said in a gentle voice.

The train sat immobile in the dark tunnel, not even the sound of breathing breaking the silence of the carriage. In the brief, screaming panic that had followed that first shot, its extremities had pulled spring-tight as the standing passengers packed back against one another, and those who only moments before had counted themselves lucky to have won seats now found they were helplessly exposed to the gun. And Jamey.

She brought the barrel to face the nearest passenger – a man, perhaps in his early forties, wearing a loose linen suit. His face was attractively built, with a hint of arrogance to his eyes, and his thick, dark hair had been cropped short to minimize the white beginning to pepper his crown. He looked to her the type to cheat on a wife out of vanity, or perhaps to leave his family in panic at the way they seemed to be draining him of his youth. And yet, as the barrel hovered before his tanned face, all that self-delusion crumpled away to reveal something so scared of

123

the darkness looming that he seemed like a boy again. A boy, albeit trapped in a tiring body, that still sought comfort from the unknown in night lights and little talismans of his mother.

There was no real strength there, only a kind of playground bravado. Hardly worth killing once the bluster was blown away.

With a small push of her fingertips, Jamey steered the gun past him to the older woman sitting by his side, a bulging carrier bag clutched on her lap. She met her judgement with more composure than the man, setting her mouth and trying to hold herself still, perhaps even gazing back at them with an edge of defiance. Yet she too seemed an unworthy target – just sad-eyed and harassed, barely able these days to look after the little she had been given in the way of feminine charms. She had no delusions to kill, only a dogged determination to make the best of her lot – perhaps by being a kind mother, or an uncomplaining friend, perhaps simply by refusing to regret the unfulfilled dreams she might once have dared to have in more naïve days.

Jamey ushered the barrel past, finding it gazing upon empty space until she lowered the hand to which it was attached to settle upon the quivering form of a young boy, probably nearing his teens. With a swift, yet unthreatening motion, the sad-eyed woman lowered her head across to place it in front of the boy's face, her hand reaching up to cradle his gaze into the soft flesh between her neck and shoulder, and Jamey rapidly nudged the gun along, feeling the first hint of a tremor in the wrist that held it.

There was no opportunity to look ahead as she proceeded meticulously along the seats, no respite in the tension for her even to glance at the other passengers in answer to the question that was growing ever more urgent

124

with each successive moment of judgement. She had to stay concentrated upon the instant at hand, hoping and trusting that ahead did not lie a person who would, in some unforeseeable way, fail the test. Her heart began to thrash painfully as she sensed the balance start to tip in the body she held tight against her, doubt beginning to weaken the taut muscles, the grip on the gun beginning to loosen. She knew with absolute conviction that the only way forward lay in not wavering from her mission, in facing each terrible trial in turn without trying to argue or renege upon her promise.

She pulled him tighter and turned him as she reached the end of the seats, growing more afraid with every thud of her heart that she might break before him, that her body might betray her and panic him into pulling the trigger. She pulled him so tight that they were breathing in unison, their bodies moulded from thigh to shoulder, and forced herself to begin the painful journey back up the other side of the carriage.

She prayed silently with each halt of the barrel, not so much to any god as to the shittiness of life and making one's way in the city, to the law of probability that let her hope that there would be nobody – nobody who was forced to travel on the rush-hour subway, at any rate – on whom it was not possible to take pity. She tried with all her might to hold herself together, promising herself that she would reach the end.

Still the train did not move, but, as they neared the last few seats, she prayed that it would not do so, that nothing would happen now to break the inexorable logic that she had somehow managed to bring to this moment of insanity.

And then, so quickly that it caught her by surprise, they arrived back where they started.

She turned her head back to gaze at him, seeing the

confusion and fear that was now pulling at his face, and, closing her grip more firmly upon his wrist, she brought the gun gently down and around to touch her own body. She felt its hardness upon her thighs, and drew it slowly up her hips, letting the cold metal scrape across her bare tummy and travel on up over her breasts until it broke free and drifted up to hover in the space between their faces. She did not look at it. She did not break her hold over his eyes even to blink.

She opened her mouth.

Jamey felt his arm resist as she turned the barrel towards herself, his eyes beginning to moisten and twitch as she let her lips touch the dark steel, and raised her eyebrows questioningly.

He pulled it away.

Her legs quivering uncontrollably now, she looked at him with all the pity she had felt for all the targets they had let live, and turned his wrist the other way. Gently, very gently, she brought the gun around to face its owner. She pressed herself hard against him, as hard as she could, then relaxed her grip on his back and moved softly away until their only contact was in the hand upon his wrist and the embrace of their eyes.

Quiveringly, hesitantly, his mouth opened.

Jamey smiled reassuringly, letting go of his wrist as the barrel slid inside, and they looked at one another for the last time – a time without duration, a moment as absolute as the creation of a universe.

A tear fell from Randall Walcott's eye.

And he pulled the trigger of the gun he owned.

Entropolis Beltway,
Seven Forty-Five a.m.

'Mr Carraway! Mr Carraway!' comes a muffled shout.

I jump in my seat, looking around as someone hammers on the window to get my attention. I find myself staring at a camera through the glass, and frown, thinking I must have lost all track of time and be at the courthouse already.

I'm not. We're still on the Beltway, still stuck in the jam. The cameraman is standing on a damned motorbike, his partner holding it steady below.

'Dan Zemansky, *Justice Live*!' he bellows, pointing at himself. 'How are you doing today?'

My jaw drops. I don't know how to deal with this. A cameraman standing on a motorbike in a traffic jam . . . asking how am I *doing* today? He's grinning, obviously very pleased with himself. *Justice Live* has to be the channel that has the chopper overhead – this is their solution to the fact that a bus in morning traffic hasn't been making very compelling viewing.

'How do you feel it's going to go in court today, Mr Carraway?' he shouts.

127

I turn to Wolsheim in panic, saying, 'Is this live? Is this on air?'

Wolsheim stands up, looking over my shoulder. The bike has an antenna on the back – it looks as if it's been adapted to relay images back, live. We are on air.

'Ignore him,' Wolsheim says. 'Let me handle it.'

He ushers me across the bench, switching positions with me, and faces the camera, blocking me from view.

'My client does not have any comment to make!' he calls in a loud, clear voice through the glass.

'What about you, Mr Wolsheim?' the cameraman yells back, undeterred. 'How do you rate your chances in court this morning?'

'I'm not going to discuss that with you,' he snaps. 'You know what I think. You people are making it impossible for my client to get a fair trial! I have filed an official complaint against you and your parent company, InfoCorps, to that effect. I think your viewers should realize that *your* behaviour, Mr Zemansky, is perverting the course of justice and denying a man his constitutional right to an unbiased hearing in court.'

I stare dead ahead, my heart pounding with anxiety. I feel trapped, cornered. Suddenly I want nothing more than for the traffic to free itself up and for us to be on our way. Compared to this, the courtroom itself would seem like sanctuary.

'We're just giving people full and impartial coverage of the news, Mr Wolsheim,' comes the reply through the glass.

'You're standing on the back of a motorbike, Mr Zemansky,' Wolsheim hollers. 'I don't know why, but somehow that's not quite my idea of journalistic objectivity.'

Zemansky laughs, looking like my story is turning out to be the most fun he's had in weeks, and shouts back,

'Do you think the viewers are going to be taken in by your show of moral outrage when they know full well that you yourself are using this trial for entirely personal ends?'

'I don't know what you mean.'

'Why are you offering your services for free, Mr Wolsheim?'

'Because my client is an innocent man entitled to the best defence I can give him.'

'Come on, Mr Wolsheim!' Zemansky laughs. 'You are in this trial for the publicity. You're making use of the media even as you condemn us! Nobody is fooled!'

'What is your point? That it would be better, morally speaking, for me to make my client *pay* for his defence? I don't really follow your logic.'

'Even if someone accused of murder was clearly innocent, you wouldn't defend him for free if we weren't giving the trial any coverage, would you?'

'Why, wouldn't you always cover the murder trial of a man you considered to be innocent?' Wolsheim cuts back instantly.

'You're not answering the question.'

'Neither are you, I notice.'

'It's not my choice which trials are covered by *Justice Live*, Mr Wolsheim, but you do choose your clients.'

'Oh . . . *please*!' Wolsheim sneers caustically. 'Is that the best you can come up with? You're just following orders. Is that what you call being a champion of free speech, Mr Zemansky?'

This is a joke. A tennis match on a court with no net and no lines. But who cares? The viewers have their drama, there is conflict and anger. They will not switch off for now. I want to speak up, to say what I truly think of the farce the two of them are playing, but I can't. I will only become an actor in it. There is no escape, no way to take any kind of stand. If I say anything, I will simply be sucked into the vortex. In the land of free speech, my only choice is to be silent.

'Eighty-seven per cent of viewers who expressed an opinion say they believe your client to be guilty of murdering Jamey Gatz – what do you say to that?'

'I say, as I have always said, that your viewers don't know the facts. Because you haven't told them the facts. Because *you* don't know the facts, Mr Zemansky. In case you hadn't noticed, the trial hasn't started yet.'

I swear I'm going to explode if this carries on much longer. I'm going to lose control and let rip. Become my own worst enemy, give Atlantis the spectacle it truly desires . . .

'You're breaking the law, sir,' a familiar voice cuts in.

I turn back to see Bergman glowering down at the journalist, poking his face right at the camera.

'This vehicle belongs to the Entropolis Justice Department,' he growls in a voice that is both loud enough to be heard through the glass and calm enough to be a simple assertion of authority, absolutely impartial to the argument in progress. 'It is an offence to communicate with prisoners travelling in this vehicle. It is an offence to touch this vehicle or in any way impede its progress. I suggest you back off from it immediately, sir, or face possible prosecution.'

Bergman. God bless the man.

I look ahead, see cars in the distance beginning to move. I can't hear what Zemansky is replying. His tone has dropped several notches. Please, I pray, please just let the bus move, and keep moving, and let me breathe again . . .

From the corner of my eye, I see the camera disappear from the window. Wolsheim laughs.

'Excellent!' he exclaims happily. 'Very nicely handled, Mr Bergman!'

Bergman grunts non-committally, his hackles still raised from dealing with the trespasser on his territory. The bus guns its engine and begins to roll forward at last, and I sink back in the seat, sighing with relief.

A phone rings. I assume it's Wolsheim's, but he glances around in surprise, denying responsibility.

'Hello?' Bergman grunts, producing a phone that looks ridiculously small in his broad hands. 'Mum! . . . Oh yeah? . . . How'd I look? . . .'

DOWN, BOY!

There's nothing we Atlantians like better than a franchise. Restaurants, shops, movies, coffee bars – the reassurance of a standard product, of knowing exactly what we're going to get for our money. No nasty surprises. We must suffer from some kind of chronic insecurity, some lack of faith in our own ability to choose.

Perhaps it suggests that people aren't really made to be free. We're pack animals at heart, we like to blend into the mass. We like to be told where we stand in the pecking order. Atlantis, however, is based on a wildly optimistic vision of human potential – a nation where individuals are supposed to control their own destinies, form their own opinions, and cut their own paths through life. If it were truly human nature to live like that then isn't it odd that democratic societies are such a minor aspect of human history? The idea is pretty self-evident, after all, so why has almost every human being in history been content to live in some form of totalitarian society? Why so few revolutions?

Atlantians don't have that comforting certitude, our society is constantly shifting and we all live in fear of being superseded. We're all petrified that other people are going to realize we don't know what the hell we're talking about most of the time. One day, maybe, we'll make the wrong choice, and our credibility will be shot. So perhaps we love brands and generic experiences because they relieve some of that pressure.

It's surprising that nobody came up with the concept of the Down, Boy! chain earlier. That men want to see naked women is one of the few undeniable truths of human nature, after all – certainly a greater urge than the one to be free. So it makes sense to offer them a standardized, guaranteed, hygienic female-flesh service. You can't go wrong.

It's a no-brainer. A Down, Boy! offers nothing but attractive young women – and occasional young men – who all conform to our democratically standardized concept of beauty, and it does so in an environment that is rigorously controlled to remove all sordidness and danger from the experience. You will never find yourself sitting near some crazy-eyed freak in a Down, Boy! He won't get in the door. So it is possible for the management to create an atmosphere of normality, just a bar with a twist, where everyone is like you and knows that they have to respect certain codes of conduct. Even women feel safe. It's a great place for a party, like taking a bunch of kids to a burger joint.

The Gossom Down, Boy! – one of four in Entropolis, when I was last in circulation – is right on the corner of 5th and Easterhouse. It felt like I'd landed on Go when Frank told me that Jamey Gatz worked there, her story instantly doubling in value.

There are basically two stories that have always, since time immemorial, been popular favourites. The first is The Fall of the Mighty – which could involve a defeat, a death or, these days, a scandal. Doesn't really matter. The point is simply that someone with power has been laid low by the world. We love that, even if we admired the guy.

The other big storyline includes all the one-off tales about ordinary folk that you could group together under the heading The Whore with a Heart of Gold. Humble, fallible people – people like ourselves, whose place in the world might seem insignificant – who do something unexpected and extraordinary. We all need to believe we have that potential. The wider the gap between the person's status and their impact on society, the better the story – because more of us fall into the territory in between. That's why The Whore with a Heart of Gold is the archetypal example, because the gap is the biggest. Frankly, in journalistic terms, a stripper is counted as only one step away from a prostitute on the unwritten scale of characters. So a stripper who saves a bunch of strangers from a maniac is clearly a much, *much* bigger story than if an accountant were to do the same thing.

I didn't make the rules.

That day I found out all I could about Jamey Gatz – very little beyond the fact that her parents were deceased and she shared an apartment with a Heather Gatz, her older sister. She had moved to Entropolis a little under three years ago. I resisted the temptation to try her at home because I wanted to see her dance before approaching her. Instead I waited until around six and then headed off to the Down, Boy!, figuring that I'd be early enough to get a good table.

Back when the first of the Entropolis branches opened, they had held a press launch which I'd covered for the *Post*, so I knew what to expect. The Gossom establishment was precisely the same, of course. The same discreet bouncer posing as a doorman – a good-looking guy, but a little too muscular and thick-nosed to look natural in a suit. The same loud, mainstream rock pumping through

134

the doors, and the same interior glowing with a permanent sunset burnish. A pretty brunette offered to take care of my coat. I thanked her and declined, but she just smiled, holding out a plastic chip, and said it was no trouble. Clearly, I realized, coats were to be checked. That was a detail I hadn't picked up on when writing my article because it had been summertime. A friendly blonde showed me to a table for one, hidden in the twilight near the back and not at all where I had been planning to sit, but again I understood that the service was not really there for my convenience. They just didn't want lone males in coats lurking around the stage and putting other parties off having a good time.

Like all the floor staff, they wore little dark green dresses – simple, sleeveless numbers that showed off their figures without getting tacky about it. The blonde had added a cropped green jacket in what was undoubtedly a discreet corporate seniority code. And they were genuinely cheerful, intelligent-seeming young women – no doubt hired for their 'people skills' as much as their looks. Probably students, probably planning careers in medicine and law.

I considered asking when – and indeed *if* – Jamey Gatz would be dancing tonight, but decided against drawing too much attention to myself. Something in the hostess's eyes told me I was already under suspicion of being a freak simply by virtue of being there alone, and I didn't want to compound her impression by asking after one particular dancer. So instead I ordered a beer and settled down to watch a lithe young dancer working up a sweat in a misguided attempt to mate her silver lamé bikini with the chrome pole. Not that I would try to deceive myself or anyone else by pretending that I don't enjoy watching an attractive woman strip, but, in all honesty, I have to say that the pole doesn't really do anything for me.

135

Frankly, it's a little big for a phallic symbol. It reaches the ceiling and, even in my wildest fantasies, I can't identify with that. Now, if they had a stubbier, half-height pole that she danced around, I'd probably find that pretty damn sexy. A case of less is more. As it is, the pole is just a chrome pole so far as I'm concerned, and I can't buy into the idea that she's getting so steamed up about it. My imagination won't stretch that far – no women *I* know get turned on by lamp-posts. No women I *want* to know, come to that.

As I expected, the place began to fill up fast from six onwards. Office crowds started arriving, pumped up and loud with ersatz camaraderie. A stag party were starting their night at one of the biggest tables, centre front. There were women mixed up here and there in the groups, disguising any unease they felt with brash laughter and relentless teasing of their male companions. Their enjoyment looked more genuine whenever a man took the stage – which they did according to a three-to-one ratio, I noticed. Such a precisely judged product, a Down, Boy! – just enough sexual equality to satisfy female clients and to let the men off the moral hook without going so far as to seem homoerotic.

The men stayed glued to the dancers, on a two-to-three basis, while the women were more inclined to look around, checking out the customers. As the evening progressed and the pole got progressively less shiny, I several times noticed myself being examined in that way, and tried to appear relaxed though I knew what I'd be thinking of me if I was them. I grew less comfortable with time – I hadn't expected it to take so long for Jamey Gatz to appear, but one adult-oriented rock track followed another, the strippers came and went, I drank more beer, and still no sign of her.

My body tensed every time a blonde took the stage,

only to slump again as I decided it wasn't my woman – the hair would be too long or too short, her build would be too petite, or sometimes she would simply move in the wrong way . . . I didn't know quite what Jamey Gatz looked like, but she had had a presence on the subway that I felt sure I would recognize when I saw it again. A way of holding herself. It wasn't something so definite that I could say with instant certainty whether or not a dancer was her, but none of them quite fitted my idea of her character. The longer I looked at each woman, the less I could picture her kneeling in that pool of blood, holding herself with that extraordinary dignity.

It got beyond nine o'clock and most of the dancers had done at least two routines. I was feeling a little drunk and depressed – my hopes only kept alive by the fact that a new face would occasionally appear, suggesting that the strippers worked overlapping shifts. Perhaps Jamey Gatz didn't start hers until late in the evening – a Down, Boy! stayed open until three in the morning, after all. But then, thinking about it, what had she been doing on the subway at six o'clock – on a train heading through Gossom – if she hadn't been coming into work? Either the shifts changed each day or, more probably, she simply wasn't working tonight – wouldn't she be expected to take a few days off after what she had been through?

I cursed myself for my stupidity – I should have tried her at home as soon as I discovered her address. She wasn't going to show, and I had wasted the whole day, giving other journalists the chance to find her before me. For all I knew, I'd already let my opportunity to avenge my humiliation at the *Post* slip through my fingers.

I got up from the table, suddenly in a hurry to leave. I was a fool not to have at least asked if Jamey Gatz was working tonight. I looked around for the waitress who had been serving me all evening, wanting to settle the question, pay my bill and get out, but she was nowhere to be seen. Snatching the little pile of till receipts up from the table, I began making my way towards the bar.

The beer had had more of an effect than I realized, taken on an empty stomach, and I was a little unsteady on my feet as I weaved through the tables, confused by the flashing lights, the loud music and the whooping and whistling of the customers. Green-dressed waitresses were hollering orders to the bar staff, standing impatiently with trays, and I made a line for the nearest gap along the brass counter. The wrong end of the bar from the cash till, I realized when I found myself watching a woman loading dirty glasses into the dishwasher, but I was too drunk to do anything except proffer my little clutch of beer bills, waiting for someone to take them from me. Which no-one did. They were all either too busy or determined to seem that way, and a ridiculous, almost tearful sense of hopelessness began to come over me. I'm not good when I drink. I needed to get out, close the door on the noise and garish lights, and let the cool evening air sober me up. Thankfully my waitress swam into view, loading beers onto a tray just nearby. I tapped her on her green jacket and she turned, frowning as I offered her the clutch of bills.

'You're supposed to settle at the table,' she informed me tetchily, snatching them from my fingers. 'The bar area is for staff only.'

I mumbled an apology, pulling a fifty-dollar bill from my wallet, and she took it with her down the far end of the bar to get change. She no longer seemed the best person to ask about Jamey Gatz, so I leaned across the counter to call down at the woman who was bending over the dishwasher, carefully enunciating, 'Is *Jamey Gatz* dancing here tonight, please?'

She rattled the rack of glasses into the machine and

138

slammed the door shut, wiping a bead of moisture from her temple as she straightened back up to look me over with a curious frown.

'I'm cleaning glasses,' she said. 'Who are you?'

In my condition her reply seemed something of a non sequitur.

'I'm looking for Jamey Gatz,' I repeated. 'She *dances* here.'

'No . . .' the woman answered slowly, an indulgent smile playing over her lips as she examined me. 'She cleans *glasses* here.'

The music reached a crescendo and stopped suddenly, a brief silence holding sway before the applause began. Jamey Gatz cleaned glasses?

'So you know her,' I concluded.

'Wow . . .' she sighed, shaking her head in amusement. 'You're not too quick on the draw, are you?'

I stared at her, my soaked synapses sparking feebly. Her hair was held back with a bandanna. It was blonde. She was young – in her early twenties. There was a soft twang to her voice, a decidedly un-Entropolitan lilt.

'You're . . . ?'

'Seventeen fifty change,' a voice cut in beside me.

I turned to take the money, nodding speechlessly, and felt the alcoholic fog lift from my brain as the adrenalin kicked in.

'*You're Jamey Gatz!*' I cried triumphantly.

'I know,' she answered with a tilt of her head. 'They already told me.'

'Can you move away from the bar area, please, sir?' the waitress requested.

'Just a second,' I responded, holding up a hand. 'I just have to—'

'Can you move *away* from the bar area, please, sir?' she repeated.

'Wait!' I snapped. 'Just *wait* a second, will you? Can't you see I'm trying to talk to her?'

'Jamey, do you know this guy?' the waitress demanded. 'Is he a friend?'

'He's news to me.' Jamey shrugged, apparently beginning to find the situation amusing until I announced, 'I'm a journalist. I write for the *Entropolis Post*.'

The smile drained from Jamey's face.

'I don't understand,' the waitress said to her. 'Can you tell me what the hell this is about?'

'No,' Jamey answered, staring hard at me. 'I have no idea what this is about, or who he is, or what he is doing in the bar area.'

'I'm here to talk to *you*!' I exclaimed, turning in frustration from her to the waitress. 'I need to talk to her.'

'Maybe so, but you can't do that in the bar area, sir.'

'I *understand* that!' I seethed. 'Will you just give me one minute, please?'

'I'm sorry, I can't do that,' she insisted, placing a hand on my arm to urge me back. 'This is a staff-only area.'

'What *is* it with you?' I exploded, shrugging her hand off roughly. 'It's a fucking *bar*! It's not sacred ground, for fuck's sake!'

'You're creating a disturbance. I'm going to have to ask you to *leave* the establishment now, sir.'

I saw her signal over to the doorway, motioning the bouncer across to us, and tried, too late, to calm the situation.

'Look . . . there's no need for that. I'm sorry – you're just trying to do your job, and so am I. I shouldn't have said that.'

I turned to Jamey, standing impassively by the dishwasher.

'You must know why I'm here, Miss Gatz,' I argued.

'I *have* to talk to you. Can you tell her to give me just one minute, please?'

'You have the wrong person,' she informed me in a conciliatory tone. 'I'm sorry. Y'all must be looking for someone else with my name.'

'The hell I am!' I exclaimed as a firm hand settled on my shoulder. 'Do you really think you can just *walk away* from this?'

'Will you come with me, please, sir?' the bouncer ordered quietly. 'We're going outside now.'

I felt his other arm pin me to him and knew it was hopeless trying to struggle. I didn't fight, but simply offered passive resistance by refusing to use my feet.

'You're going to have to talk to someone!' I called to her as he began physically dragging me away from the bar.

'I have nothing to say,' she shrugged. 'I'm sorry.'

The bouncer swung me around like a doll, lifting me off my feet and lugging me off towards the door. I turned my head to call back 'That's not going to work, Jamey!' and saw her raise her hands in a curious gesture of surrender to the fates, smiling attractively. Then I was floating through the tables, aware of eyes watching me from every direction, and muttering 'OK . . . OK . . . I'll walk.'

It was too late for that. The bouncer was finally having some fun, finally getting to use the muscles they had hired him for. He carried me right across the bar to the main doors, pushing them open with his free hand. One knocked my shoulder as it swung back, and he dropped me roughly once they had closed behind us, grabbing me by the collar and throwing me up against the wall. I saw his fist go back to pile into my stomach. I folded over from the impact, and he threw me back up to the wall, bringing his nose up against mine.

'I don't want to see you again, you little fuck,' he warned

141

me with exuberant aggression. 'Do you understand that, Fuck?'

I nodded agreement, unable to speak, but it wasn't enough for him. He was excited now, unnecessarily shaking me for a response.

'Do you know what you are?' he demanded, bringing his fist back for a second go.

'*A little fuck* . . . ?' I gasped desperately, hoping to ward off the blow.

It worked. He smiled with satisfaction.

'Good,' he snarled.

He wrenched me away from the wall and opened the second set of doors to hurl me out onto the sidewalk, watching me roll to the ground and come to rest. The coat-check girl appeared beside him, holding my coat, and he threw it onto the street before me.

'*Always* remember that,' he called out before letting the door close between us.

I have done, as a matter of fact.

If I think of myself as a little fuck, it makes sense of practically everything.

Wessex Boulevard,
Seven Fifty-Five a.m.

The traffic is heavy, but moving. I'm aware of the *Justice Live* bike hovering around us, but he doesn't have time to get any close shots. We will be there soon, I realize with a lurch in my stomach. The lynch mob will already be waiting for me, checking their cameras and microphones, jostling for position. And no doubt more than a few ordinary citizens come to jeer and spit. Jamey's fan club.

Seriously fucked-up individuals. I've seen some of the web sites devoted to her, and these people are insane. There is at least one entire site based around her time as a stripper – people write in with their recollections of seeing her on stage, describing her dance and exactly how she took her clothes off. There are even pictures of her in various stages of undress. And, so far as I can tell, they believe it.

But Jamey never stripped in her life. These people never saw her and there is no way on earth any of them could ever have taken a photo. The whole stripper myth is something that I am responsible for. I allowed it to get started simply by choosing to say that she worked in a Down, Boy! without specifying that she cleaned the glasses there. It wasn't a lie, but obviously I knew people would incorrectly assume she was a dancer. Instantly, it became such a major factor in her image that even Jamey herself ended up having to play along, realizing that it was far too late to change the story. Had she turned around, after so much had been said and written about her as some kind of post-feminist role model, and told everyone that she just cleaned glasses . . . they would have blamed her for the lie. They would have felt betrayed and accused her of manipulating them – she was smart enough to see that. She knew she had no choice but to let it ride.

And, curiously, it's not as though I haven't seen the truth written. Other people, mostly actual dancers from the club, have come forward saying that Jamey never stepped on stage – but the information refuses to sink in. People don't want to hear it, and they just wipe it from their minds, writing off those testimonies as the product of jealousy.

The truth will always be whatever people want to believe. Clearly. How many times are they going to believe that a new diet works, that they can lose their unwanted pounds fast and painlessly, just as the magazine cover promises? How long can they carry on believing that, and buying the magazines, when none of the other diets worked? Endlessly, it seems.

We're not creatures of reason. We're just not. We can map every inch of the planet, put a man on the moon, and send all our children to college, but that does not make us creatures of reason. There is no such creature, and there never could be, because life is not about reason.

Life is about passion.

Life happens because of passion. Our first thoughts and desires in this life are pure, undiluted passion – the catastrophe of a baby's discomfort, the urgency of a mother's breast, the automatic, irresistible desire a young child has to break a toy. So what exactly are we pretending to believe here – that we emerge from some cocoon at the end of childhood as rational, emotionless adults?

The very fact that we can even *think* we're creatures of reason proves that we're not. It's just a myth we've invented. A wonderful piece of propaganda to justify all the shit we inflict on the world. A story that is all about us, and so whatever we choose to do we turn out all right in the end because we are heroes.

It's all bullshit. No man ever steps into a courtroom to face a judgement free of bias, based purely on the facts, protected by the very laws that will also serve to punish him. No-one. He is judged the second he shows his face, and what follows is an attempt to influence that judgement one way or the other by rhetoric and emotional blackmail. The same facts will condemn a black man that will free a white one, for fuck's sake – *everyone* knows that!

Creatures of *reason*? There are untold amounts of shit going down today – injustices rife in the very heart of our society, crime at its highest levels, promises being broken and deals being struck, lies on every package in the supermarket and in every advert that the nation's children are watching right this second, and where are the cameras? What is the centre of everyone's attention?

This bus. Me. The last remaining character in a story that will change nothing in anybody's life, that ended over six months ago when Jamey Gatz died, that was totally irrelevant to everything else anyway. That's what everyone wants to hear about.

And I know exactly why. I had it explained to me by the man at the very top of the media mountain, McQueen himself, the day I made the deal on Jamey's behalf. The last day I was free. Hell, I can't hate *him* for any of this, even if he is the closest thing this circus has to a

145

ringmaster, because he *did* tell me the truth. The obvious, irrefutable truth if one does actually apply a little bit of reason to the way society operates. And I should have listened, and I should have understood what he was implying, what he was, I think, trying to *warn* me about . . . but I was too stupid, too wrapped up in my own bull-shit to listen.

I understand what the point of this is. McQueen told me that day what society is all about, and I know that is what is happening right here, right now. I know, just as Jamey finished by knowing, precisely what my options are.

And, like her, I am not going to play the game any longer.

I'm not.

If I can demonstrate today one little bit of her courage, I will regret nothing except the fact that I ever forced her to play in the first place.

And nobody will understand what I have done, or believe me if I tell them, except ironically McQueen himself – no doubt half-watching this right now in his quiet, tasteful office looking over Central Park as he makes his phone calls and does his sums. And maybe he will smile that melancholy smile, and nod softly at the television screen in a small gesture of respect before calling for tea and moving on to other stories . . .

Miss Gatz

Jamey left work at a quarter past three. She paused to look for a taxi, pulling her jacket collar tight against the morning wind, then set off down Easterhouse. The avenue was pretty well deserted at that time of the morning – beyond the occasional car, the only movement lay in the silently blinking neons of closed shops and the drunken reel of the day's litter. A lot of women probably wouldn't have felt safe walking down it at that hour, even though this was not a bad part of town. I let her get a couple of hundred yards away from the bar before I crossed the street and began catching up with her, my hand placed on my still-aching belly.

'Ten thousand dollars,' I called when I was only a few paces behind.

She wheeled to face me and I stopped walking so as not to alarm her. Her expression turned from surprise to irritation as she recognized me.

'Do they pay y'all overtime or is this just dedication?' she sighed in that softly lilting voice of hers. It came across more powerfully now that we were away from the noise of the bar – an accent that could only come from a place where people had time to talk and rarely took the

147

fastest route to saying something. The sort of people Entropolitans find amusing.

'Freelancer,' I smiled, shrugging. 'I get paid by the story. The hours are whatever it takes to get it.'

'Well, you don't seem to me to be getting it at *all*,' she countered. 'I told y'all I have nothing to say. You're wasting your valuable time.'

'You don't deny that you are the subway heroine, the woman who shot Randall Walcott?'

She rolled her eyeballs in despair, her shoulders slumping with exhaustion.

'I surely *do*!' she groaned. 'I'm sorry to disappoint, but I am no heroine, and I did not *shoot* that man! Lord knows *what* put y'all on my trail, but you're no hound dog, OK? You've got it *wrong*! Now, go on home, Rex.'

She spun round and strode off without waiting for an answer. I smiled – she was a good actress. If I hadn't known beyond any doubt that she was indeed the woman everyone was looking for, I'd have probably been inclined to believe her. In part, of course, that apparent sincerity came from the fact that she was telling a literal truth – she hadn't shot the man, and, as I was also to understand later, she didn't feel at all heroic for the part she *had* played in his death. But at the time I just thought she was lying.

'There's ten thousand dollars in it for you!' I called after her. 'That's a lot of clean glasses. I know it's you, Miss Gatz – I *saw* you on the subway!'

'Is that a fact?' she scoffed over her shoulder. 'Maybe y'all need some glasses yourself!'

'I'll just write the story without you, then, shall I?' I challenged, starting after her.

'*What* story?' she called back, refusing to break her pace. 'There ain't no story, mister!'

I quickened my pace, breaking into a trot and catching up with her.

'Look! I just want to talk, for god's sake!'

She stopped unexpectedly, forcing me to skid to a halt and turn to face her, repeating, 'I just want to *talk*!'

Jamey threw up her hands in exasperation, shouting, 'Well, do like everyone else in this town and join a god-damned *therapy group*!'

'You can't walk away from this, Miss Gatz,' I informed her in a patient but firm tone of voice, wincing from the pain in my midriff. 'Like it or not, you're going to *have* to talk to somebody sooner or later. If I found you this quickly, others won't be far behind. You're news. You're a good story. The media isn't going to let go of that story just because you're publicity-shy and, believe me, it can be written with or without your co-operation.'

Something changed. She began to look hunted, her self-assurance cracking as she felt the net close around her.

'Well then, y'all don't need me, do you?' She smiled sarcastically.

'Of course I do.' I grinned back, attracted by her stubbornness even if I was obliged to break it down. 'That's where the money is – in an exclusive interview with you. If you're smart, you'll see that you can't kill the story, so your best option is to co-operate, let me write the story as you *want* it to be written, and earn yourself some good money into the bargain. You have to understand that the more you run, the more people will be on your trail. Chances are that tomorrow or the next day there'll be twenty or thirty guys on your doorstep, all shouting questions, taking pictures, and prepared to write whatever bullshit they can think of to fill in the blanks. Once that happens, you will have *no* control over the situation. But I'm offering you a form of *protection* – by letting me have the story, you can draw the heat off. We'll go to a nice, calm hotel where nobody will find us, and you can take the time to tell the story in your own words. Believe me – I'm a blessing in disguise.'

Jamey looked to one side, cursing silently. I suspected she knew she was beaten.

'Good disguise,' she muttered.

'I'm not a bad guy,' I told her. 'I'm only here because I admire what you did.'

She looked flatly at me – a cool, appraising regard that flaunted convention. Maybe it's just a city thing, but I'd be incapable of looking someone in the face like she did me at that moment, sizing me up as the seconds ticked by. The wind charged down the sidewalk, scattering the litter and whipping her hair around her cheeks. A car sliced by, far exceeding the speed limit, and I remembered why I'd found her so beautiful on the subway. Something about her stillness, her composure standing there on the all but deserted avenue at half three in the morning struck me as magnificent in the same way that you can be suddenly struck by a formation of clouds, or light coming through leaves – things that may have been there the minute before, but which you looked at without seeing.

Hers was not a fashionable look, too athletic and hard for it to be the face of a perfume or fizzy drink. It's a paradox that today the sexes are supposed to be equal, but our ideal of femininity is this characterless and vapid beach-babe beauty. Look at the statues and paintings from great cultures of the past, paternalistic societies at the peak of their power, and the women are all proud and vigorous. They symbolize the nation's inner strength, while the men simply represent its muscle. Jamey Gatz belonged to that tradition – her profile built around the twin strengths of her nose and chin, a little Slav-looking in her irascible beauty. Quite the opposite of how we categorize blondes.

Maybe that's why her beauty shone brightest in adversity – against the backdrop of horror in the subway carriage, or now as she felt herself cornered by my argument.

'You don't much have an idea what I did,' she announced. 'And I surely don't know that you're capable of understanding – y'all talk about what happened on that train like it's so cut and dried. Like we should all cheer because the bad guy died . . .'

It was probably the wind, but her eyes glistened and she looked aside. I knew to keep my mouth shut, sensing she had not finished.

'Damn . . .' she sighed. 'Why does everything have to be talked about? It's not like it really *matters* to anybody. They're just going to keep on living their lives just the same, so why can't I?'

She turned back to me with an urgent emphasis, frowning.

'I know what you want, and I know what you'd like me to say, but it wasn't that way at all . . . you'd have had to have been there and seen how sad that poor man was before you could understand. And I'm not willing to tell you he was bad or crazy, so it's just going to mess up your *story*! What you've all written already is so damn far from any kind of truth that there's no *point* in me talking to you now, don't you see? So can't you just let it lie?'

'Maybe you could have stopped that happening if you'd talked about it,' I pointed out. 'How else are we supposed to get it right?'

She raised an eyebrow and laughed.

'You think I was born yesterday?' she exclaimed. 'You people were *always* going to tell it the way you did! Don't you think I *knew* that? It's business – you've got newspapers to sell! Y'all are about as likely to tell it my way as

151

movies are going to stop having happy endings! And you must *really* be thinking I'm stupid if you expect me to buy that you have my own best interests at heart, mister!'

I ignored the criticism like anyone can who works in a profession that people generally claim to despise while being only too happy to use what it offers, and replied, 'If you know so much, Miss Gatz, you *have* to know I'm right about the fact that you cannot walk away from it now.'

Jamey looked briefly as though she was going to disagree, but then groaned in exasperation and dropped to her haunches as if drained of the strength to stay standing. She gazed down at the sidewalk, shaking her head, and I knew that I was that close to winning her over. I felt just a step away from avenging my humiliation at the *Post* – she'd practically argued herself around to accepting the inevitable. Her wild hope that this would all blow over if she ignored it had turned out to be in vain, and I just had to make sure it was me rather than someone else she surrendered to.

'You're not going to get a better option,' I insisted. 'And I'm not as bad as you seem to think I am. If you come with me like I said, I can at least control the situation for you.'

'What?' she scoffed, not looking up from the sidewalk. 'You want to be my *manager* now?'

'You might find you need one. Things can get out of hand very fast in my business. You're probably aware of that, though, right?'

'Lord almighty . . .' she sighed, clasping her fingers behind her head and resting her elbows on her knees. 'What do you get for helping people?'

I thought fast, and answered in relaxed fashion, 'Oh . . . forty per cent.'

Jamey stiffened. Her fingers sprang back open and she

gaped at me in amazement. For a second I assumed that I'd hit too high and was about to suggest reducing my cut, but instead she gasped, 'I wasn't talking about *you*, for crying out loud!'

'Sorry . . .' I answered. 'Misunderstanding.'

'But that said, I *never* heard of forty per cent, either,' she snapped back. 'My agent takes ten.'

'Your *agent*?' I frowned.

'What – did you think cleaning glasses was my vocation?' She laughed dryly. 'I'm an actress, like it seems practically every other woman behind a bar is in this damn town!'

'An actress. Really? Would I have—'

'No,' she cut in before I could finish, letting her head drop wearily back down. She cupped her chin on her palms, letting her knees take the weight, and continued in a musing voice, 'But maybe soon – I'm in the running for this movie. A good part, too. Damn!'

She shifted her weight to sit despondently on the sidewalk, sighing. 'Things were *just* starting to work out right – now I *know* you're going to screw it up for me!'

'Of course I won't,' I replied hurriedly, my heart leaping at the implication that she had accepted the inevitable. I could live with ten per cent – it wasn't about the money, anyway.

'You'd better not,' she warned softly, staring forward at about the level of my thighs. 'You'd better not.'

A fresh gust of wind set the litter scampering again, a page of newspaper tumbling past me to plaster itself against her shin. She let a desultory hand drop to peel it off and send it on its floating, scraping journey down the avenue.

'So be it,' she accepted, looking up at me with an air of decision. 'But turn me over and, believe you me, I *will* make you pay, Mr . . . ?'

'Nick.' I smiled, holding out my hand. 'Nick Carraway.'

She closed her palm around mine. My neck prickled at the touch of her skin, warm and soft in the sharp morning air.

'Well, Nick?' she asked. 'A gentleman would help a lady up . . .'

CAPITOL AVENUE, EIGHT TEN A.M.

Soon. Very soon now. These last minutes of peace will slip through my fingers like water, and we will be there. The stars of the show, the crowd pressing in, cops trying to hold it back, shouts from every direction, twisted faces, placards, microphones and flashes . . . I know what to expect. I've seen it a thousand times. I've been seeing it all my life. Adulation or hatred, a premiere or a lynching . . . they are very similar. More so than people would like to think.

It doesn't mean anything. It's not me they hate.

It was harder for my mother. She was in uncharted territory, the star of one of the first TV shows to hit that reptilian core in people's minds where the desire to believe overwhelmed the knowledge that it was fiction. I remember thousands of letters every week either addressed to her as Marcia Hudson, or using her real name but talking to the fictional character. Her on-screen children were sent Christmas presents by the vanload. There were get-well-soon cards for fictional illnesses, flowers for anniversaries, valentines, and collars for the dog. And so many requests for advice that my mother –

who in reality probably didn't even know where the Hoover was, let alone any handy tips on using mayonnaise to remove water stains from your coffee table – had a series of cookery and good-housekeeping books published under her name. Nowadays it seems a banal example of cashing in on success, but at the time I think my parents genuinely didn't know how to handle the situation. It was a new phenomenon created by a new device, and as the fiction of *Meet My Wife* spilled further and further out from the weekly show, there were no guidelines about where to draw the line. I think they were both terrified that if she called a halt to the madness and reminded everyone that Marcia Hudson was a fictional character, and that she was nothing like her when the cameras stopped rolling, they would kill the goose that was laying the golden eggs.

She felt that she had to be Marcia Hudson whenever anyone was there to see, as though every eye in the world was a camera. To the extent, I suppose, where I myself no longer knew who my mother really was, this person who kept changing character. But I knew that all the children at school were jealous of me because I had the best mother in the world.

The best mother in the whole damned world.

I remember the awe it inspired on the occasions when she made it to a Parents' Day or to pick me up from school in person. How I loved those moments – not just for the envy I inspired, but because she *would* be so perfect, so like Marcia Hudson. Her smile would dazzle me, and she would ruffle my hair just like she ruffled Jimmy Hudson's hair on TV.

Probably more than anyone else, I didn't want the lie to end either. I wanted Marcia, not the woman who cried, and took pills, and smelled of whisky. It was only after she was gone, when the dazzling smiles had faded from my memory, that I found myself treasuring the previously insignificant moments when we had been alone, and she had tried to be a normal mother who asked me about my schoolwork and helped me tidy up my room.

This is easier. I understand what is happening today, and I know what is real and what is illusion. I am Nick Carraway, a man I do not in any way admire, perhaps even the villain in all that has happened, but I am not the monster they need me to be. I know that, and it will be all right. It will not hurt me. It will not even scare me, because I understand better than they do why they hate me so.

How perfectly I antithesize their heroine. I am a man, and she is a woman. I am the corrupt product of this city – their city, their product – where she is pure as the country air she breathed. Ambition versus decency. Mine has been a life of lies and manipulation, where she only spoke the truth. I grew amid wealth and glamour where she knew only simple, honest things.

What they hate about me is everything they hate about Entropolis, about their own lives, about themselves. Only they don't know that. They can't know that. If they knew it, their hatred would wither.

And, as cardboard as are the characters Jamey and I have been allotted, there is an element of truth in it all. Of course there is. I do think I would be different if my familiarity with the world beyond this city as a child had not come through books and films. So many of us grow up that way – knowing what a cow looks like, just like we know about tigers and coral reefs, and able to imitate an owl without ever having heard one, and you can't tell the difference between us and the others once we are all adults making our way in the world, but it must make a difference.

Why, until I was old enough for my sense of awe to

have already become irretrievably blunted, I never even saw the stars. It's extraordinary, when you think about it. We know they are there, of course, and what the cosmos looks like, but there is never a night when the glare and haze of the city does not block it from our view. Our night sky is a dirty orange. On the clearest evening, it stops at about the height of a passenger plane. Occasionally, one or two bright points of light might make it through the neon dome over Entropolis, but never a constellation.

Nothing like a universe.

So how can any of us who are born and raised under that have a sense of proportion? Of significance? Of something . . . beyond our lives.

Then someone like me meets someone like Jamey. And we are similar in many ways – both young, both sharp-minded, both aware of our own faults, both ambitious, both stubborn in our own ways. And both attracted to each other, for all the antagonism that poisoned any chance of that attraction becoming love.

But how big a chance was it? That's what I want to know.

What could a boy who had grown up under a starless sky offer a girl who had been raised in a place with not just one universe, but two?

The most important thing when you have a good story is to keep it exclusive. If it centres, as Jamey's did, on a particular individual, you have to keep them away from the competition until you are ready to run your piece. That can take a day or two – the time needed to interview them at your leisure and follow up the information they give you. The *Post* used to keep an apartment just for that purpose, but I, like most papers, was using a hotel. It's called a babysit.

A babysit is a weird experience – you suddenly find yourself living with a total stranger twenty-four hours a day, kind of like a hostage crisis without the guns. You only go to this trouble if the story is big, so the babysit is a strange, quiet time before the storm breaks, and the person usually doesn't want it to end. They come to see you as their protector, even though you're precisely the one who's going to give them up to the nation.

I'd chosen the Cadogan Hotel because it was respectable and discreet, and had booked the Family Suite that afternoon, stocking up with supplies for a couple of days. It was way over my budget, but I'd never heard of maids passing on tips from the Cadogan, which they do in some of the most expensive places. Celebrities often don't seem to get that. They think that the more they are paying, the better protected they'll be. But the staff in those establishments aren't paid any better than people who work elsewhere – they just have greater reason to be envious of the customers. And simply because the management in some joint knows how to lick celebrity butt it doesn't mean they have any control over their employees. So if you want to protect your privacy, go somewhere that isn't too fashionable or extravagant, don't be arrogant with the staff, smile, and tip everyone generously. They might not sell you out.

We took a cab to the Cadogan. It was hard convincing Jamey to come as she was insistent about having to go home first. She said she had to tell her sister what was going on, but I eventually talked her round to phoning from the hotel once we got there. Or, given the hour, the next morning. I didn't say that there was a pretty good chance that by then there would already be a small army of journalists camped outside their apartment.

All the way there in the cab, I was feeling as skittish as a puppy, totally pumped up on the thought that I had

159

pulled off my coup. It was hard for me to keep still or make polite conversation, not that Jamey seemed to be in a mood to talk. She was just staring out at the night-time streets, her face flashing light and dark as it was caught by the headlights of cars coming the other way. She had said nothing since we got in the cab.

'Who told you?' she asked finally, not looking my way.

I frowned at first, then understood.

'I just found out. It's my job to do that.'

'Was it Detective Bosch?' she continued. 'He *promised* me he—'

'Who's Bosch?'

She looked at me, narrowing her eyes.

'He gave me his card if ever I needed to get hold of him,' she whispered. 'Why don't we give him a call?'

'It wasn't this guy Bosch!' I insisted. 'Do you know how many people in a precinct have access to information like that? You *can't* keep it a secret. But I have to keep my source's name confidential . . . I'm sure you understand.'

'No, actually,' she snapped. 'I don't understand. Why does your informant have a right to keep his name quiet, but not me? Can you explain that to me?'

I started to speak, and then realized that I couldn't. I had nothing to reply to that. She saw me give up just by watching my eyes, and burst out laughing.

'Got you there, haven't I?' she announced, her mood suddenly changing.

'Yes,' I admitted, as gracefully as I could. 'You've got me.'

She smiled and turned away to watch the city go by again. I felt it was up to me to make the next move, to give something back in acknowledgement of her having defeated my whole argument.

'Listen – I should phone Heather when we get to the hotel,' I suggested, keeping my voice low so as not to be overheard by the cab driver. 'There may be journalists there by tomorrow morning. But it's best if you don't tell her where we are.'

She turned to stare at me in surprise.

'How do you know my sister's name?' she frowned. 'I didn't tell you her name.'

'It's my job to know things.'

'What else do you know?'

'Not much. She's three years older than you, but I couldn't find out what she does for a living. The apartment is in your name, I noticed.'

Jamey turned away, her mouth set hard, and then flashed back, 'Can you leave my sister alone, please? She's got nothing to do with this. You've no right to go prying into her life.'

'Who's prying?' I defended myself. 'It's not like I went through the trash.'

'Because you *do* that? You go through people's *trash*?'

'No . . .' I hesitated, suddenly realizing how tacky it must sound. 'Well . . . it's been known to happen, actually, yes.'

'Lord help me,' she sighed, looking away again. 'I'm going to a hotel with a man who does garbage inventories.'

I suddenly felt very small, my pride at having bagged her deflating on the spot.

'It's not something I do on a regular basis,' I defended myself. 'Only in exceptional circumstances.'

'Oh, well, that's different.'

'It's an accepted technique,' I argued. 'You can find out a lot about people that way.'

'I'm sure you can. Why, I bet garbage collectors know a thing or two about human nature.'

We fell into silence again – she checking out the queue outside a late-night club as we waited at the lights,

161

me staring tongue-tied at her neon-bathed cheek.

'Is there no *law* protecting people's garbage?' she asked finally, turning back to face me.

'Garbage enters the public domain the moment it is left out for collection,' I explained, suddenly ashamed of my intimate knowledge of refuse legislation. 'It has no rights as such.'

'Garbage has no rights. You sure know your stuff, don't you?'

She laughed at me, bringing the discussion to an end, and her air of defiance suddenly disappeared as though she had got a handle on me now and knew how to deal with the situation.

'Will there really be journalists there by tomorrow morning?' she asked softly.

'It's possible . . . but I doubt it,' I decided. 'I think I probably have the jump on everyone in finding you.'

She raised her eyebrow, whispering with mock admiration, 'You mean . . . I'm with the best?'

'Maybe . . .' I grinned.

'Well, in that case we can leave Heather to sleep in peace, can't we?'

I will say this for Jamey Gatz: she never wanted to get involved in the first place, but once the decision was out of her hands she played the game. I told her we were booked into the Cadogan as Mr and Mrs Kevin O'Neil, and she playfully took my arm when we approached the front desk, looking at me with mock adoration as I spoke to the receptionist.

I really liked her for that.

I doubt he was fooled, given our lack of luggage, but he had perfected the art of keeping his face free of personal judgements, greeting us with impeccable neutrality.

Once upstairs, Jamey took a bath, reappearing twenty minutes later in a great big bathrobe, her damp blonde hair scraped back behind her ears and her skin burnished with a sunset glow from the heat of the water. The Family Suite had two bedrooms, and a large living area with a pair of couches in it. She must have realized I was appraising her, because she tilted her head ironically as she settled down on the couch, cross-legged with her feet tucked under her thighs, and made a consciously exaggerated show of covering up any exposed flesh.

How we ended up on the subject of her home town I cannot remember. I wasn't interviewing her at that point – I could afford to wait until the morning, and still have time to write the story up and get it to Kevin O'Neil for the next day's edition. It was gone four a.m., but neither of us seemed ready to go to bed, so we ended up talking for an hour or so. When she was in the mood, Jamey could really talk – fast talk, skipping from one subject to another, her mouth barely able to keep up with her thoughts so that you had to be on the ball to follow the connections.

We talked a lot about her acting ambitions. She'd been working in bars for almost three years now. It wasn't that she had been unable to get offers of work as an actress, but she was holding out for a good part, and at last it looked like her stubbornness was going to pay off. She was on the final shortlist of actresses for a big role in the next Tom Harris movie – and it was a good part, just as she had wanted. She didn't seem to have any great desire to be a star, she simply wanted to be able to do the work on her own terms, but I guess she realized that the two usually went hand in hand. It wasn't certain by then, although her agent was all but telling her that she had been chosen, yet I found myself becoming convinced that she would succeed – if not this time, then the next. She had a force of character that made it seem inevitable in the end, even without having seen her act. A kind of glow that some stars have. She told me about the role, but I was only half listening – partly it was tiredness maybe, but mostly it was that I couldn't stop thinking how beautiful she looked as she talked about it.

The curious thing about Jamey was that she was at once one of the most controlled people I've ever met, and the most passionate. Your first impression was of somebody relaxed, somebody who was quite detached from life, observing it with an almost amused eye. She could seem arrogant that way. But you only had to get the conversation onto something she cared about for the passion to come through, for an almost scary amount of energy to bubble out from that cool exterior. And when it came out it seemed to charge her whole body, taking possession of her eyes, her hands and her mouth in the desperate urge to communicate itself. She would completely lose that sense of detachment, and barely be able to contain her enthusiasm, almost like a child. And then, when it had spent its fire, she would laugh at herself and regain her air of wry observation.

It was extraordinary, and for a long time I found it impossible to reconcile the two sides of her character. It was only much later, when I had no more contact with her, that I realized that there was no contradiction there – a greater level of passion simply needed a greater level of control. Most of the time she was keeping her passions under control, and that was what made her so determined, so unstoppable. She was a permanently smouldering fire, able to spark alight the moment she let the air in.

I think I must have said something about her becoming a star one day, because somehow we got from her acting onto the subject of the lake.

Her home town, Otterway, is situated high in the Seskatchuan hills and built on the edge of a meltwater lake. The peculiar quality of this lake, due to some combination of mineral deposits and atmospheric conditions, is that in winter it freezes over with a silvered, looking-glass sheen. The worst of the weather stays blocked on the eastern face of the hills, and Otterway, nestling in a bowl below the peak on the western face, never receives much snow. So for most of the winter the lake remains clear – a silver sheet of ice mirroring the sky above. In the daytime it reflects the clouds, and at night it reflects the stars. Two universes.

That's what I like to think of now: Jamey at five in the morning, curled in a white flannel ball on the couch, smiling as she recalled the times she used to go out onto the lake as a child. She would walk on the clouds, jumping from one to the next over the reflected blue heaven in between, playing stepping stones on the herds of little cumulus drifting below her feet. God, I wish I had seen that. I wish I could have seen Jamey Gatz as a little girl, all scarfed and bundled, her chunky boots picking out a path across the sky. I wish I could go back in time to have us meet as children, and walk out across the clouds with her.

Instead, I have to remember us as adults, walking on the lake at night. Where, as the court will hear, I murdered her.

InfoCorps

I re-emerged a few hours later to find Jamey already up. It may have been the sound of her voice that woke me – she was in her bathrobe, sitting cross-legged on the floor, talking on the telephone. The conversation, I think, had already been going for some time.

'Do what we normally do,' she was urging patiently. 'It's no different, honey . . . I know, I'm sorry . . . just for today, OK? . . .'

I waved good morning in passing on my way through to the bathroom. I took a long shower, standing semi-drugged under the jets until I felt the water had washed the worst of the drowsiness away, then shaved and returned to my bedroom.

'The top drawer in the freezer . . .' she was saying. 'Turn the dial *all* the way round and then wait for the light to . . . with the gloves, that's right . . .'

I heard the muffled conversation come to an end just as I finished dressing, and came out to find she had disappeared into the bathroom. I ordered a breakfast to be delivered to the suite and then rang a photographer friend of mine. I'd need a few portrait shots of Jamey to go with the interview, and he was someone I knew I could trust –

if only because he considered it hack work, a rent-paying sideline to his art, and was more likely to want to keep quiet about his involvement than start hawking tips around town.

He arrived mid-morning, giving Jamey and me a welcome break from the interview, shot off a reel of film and left it with me. Easy damn money, frankly.

Certainly compared to my end of the deal. Normally, I was pretty good at interviews. The trick is not to talk too much. When I first started I used to be nervous and keep firing questions at my subject, barely letting them finish what they were saying before moving on. Hopeless, frankly. The art of good interviewing, as I eventually understood, is to pass that pressure onto the other person – if you don't pick up the conversational ball when they drop it, they feel obliged to do so themselves, and the more a person talks, the more unguarded their comments become. Human nature. It takes nerve, though, because if the tactic fails the result can be hideous.

I don't know quite what went wrong in Jamey's case – whether I was destabilized by her in some way or her nerve was simply greater than mine – but I couldn't take the silences. Once she'd answered a question to her satis-faction, no amount of stonewalling on my part seemed to pressure her into expanding upon her response. We'd just sit there, she staring expectantly at me with a raised eyebrow, waiting for another question. And I cracked every damn time. I couldn't hold her gaze in silence – those green eyes seemed to bore through my defences and force me to surrender the point.

It's harder, of course, when you find someone attrac-tive, but there was more to it than that. Without being in any way arrogant, she was blessed with a remarkable degree of self-possession. She appeared to have no in-security, no need for anyone's approval, and you could not make her step over the line. Her answers were sharply observed, but retained an infuriating element of discretion – they met you halfway every time, providing you with the information you requested but politely deflecting any attempt to elicit a judgement upon anyone or anything but herself. Even Walcott.

She had nothing but sympathy for the man, and even her sympathy was guarded in the sense that she didn't presume to comprehend him. It was inconceivable – the guy had shot a man dead, pointed the same gun straight at her with, as she herself granted, the firm intention of firing again, and yet she refused to describe him as a maniac or a lunatic.

God knows I tried – my back-up tactic, when stonewalling doesn't work, is to offer people opinions and comments that they can agree with. If you ask 'Would you say that X is true?' and they grant the point, then you're morally entitled to cite opinion X as if they had said it themselves. The subtlety is that you put it in single quotation marks rather than double ones, which would imply direct speech. It's an old trick, and generally never fails, but Jamey wouldn't even give me that much. She was alert to my every subtle change of emphasis if I tried to bounce her own comments back at her, refusing to let me channel them as I wished and forcing me, over and over, to accept her original statement. She was so sharp I could have sworn that she'd been interviewed before.

It didn't occur to me at the time to ask her outright where she had got that skill from. I just imagined her precision of expression was innate. It wasn't, as it happened, but nor was it that she had any experience of being interviewed.

Slowly, however, I gathered enough material to write the story as it should be written. By the end, and much against her will, I had forced Jamey to give me a detailed

168

account of the subway shooting and an apparently thorough biography of her own life, from childhood to the last boyfriend. It was a painful process, a battle of attrition. Almost like mental rape.

I had the story written up by three in the afternoon. And I tried to write something she would appreciate. I wrote a version of the facts that was a true reflection of her own opinion – not just out of professional pride but also because, more than I could recall on any other story, I found myself wanting to please her.

I made her promise not to leave the hotel, and left for the *Post* so as to be in plenty of time for the morning edition, making a short detour to get the film developed. Not that I didn't trust my friend to take good pictures, but I wasn't going to walk into the *Post* without looking at the photos I was selling twice in the same week. Even as it was, it took some nerve to go back there just forty-eight hours after I had been so thoroughly humiliated. I paced up and down the street outside, smoking a final cigarette, before I worked up the courage to go in.

I didn't have an appointment, but the security guards knew me well enough – I just told them I was going to see Kevin and they gave me a badge. The elevators that served the *Post* and everyone else in the top half of the building were rigged to rocket straight past the first twenty floors without stopping. It was not a pleasant experience if you were hung-over or, indeed, just nervous – your bowels lurched physically with the G force of the leap, your ears popping mildly as you approached the late teens. It cannot be good for the body or the soul to work in such a place, beginning every day with that violent wrench skywards. You don't have to believe in New Age karma crap to see that it just isn't *shanug* to be whisked up there only to spend the rest of the day in a vast, neon-lit eyrie where the windows cannot be opened and the air is thick

169

with the radiation of hundreds of computers. One day people will look back with horror at things we accept as normal, I'm sure.

As I crossed the newsroom floor, I sensed an unmistakable frisson run through my erstwhile colleagues. The Kandonese holiday snaps episode was still fresh in their minds, undoubtedly the high point of their week, and they could not help smiling as my return reminded them of it. No doubt they were surprised to see me back there so soon, daring to show my face when my professional rep was in tatters. I saw Macauley Connor eyeing me arrogantly as I approached his desk, these days placed in glorious proximity to Kevin's glass-walled office.

'Kevin in?' I asked, smiling defiantly at him.

'My god!' he laughed. 'You're just a glutton for punishment, aren't you, Nick?'

'Maybe. So . . . still on the subway heroine story?'

'Sure, we're following it up.' He yawned lazily, adding with a malicious twinkle, 'Carrying on your good work.'

'Forget about it – I've beaten you to her.'

'Oh, you have?' He grinned. 'You're sure this time, are you? She's not going to turn out to be . . . *black*, or something?'

I smiled sarcastically, feeling all my former rage boil up inside me again. One day, I prayed, it would be Connor's turn to fall.

'You're wasting your time,' I announced. 'I'm babysitting her. I have the exclusive. Come and see Kevin with me, if you like.'

'Is he expecting you?'

'No, but he better find the time if he doesn't want the *News* to get the story.'

'*Oooh* . . .' He pursed his lips, getting up nonchalantly from his chair. 'We're a little riled about all this, aren't we?'

170

'Not any more,' I answered.

Kevin received us after he finished a phone call, nothing in his manner suggesting that he intended to rub my nose in the fiasco of two days ago. Apparently that was history, so far as he was concerned. Or it may have been that he had no stomach for teasing me that day – his skin was pale, with an unnatural, waxy sheen. There were dark rings under his eyes that the baseball cap only helped to accentuate by throwing his face further into shadow. By rights, the man should have been in hospital. Or a morgue, to be quite honest. Yet he was still the same nervously energetic Kevin O'Neil, bouncing up from his chair only a fraction of a second slower than usual, a brief twitch in his cheek betraying some internal jab of pain as he did so. Macauley Connor wasted no time in announcing my reason for coming, that same wry tone informing me that he still remained to be convinced.

'You're babysitting the subway heroine?' Kevin repeated, fixing his sunken gaze on me. 'I'm impressed, Nick. How much would you be asking for her?'

I took a deep breath and stated my price. There was a heartbeat's pause before Connor burst into laughter, announcing, 'You really have lost your fucking mind!'

'Be quiet, Mac,' Kevin cut in, narrowing his eyes. 'You know the price scales, Nick – you know I'd normally pay half that for this story . . . so what is it? What's the thing?'

I smiled. This was the moment of truth – I was pricing Jamey Gatz right into the realm of a politician's mistress or a squeaky clean pop star confessing to a penchant for drug-fuelled orgies and devil-worship. The kind of story that will run and run, changing the cultural landscape. It wasn't that I was greedy, so much as that I needed to make them pay to undo the humiliation that had been inflicted upon me two days before – but I genuinely believed Jamey was worth it. I reached into my bag and

171

produced a doctored copy of her story, with all the names and places left blank.

'Because she's the subway heroine, obviously . . .' I began calmly, handing it over to him '. . . and she happens to be young, beautiful and intelligent. But mostly because she works in a strip club.'

There was an impressed silence. I imagined how Macauley Connor must have been feeling, knowing I had beaten him to this. Kevin nodded slowly, taking the copy.

'Could you give us a minute, please, Mac?' he whispered.

Once we were alone, I sat in silence as he looked over it. One of the things that had always irritated me about Kevin when I worked for the *Post* was the way he seemed to skim through everything you gave him rather than reading it. He'd turn the page when you knew he shouldn't have even got to the end of the first paragraph, usually grunting non-committally as he did so. He did that now, perched on the edge of his chair like he didn't plan for this to take so long that it would actually be worth him getting comfortable. He flicked past the second page after a matter of seconds and skimmed to the end, putting it down on the table with a final grunt.

'Fantastic story,' he announced, relaxing back into his chair. 'Perfect combination – violence, beauty, heroism and sex.'

I tried to suppress my smile, but my facial muscles were not strong enough to hold it back. Kevin saw it, raised a hairless eyebrow and tapped the papers before him with his index finger.

'But crap journalism,' he finished.

The smile drained from my face, and my lips opened to mouth a protest.

'Come off it, Nick!' he continued. 'It's bollocks. What the fuck is wrong with you? What's all this crap about her

172

being an actress? You told me that she's a stripper – which is a *great* fucking angle, no mistake – but then you only mention the strip club one time in the whole fucking article!'

'She describes herself as an actress.'

Kevin burst out laughing.

'I'm sure she fucking does!' he squawked. 'Wouldn't you? It means fuck all – actors are just unemployed people with a union! Maybe this girl will win an Oscar one day, but right now what she does for a living is work in a strip club! She is a stripper! Walcott was overcome by a lap dancer!'

I was about to correct him on that when a thought suddenly struck him. He raised his palm like a traffic cop to tell me to hold my tongue as the other hand placed words in the air, writing a headline.

'THE LAP DANCER OF DEATH,' he announced with a huge grin. 'Now *that* would go on my wall. But this . . . this is . . .'

He picked up my papers, waving them despondently and letting them drop to the desk.

'Do you have a *thing* for this girl, Nick?' he asked casually.

'No . . . no, she's not . . . no . . .'

Perhaps it was the simple fact that I was deigning to deny his comment, or perhaps my eyes betrayed some feeling I was not aware of, but Kevin's hands slapped to his cheeks and he gasped, 'Oh . . . my . . . god, you *do*! You have a *thing* for her!'

'What? What are you . . . no . . . why?'

'You've been all alone with her in some hotel room for the last day or two, and she's got to you! You are a reporter with a *thing* for his subject, Nick!'

'Bullshit!'

He slammed a hand down on my copy, his eyes on fire.

173

'This is not an objective piece because you want to *fuck the news!*' he accused me. '*Or maybe you fucked her already! Did you fuck the news?*'

'*No!*'

We both looked around through the glass walls, suddenly aware how loud our voices had become. A few heads had turned our way.

'*But you want to, don't you?*' he continued in a lower tone, hands gripping the table. 'That's why you've written this crap! This . . . *manure* here is a fucking love letter! She's got you wrapped around her little finger – turned you into her PR agent! How could you be so naïve? Can't you see what she's like? She's sexy, but she's also able to blow a man's *head* off, for fuck's sake! She's like some kind of nympho hit-woman!'

I stared at him in amazement, hardly knowing where to begin with a reply, but he was rolling. He wiped the sheen of sweat from his brow, his eyes alight with fever.

'She's like a . . . *black widow*!' he yawped. 'She'd consume any man who got too close to her, like a praying mantis with tits! My god, can't you see the angle here, Nick?'

'Don't you think you're a little out of line?' I suggested. 'You haven't even met this woman!'

'I don't *need* to!' he snapped. 'Why do you think I'm an editor? I *know* the stories, Nick! I know them all, and she is the oldest damn story in the world! The oldest, and still the best! She is there on page fucking one of the Good Book, isn't she? She is the seed from which everything else springs – all other women, and everything that men have ever done to those women, is a reaction to *this* woman! *The one we all fear and desire!* And you're trying to tell me the angle here is that she's a fucking *actress*?'

I was speechless in the face of his apparent loss of sanity. The man actually seemed to believe what he was

174

saying. Too many years of pandering to the basest instincts of the *Post*'s readership had finally shattered his reason.

It was as though the daily quest for the ideal story had overwhelmed his grip on reality and his overheated imagination had fallen back on mythology. The real world for him was now one peopled with monsters and nymphs in human guise, a maelstrom of bestial urges hidden behind the façade of ordinary men and women going about their humdrum lives.

'I don't *need* to know this girl personally,' he insisted. 'All I need to know is how she fits into the grand story. And *that*, my friend, is something I understand about her better than you do yourself, judging by this crap you've written.'

'Maybe that's because I didn't want to portray her as a character in a grand story, but as the person she really is,' I answered dryly.

'You can't do that! That's not our job! And anyway, what exactly would that be, Nick? What the hell is a *real person*, for heaven's sake?'

'Ummm . . .' I smiled, wondering if anyone else knew just how seriously he had lost the plot. 'Somebody who's actually *there*, Kevin. Like . . . you. Or me – I'm a real person!'

'Well which Nick Carraway do you mean, Nick – you as you see yourself, or as *I* see you? They're different! You as defined by your words and actions, or as defined by all the things you think and feel? Is it how you fear you are or how you would *like* to be? Come on – there's no such thing as *the real person*!'

'When did you get so philosophical all of a sudden?' I laughed, finding his whole way of thinking quite unlike the Kevin O'Neil I knew.

'Well, there you go, Nick – what do you know about

175

me?' he answered. 'Maybe I've always been like this, but you never saw it, or maybe I'm different now because I've got a fucking tumour in my head – who knows? Who fucking *cares*? It doesn't matter! However well you or anyone else might know me, I wouldn't recognize myself if I could see me through your eyes, would I? So don't be so *childish* as to tell me you've written the *real* version of this woman here! I want the *newspaper* version of her, for fuck's sake!'

'The Lap Dancer of Death . . .' I sighed, knowing exactly what he was looking for.

'Yes! Why not? Newspapers are just one more point of view, Nick, one more reality as valid as any other. Our job is to give an angle that *everyone* can connect with, to offer people a *communal* story where we all know the characters! It is *not* our role to write the fucking Authorized Biography of everybody we cover.'

Of course, he was right.

I knew that, even if I had never put it into words. I nodded my head softly, and took back my copy, placing it in my bag, but leaving my hand in there.

'I understand why you wanted to write something this girl would approve of, Nick,' he offered in a gentler tone. 'We've all been guilty of letting our admiration for people get in the way of the journalism. But it's not going to happen – this girl has been noticed, and she's a fucking *heroine*! She has a great role to play – people will love her! She *is* exceptional – in my whole career I could count the number of women we could write this kind of story about on the fingers of one hand! But that *is* the story, Nick. I will pay you for her name, but I won't give you one fucking dime for your version of her story.'

My hand was still inside my bag, fingers playing over the contents. Suddenly, as though not responsible for my own actions, I pulled out the other sheaf of pages I had in there.

'Then you'll be wanting this,' I said, handing them over to him.

The truth was that I had suspected all along that he would react this way to my original version of the story. I'd genuinely wanted to sell him a story that Jamey would approve of, but I had prepared the other version just in case that didn't work out. It wasn't so different, just a question of the emphasis being changed slightly, of the light falling on her another way. The facts were all the same, but the words had another tone.

Kevin took the pages, a curious smile playing over his lips, and began to read them at his customary lightning speed. The smile broadened as he made his way through, his fevered countenance seeming to cool. He came to the end, and looked up with a twinkle in his eye.

'Well . . . you're more on the ball than you let on, aren't you?' he grinned slyly. '*This* person I can put on the front page tomorrow. *This* is someone who will capture people's imagination!'

I suppose I should have been pleased, but I wasn't. It was a defeat. I'd tried to write the story Jamey's way, and failed.

'What about my price?' I asked. 'Am I still aiming too high for you?'

He raised an eyebrow in surprise.

'I never said you were,' he answered, gazing intently at me. 'In fact . . . what if I said you weren't aiming high *enough*?'

'I guess I don't mind if you want to pay more . . .' I laughed dryly.

Kevin wasn't laughing. He sat back in his chair, removed his baseball cap and wiped his sickly skin with his sleeve. He looked at me with a strange air, as though sizing me up for the first time.

'What sort of a deal have you got with this girl?' he asked eventually.

It was an unexpected question and I was immediately on my guard, worried that I had overlooked something and was going to find myself being sidelined. It seemed wise not to answer him too explicitly.

'I'm looking after her interests,' was my wary reply.

'Not just for this interview, then?' he continued, still with that unfamiliar regard.

'It depends what happens,' I answered carefully. 'Why?'

Kevin replaced his baseball cap and let his chair tilt backwards.

'Things work differently these days, Nick,' he mused. 'You left the paper when we had only just joined InfoCorps, so the change wasn't really noticeable, but you need to understand what we're *part* of these days – it's more than a question of being owned by a big company. We are integrated now.'

'Precisely why I left.' I smiled.

'But you were wrong!' he declared, sitting back upright and leaning across the desk towards me. 'It's not a *bad* thing! Sure, I don't like *everything* about it, but I can't deny the advantages – you cannot imagine how much more *weight* we have now!'

Suddenly, he was up on his feet, throwing his arms up and exclaiming, '*Anyone* who deals with us knows that they are dealing with InfoCorps *as a whole* – one company that on its own is bigger than the entire media sector of most of the countries it operates in, Nick! They don't fuck with that!'

Oh my god, I found myself thinking, the man had been turned into a Born Again Cretin. He had undergone a late-life conversion to the Corporate Gospel and become a more fervent believer than those who had been raised in it from childhood.

178

'Newspapers! Magazines! Books! Photo agencies! Ad agencies! To say nothing of TV on cable, satellite *and* terrestrial channels! Whole sodding *movie studios*, Nick! Can you imagine the mass that gives you? *Nobody* fucks with us these days! They know that by fucking with the *Post* they could find *all* of that against them! Even in its golden age, the paper *never* had anything like that kind of punch!'

I frowned, not really understanding where he was going with this beyond perhaps hoping that I would fall to the floor and accept McQueen as my saviour.

'Well, I'm glad for you, Kevin . . .' I shrugged. 'But it's still not my idea of fun.'

'I'm not trying to get you back on the staff, for fuck's sake!' he exclaimed, lowering his arms. 'No offence, but I can pretty much take my pick of the city's journalists, Nick. I'm talking about your *story*! *The girl*! Do you realize what InfoCorps could do with someone like her? She doesn't have to be just a one-day story – InfoCorps can take anybody it wants, and make them a celebrity! All it requires is a fucking memo . . .'

'Sure . . .' I agreed, slightly riled at the idea of Jamey being the subject of such a memo. 'So McQueen decides to make her a star – he doesn't need *me*! Once you buy the story, everybody will know who she is – I can't babysit her after that. I don't see what you want here.'

'Listen!' he ordered in a fierce whisper. 'You know as well as I do what happens when somebody hits the head-lines – it's fucking chaos, isn't it? Everybody suddenly wants a piece of them! They go from complete anonymity to having their apartment staked out by fifty fucking photographers – they can't go anywhere, they can't open their mouth without finding their words repeated and twisted a hundred times over, they can't even trust their friends! It's total anarchy – the person's life is turned

179

upside down, they're pumped until their news value runs dry, and then dumped as soon as the next big story comes along. Is that what you want to see happen to this girl?'

'No . . .' I reflected. 'But I don't see how it can be stopped. That's the nature of fame . . .'

'No! It doesn't have to be!' Kevin proclaimed. '*We* want to do it differently! The advantage of being a big media group is that we can *contain* a phenomenon like that, stop it from getting out of control and harness the energy in a more constructive way! Celebrities have managers, right? But what if *we* were the management, do you see? If you chose to sign an exclusivity deal not just with the *Post*, but with the whole of InfoCorps, then we could assume responsibility for her image across the entire range of media! Instead of this insane circus that is only going to leave her burned out by her moment of fame, we can offer her a carefully managed elevation to celebrity status – one that will last long after her original *story* is no longer news! She'll do the press, TV and radio interviews, but not so many that the public gets tired of her, and then, once her fame is established, we'll see how best to use it *constructively*. Maybe she can even do some acting, if that's what she wants! Whatever we end up doing, the important thing is that she will be an InfoCorps client with a guaranteed level of exposure and a steady income based on her publicity value – it's a whole different way of working, Nick! We don't believe that people in the news should be considered disposable commodities.'

I couldn't believe this was Kevin O'Neil talking to me. The journalist whose instincts I had the most respect for in the business, sounding like some unholy cross between a press agent and a management consultant. Everything he was saying made perfect sense, of course – as soon as he explained the InfoCorps strategy of managing the news, it had an air of logical inevitability about it. If everyone already accepted that movie stars and other celebrities used the news media as a form of advertising, then why not make the equation work the other way round – why not use the news as a breeding ground for career celebrities?

And why shouldn't a media company – whose business was to sell a product, after all – build itself a roster of marketable individuals like any normal company has its brands? Hell, why not copyright them and stop the competition from having access to your most valued commodities?

Sure. You could do it with politicians, even. One day, I suddenly suspected, elections would come down to being a ratings and circulation battle between two rival media groups. There was something logical, almost inevitable about that being where society was headed.

Hell, I wasn't naïve enough still to believe that the news had some kind of sanctity. But part of me, I suppose, *was* still the child who had stood outside the printing press on those nights with my father, my hot breath steaming the glass as I stared in at the fabulous, tentacular black machine, spinning and weaving rolls of paper into the stories of the day. I know it probably never existed, that sordidly romantic world of hot news and cold coffee – I think I knew that before I ever set foot in a real newsroom – but that was what sparked my imagination in the first place, and I'm sure I'm not the only one of us to warm my hands on a spent fire, am I?

How many people fall in love with the person they only *want* someone to be?

'I'll think about it,' I answered.

'How can you think about it? You don't even know what kind of figures we're talking about yet!'

'It's not just a question of money, Kevin,' I retorted tartly.

181

'Oh *god* . . .' he groaned, sitting back. 'You're still on your little trip about not selling your soul to the Big Bad Corporation, aren't you? When are you going to grow up? What are you hoping to prove? While you're wasting your time fighting some futile battle with your conscience, the world is moving on, Nick! Everyone else has realized that it's not a question of good guys and bad guys – a corporation is made up of people just like you, no better and no worse! It's just a big company, for fuck's sake! Can't you see yet that all you are doing is marginalizing yourself, making yourself irrelevant because you won't accept that things *change*? I am just trying to *help* you here!'

It was hard to stand my ground before his onslaught, especially when I wasn't even sure quite what principle I was supposed to be defending. Kevin had always been a forceful character, but nowadays he spoke with the certainty of someone who knew he was on the winning team. Over the last couple of years his natural authority, founded upon an absolute faith in his journalistic instincts, had been grafted onto a foreign trunk – he spoke as a businessman nowadays, convinced that nothing could stand in the way of the market forces that InfoCorps had harnessed, and yet that wasn't really him speaking. It wasn't really him sitting across the desk from me, but a clone of McQueen. Like he said, he had been integrated.

That was what I objected to most, I suddenly realized – the sense that the person I was really dealing with was somewhere behind the scenes, too aloof to even acknowledge me.

Yet I was the one who had something he wanted. I should have been calling the shots here.

'I might be prepared to consider a deal,' I announced cautiously. 'But I want it to come from McQueen himself. I want a meeting.'

'Get real, Nick!' Kevin laughed. 'McQueen doesn't deal with the details.'

I paused for emphasis before replying, telling myself that I was in the right. InfoCorps was a person, and everything within the corporation flowed down from him. My objective in all of this, it was suddenly clear, was to make that person pay attention.

'That's exactly what I don't like, you see, Kevin. It's not very satisfying to be considered a "detail" – I don't see why I, or my client, should accept being treated that way. I came here to sell *you*, Kevin O'Neil, a story – I assume we have a deal on that, don't we? Now, if InfoCorps wants to take it further, then I want to hear that from the man I'm *really* dealing with for *that* deal. In person. There's nothing unreasonable about that – I'm sure *you* talk to him on a daily basis, don't you?'

'Most days,' he admitted.

'So you would talk to him about this?'

'Of course.'

'Well, you're integrated – how valuable do you think she is to him? I'm not trying to raise the price – I just want to be treated with some respect.'

I gazed questioningly at him, waiting for him to comprehend that I would not be railroaded in the direction the corporation guidelines had stipulated for a deal such as this.

'You're better off dealing with me,' Kevin warned. 'I'm just a journalist like you. Negotiating is what *he* does for a living.'

'I don't care.'

'He's out of town today. And tomorrow.'

'Not my problem.'

'But I can't run this story tomorrow morning if it's going to be another twenty-four hours before you can even meet him! By then all hell will have broken loose . . .'

183

'You had better run it tomorrow morning . . .' I threatened. 'Or I'll take it elsewhere.'

'Why are you being like this? This isn't constructive, Nick!'

It wasn't, I knew. I had no idea how I was going to handle the chaos that would break out once everyone knew who Jamey Gatz was. Kevin had been quite accurate in his description of the anarchy a good story generates as the entire industry tries to get a slice of the action. I figured I would just have to stonewall for a day – but that pressure would be on McQueen too, after all.

In fact, it was better this way.

It was tempting.

The media was a small world, for all its reach, and it would not be long before word got around that I, Nick Carraway, had forced McQueen himself to deal with me in person. From that moment on, my reputation would be settled. No-one would laugh at me again, and every editor in town would open his door to me.

I told myself that it was the best thing for Jamey, just like Kevin argued – what was the alternative, after all? Even though I'd kept telling myself that I was simply doing my job, the knowledge that by stripping her of her anonymity I was throwing her to the wolves *had* started to bother me over the last few hours. The woman had this damned gift for puncturing the old 'It's nothing personal' defence, it seemed. First Bosch, and now me.

Maybe, I thought, I could protect her by doing the InfoCorps deal.

I reached into my bag, producing the film and the undoctored copy of the exclusive, with all the names and details supplied.

'You can tell McQueen to ring me.'

Entropolis Law Courts,
Eight Fifteen a.m.

Bedlam. I cannot see how we're even going to get off the bus. The police have put barriers on the court side of the street, but the crowd fills both sidewalks. We stop right below the steps and people immediately start climbing onto the barriers to see inside the bus, hammering on the windows and shouting. The ones on the other side of the street flood across and in moments the entire vehicle is surrounded by an enraged mob. Inside, it sounds like it's raining stones.

There aren't enough cops. Nowhere near enough.

The people all look the same even though they are of all ages, as many women as men, their faces all displaying the same anger, the same hatred. How can they despise me so much, someone they do not know, over a woman whom they never met? I hear my name being shouted, so many obscenities and accusations that they fuse into a single roar, an unrelenting thunder roll of enmity. Their hands pound upon the steel and glass with such passion that the whole bus is shaking like an aircraft in the instant when its wheels hit the runway and the jets begin to reverse, except here the shuddering howl does not fade in

185

intensity and no blessed calm will come to release the knot in my belly.

I see Bergman looking at the other guard, a trace of panic in his frown, and the other man says something that I cannot catch over the bedlam, but which does nothing to reassure my keeper.

Some people are brandishing placards with pictures of Jamey, I see T-shirts bearing her face and home-made banners wishing me ill. And then an egg explodes on the window right in front of me, making me jerk back in shock. It gives the mob a new form of expression, and unleashes an instant barrage of projectiles – drink cans and rolled newspapers, unidentifiable pieces of food, packaging, coins, and more eggs – some of them have come prepared, armed for this moment. The daylight in the bus dims as the windows are covered within seconds, splattered all around with a dirty yellow vomit, and I can no longer see so clearly what is going on outside.

Perversely, it gives us a sense of greater security, closing us off from the storm, and we are able to think and speak at last. Wolsheim shouts over to the guards, 'This is . . . I can't let you take him out in this.'

'We can't take him out?' Bergman laughs. 'You think *we're* going out there?'

He sits down, throwing up his arms in exasperation.

'Take me back to prison,' he sighs. 'These people are dangerous.'

Wolsheim and I follow his example, sitting down in silence. Outside, the furore continues unabated, unidentifiable objects still pounding the windows, if less frequently. But, to my surprise, I find I no longer mind. The truth is that I'm not exactly unhappy to be trapped in the bus, and the madness going on out there only accentuates the peace and calm in here. Within this box, it's like the eye of the storm, unnaturally still. And best of all, the crowd's enraged attempts to get at me have ironically had the reverse effect. For the first time since we left prison, I am hidden from view . . .

Heather

The question I've asked myself a thousand times since then is whether or not I was to blame for what happened that next day, the day Jamey's story appeared in the *Post*. She blamed me, that much is certain.

And maybe she was entitled to. It could have been avoided. And she did come to regret the revenge she took on me in the heat of her pain, which is almost a kind of forgiveness. For her own part in it, however, she would never forgive herself.

I recall most of that day as a horrified, numb haze. A day of tears and despair through which I sat in stunned silence. Ironically, it started as being quite the opposite – I have never in my life, before or since, done so much talking as I did in the early hours of that morning. The first call came through on my mobile shortly after five a.m. I either didn't hear it ringing on my dressing table, or incorporated it into some inebriated dream, because the caller left a message. It was the night editor of the *News*, who had obviously just seen the first edition of that day's *Post*. The story carried my byline on it and he knew I was freelance, so it was only to be expected that he sound a little disappointed that they hadn't been offered a chance to outbid Kevin O'Neil for it.

Even Jamey had lightened up about her situation when I showed her the cheque Kevin had given me, and we'd celebrated by keeping Room Service busy that evening. She'd been on the phone when I got back, talking someone – her sister, no doubt – through the different shelves of the freezer. I stood impatiently by, waiting for them to agree on the precise contents of the different bags and aluminium containers, before I could take it no longer and held the cheque under her nose. She tensed and snatched it from me in disbelief, but her voice didn't waver in its patient delivery of instructions, like she was used to switching her brain off in dealing with her sister. She looked up at me with a smile, crooking the phone under her chin to applaud me silently, and nodded enthusiastically as I mimed pouring out a bottle.

It had been a good evening, like we were friends.

There were three more calls on the mobile that morning before one finally cut through the fog of my sleep at around six a.m. – the first of the TV channels, PCS, had picked up on the story and wanted Jamey to appear on their lunchtime bulletin. From then on, they would start coming thick and fast as everybody woke up to find themselves hungry for a slice of Jamey Gatz.

Having often experienced the other side of this kind of phenomenon, being one of a hundred callers, I knew what to expect. I was easy to get in contact with, even if no-one knew where I was. By seven o'clock the calls were coming from every direction: PCS, ABS and BNS by now falling over each other to get Jamey onto their lunchtime slots, pushy young women with honeyed voices dangling star anchor names in front of me and promising top news billing for my client; both cable news channels, CNTV and N24/7, were determined to scoop her up for themselves, hitting me with a barrage of viewer demographics in an attempt to convince me that they, and they alone, were platforms worthy of carrying a major Jamey Gatz interview; most of the radio stations wanted her there and then, on the phone right that minute for an on-the-spot interview.

The poor girl wasn't even awake yet. I soon forgot my need for coffee, and began fielding the calls with a professionalism that seemed to come from nowhere, already honed to perfection. I aped the pleasant, tight-arsed style of the PR managers who had so often frustrated me in the past, taking down everybody's details and promising to call them back, but giving nobody satisfaction. I was like the kid with the bag of sweets, taking bids over who was going to be my best friend.

It was not long, however, before the callers started to blur and I could no longer remember who had offered what. After an hour I was getting repeat calls from people I had spoken to earlier, the urgency of their invitations sharpening, and I realized that I could not keep stalling them indefinitely. I needed a plan of action, but I had no idea as yet how to sort through the cacophony of requests, nor was there any respite in the calling in which to sit down and think. My head was spinning with voices. In the world beyond, I knew that something similar would be happening to all those who could be found to have a connection to Jamey Gatz – relations, employers, and schoolteachers would be being rung right now. It was as though a master switch bearing her name had been flicked, channelling the entire force of the media's curiosity through her. Like substations on a power grid they would provide connections to other names, other forgotten acquaintances, who would be rung in turn and squeezed for a quote or a name until the current had lit up a whole network of people, setting Jamey's entire life flashing and ringing to the sound of telephone bells.

By the time she appeared from her bedroom, around eight, my brain was fried. I was talking to someone from the *Spud Braynaum Hour* who was desperate to get her on air for a phone-in session with the public; newspaper correspondents from all over Atlantis had got on the case by then, catching up with their Entropolitan colleagues; no fewer than three independent documentary-makers had thought they were getting the jump on everyone by proposing to do an hour-long profile of her; and Lola Colaco had called.

That one really surprised me. The call didn't come from Lola herself, naturally, but it wasn't from some lowly *Lola Colaco Show* researcher either. It was from the show's producer – about as close to Lola in the flesh as you could get, with the possible exception of her cosmetic surgeon. And Lola wanted to do a special. A *Lola Colaco Special* was not something you turned down, and he had made no attempt to disguise his incredulity when I asked if I could call him back, but by then I was in a state of complete panic, the intensity of the thing too much for me to handle. Jamey was an even bigger story than I had anticipated – the combination of heroism, beauty and a frisson of sex injected by her job description proving an irresistible combination to every branch of the media. It felt like I'd just driven a food truck into a refugee camp.

To be honest, I was beginning to realize just how far out of my depth I was – one guy versus an entire army of pushy journalists, angry editors, stressed producers, and sweet-voiced young research girls who hoped eventually to become one of the above. It was too much. So much so, in fact, that I was starting to wish I had let Kevin talk me into making that one-stop deal with InfoCorps the day before. There came a point when I very nearly called him up to say I wanted to do it right away, my fingers poised over the buttons on my phone, but I held myself back.

Calling now would be tantamount to admitting defeat – it would be an act of desperation and I wouldn't be setting the terms of the deal. However impossible the situation might be, I had to find a way of holding out for another twenty-four hours until the meeting with McQueen himself could happen.

Halfway through the Spud Braynaum call, the room telephone began ringing. It was too early for reception to be bothering us, which meant the call had to come from outside. I had no idea who could have traced us there already, or how, but I had no intention of answering it. I let it ring for about a minute, sighing with relief when it stopped, but by then the noise had woken Jamey and she appeared in the doorway, a charmingly befuddled look on her face, just as I was winding up the conversation on my mobile.

I didn't want her to think that I was anything but the master of the situation, however far from the truth that might be, so I smiled and turned off my phone to give myself a few minutes' respite from the chaos. The relief of knowing that the damn thing wasn't going to ring again relaxed me almost immediately.

'Who was that?' she asked, leaning sleepily on the door frame, dressed in T-shirt and knickers.

'Congratulations,' I applauded her. 'Providing the President doesn't die over the next few hours, Jamey, you appear to be the single most exciting thing happening in the entire world today. All the main TV channels, all the newspapers, radio . . . and now Lola Colaco wants to do a damn special on you, for heaven's sake!'

'That was *her* on the phone just now?' She yawned.

'I didn't answer it.' I shrugged. 'I was on the mobile.'

She pushed herself dopily off the door frame and me-andered her way over to the bathroom.

'You would not *believe* how desperate people are to

192

talk to you!' I called after her as she closed the door. 'Your apartment is probably being besieged by about a hundred hacks right now!'

I heard a tap start running and then stop almost immediately. There was a moment's silence and then Jamey burst back through the door, her face suddenly awake.

'Damn!' she snapped, making a beeline for the telephone. 'How could I have been so stupid?'

She punched a number on the phone, slamming it down almost straight away.

'*Busy*,' she announced, making it sound like some hill-country curse. She rushed back into her bedroom, shouting, 'I have to go to my place right now.'

'No way!' I answered. 'I told you – everyone will be there!'

'I need a cab!' she replied, pulling on her jeans. 'Order one, will you?'

'Jamey . . . I can't let—'

She wheeled around to face me, eyes blazing.

'Just order me a cab!'

The argument ended right where our gazes met. No matter that it was the last place we should go, there was no discussion possible – all I could do was accompany her and hope for the best.

I was far from being able then to imagine what the worst might be.

Jamey commandeered my phone as soon as the cab had set off from in front of the Cadogan, her manner so brisk that I barely dared interrupt her furious pressing of the buttons to tell her that it was still turned off. She shoved it back into my hand with a small curse after I apologetically offered to enter the security code, her customary politeness quite lost in the face of whatever urgency had suddenly gripped her this morning.

It seems now as though it should have been obvious to me, but at that moment my thoughts were scrambling uselessly over each other as I reached for an explanation, spinning like wheels in mud, and I didn't feel it was my place to ask her outright what all this was about. I was there on sufferance – she hadn't wanted me in the cab, and only gave way so as not to waste time on what was clearly a side issue to her. I was simply one of a dozen factors conspiring to hold her up, from the snarled morning traffic to the zip that stuck on her jeans, all of us treated to the same exasperated scowl and barely audible malediction.

Contemplating that pretty face from the corner of my eye, it felt like I had plunged my head into a cold basin – *this* was the woman who could have dealt with Randall Walcott, I realized. This creature with steel in her gaze, not the tired, confused person I had met the day before. She was the same, but her character had suddenly sharpened as though a lens had just been pulled into proper focus. I was both fascinated and terrified by her, amazed that only minutes ago I had been thinking she was in my charge, reliant upon me to take decisions on her behalf. Nobody could dictate to this person, I now understood, not even someone holding a gun.

And that was when I had the first inkling of foreboding at the thought that she had agreed to trust me with her life so far as she had, realizing for the first time that I might have bitten off more than I could chew not just with the story, but with the woman herself. She had something of the scorpion about her, a sense of coiled threat that set my skin tingling as I sat there beside her.

And yet even then, as my every instinct warned me this was not somebody whose wrath one would want to incur, the same instincts were drawn to her like a gaze to a flame, fascinated by her beauty.

She kept trying her home number without success, her jaw muscles flexing under her skin as she got a busy tone again and the cab picked its way across town in fits and starts. The driver was picking up on her tension and becoming steadily more irate each time the cross-traffic blocked his turn to go through a light, beginning to honk aggressively and slap the wheel in exasperation. There's something of a boxing match about morning traffic, the city like a ring in the early rounds as the combatants circle and feint about each other, trying little jabs and ducks to find a way through their opponent's guard, but no blows being landed. A couple of times he yanked the cab down side streets, racing along the little channel only to lurch to a halt as he came up against another raised glove, until he finally crossed Edgeware Boulevard and broke free. The traffic from that point on was all heading in the other direction and he had a clear run into West Gossom, darting from one light to the next in a fluid combination of punches.

I saw the mob ahead as we turned down the top end of Jamey's street – a great clot of people and vans a couple of hundred yards away – and told the driver to pull over. Jamey's hand went for the door, but I caught her arm, saying, 'Are you crazy? You can't just walk into that!'

'I have to see my sister,' she announced, pulling against my grip.

'You won't even be able to get to the door, for god's sake!'

'You don't understand,' she snarled, breaking free her arm. 'Heather needs me. I shouldn't have left her alone.'

'Try ringing again!' I pleaded, dreading the consequences of her stepping out of that car and into the view of the massed horde of journalists. 'Just try once more!'

She looked ahead to the dark mass outside her building, bulging dangerously off the sidewalk into the flow of cars, and picked up the phone again, pressing the redial button without any conviction in her expression.

Suddenly, her body stiffened and she held her breath. I sighed with relief, knowing she had a ringing tone at last.

'Get her to come out,' I instructed. 'Tell her where we are and we'll just have to do our best to—'

'*Heather?*' she clipped, cutting me off with a glance. 'It's me, honey . . . it's me . . . it's Jamey . . .'

I frowned as I heard a tin howl from the distant speaker, sounding almost like some abandoned infant animal. It was not a noise any normal person would make.

'I'm so sorry . . . I'm *so* sorry . . .' Jamey was whispering gently as the howl continued. 'I was stupid. I didn't think this was going to happen. I'd never have left you alone if I thought it would be like this, believe me, honey . . .'

I understood, finally. The snatches of conversation I had heard at the hotel, Jamey's reluctance to be away from her home, her unwillingness to discuss her family – it all resolved itself into a clear, quite obvious explanation as I listened to the tin waves of grief crashing against Jamey's ear and her calm, practised efforts to soothe her sister's anguish. I realized now that I hadn't really been paying any heed to the clues that were presented to me, wrapped up as I had been in my own grand plans. If I had, I would have suggested we do something about her earlier. Bring her to the hotel or something. It wouldn't have been too much of a problem.

But now she threatened to mess up everything.

As Jamey slowly, patiently managed to calm her down, I decided that the only answer was for me to go in and bring her out. Jamey could not enter the building, that was clear, but there was a good chance that nobody in the scrum of journalists outside it would know me by face. If I could get her downstairs and out of the building, Jamey

196

could be ready with the cab to whisk us away from there. We'd be lucky to lose anyone who was quick enough to get on our tail, but once we were back at the Cadogan it would be possible to hold tight until I hammered out a deal with InfoCorps that would take care of everything.

I wrote her a note, explaining my plan. She frowned sceptically as she read it, shaking her head and pointing to herself, but I snatched the note back and wrote YOU CANNOT GET IN THE FUCKING BUILDING, under-lining it three times to make my point.

She winced as she thought it over, clearly unwilling to trust me with the mission, yet all the while keeping up that same soothing patter over the phone. I waited, gazing determinedly at her, until she finally began to explain to her sister that a man would be coming in a minute, a friend . . .

I still believe my plan was a good one. The only way I was ever going to get Heather out of the building was to provide a distraction – when the moment came for her to make a dash for the taxi, the journalists all had to be looking in the wrong direction. For that to be possible, they had to believe *I* had information of some kind.

'Has there been an accident?' I asked a young guy on the edge of the posse, picking him because he looked as nervous about the situation as I was.

He couldn't have been much more than a month or two out of college by the look of him. A handsome kid who had probably edited the student rag and taken himself for a real journalist until a few weeks ago. Now he had the hunted appearance of someone who was intentionally having the arrogance beaten out of him, sent on this thankless assignment with an explicit, barked order to get some kind of exclusive angle on the story. He was para-noid, aware that most of the other guys there knew each other, hogging the front positions and swapping the little information they had amongst themselves. He was probably starting to have serious doubts about his choice of profession, hating the people he worked for and missing the good old days when he wasn't in competition with a hundred other guys for each little crumb of story.

I might have felt sorry for him if I didn't know that in a year or two he'd probably be up at the front with the rest of them, freezing out some bright young kid just like himself.

'Someone lives here, that's all,' he announced unhelpfully, figuring me for a nosy passer-by.

'Well, sure they do,' I frowned. 'Me, for instance.'

He stiffened, suddenly daring to hope that he might be in with a chance of getting back to the office with something, after all. He stepped marginally away from the pack, placing a hand on my elbow to take me aside as he asked in a low tone of hurried confidentiality, 'You live here? Do you know a *Jamey Gatz* who also lives in the building?'

'I dunno. Maybe.' I shrugged. 'I don't really know any of the other people by name. What's he look like?'

'She,' he corrected me. 'Blonde. Good-looking. About twenty-five years old.'

'Uhh . . . the blonde?' I answered warily, knitting my brow. 'Sure. Yeah, I see her around. Spoken to her a few times and stuff.'

His eyes were lighting up like pinball mushrooms by now, thoughts *ding-ding-dinging* around his head. A quote, he was thinking. He had to get a quote.

'Have you seen her in the last forty-eight hours?'

'What?' I laughed. 'How the hell do I know? God, yeah . . . maybe . . . let me think.'

I paused to mull it over, keeping him on tenterhooks as I worked my way back through the last two days.

'Sure, that's right!' I announced triumphantly. 'Night before last I seen her.'

'*The night before last?*' he repeated. 'Are you sure? What happened?'

'Sure I am. She seemed kind of upset. I remember now. Is she in trouble?'

'No. She's not in any trouble, but I'd really like to hear about what you saw, Mr . . . ?'

'Wilson. George Wil— why do you want *my* name now?' I asked suspiciously. 'What do you need that for?'

'For the paper.'

I stepped back, raising my hands. From the corner of my eye, I could see other journalists beginning to take an interest in our conversation.

'Hey,' I warned. 'I don't want to talk to no *paper*. I'm late for work as it is, OK? I don't want to get *involved* in something.'

'You won't be getting involved. It's just so I can say who you are.'

'I don't want you saying who I am.'

'Well, I don't have to, then. Really I just want to hear what you saw.'

'Why should I tell *you*? I dunno who the hell you are or . . . or what this is about . . . you know? Huh? Hey, I'm nothing to do with this!'

'I'm not saying you are, Mr Wilson!' he laughed. 'I'm writing a story about Jamey Gatz, that's all!'

'OK, maybe, but . . . what's in it for *me*?'

'Well, nothing, but it doesn't *cost* you anything to—'

'Right. That's what I figured,' I announced, brushing past him. 'So can I get into my damned building, please?'

That was not going to be easy, I knew. The trick with a pack of journalists is simply to keep moving – they're all in competition with each other, so if you are forceful enough the ones in front generally let you squeeze by so that they can slip in and shut out the guys behind. You just mustn't ever stop and let a circle coagulate around you. It's scary because you can't see where the hell you're going and everyone starts barking questions at you, but they'll stop just short of physically blocking your path. By now word had got around that I was a guy with a quote, or maybe even a whole angle on the story, and I found myself batting my way through a swarm of dictaphones. I could barely hear what any one person was asking over the cacophony of questions, and didn't hesitate to elbow and shove them out of my way, fulminating about how I thought this was supposed to be a goddamned free country and didn't a guy have a right to enter his own damned building? I fought my way up the stoop to the door, people packing unsteadily onto the stairs around me as I prepared to punch in the entry code.

'For god's sake!' I shouted angrily. 'I'll be down again in a minute, OK?'

The implication that I'd be willing to speak once I'd changed my shirt, or done whatever it was that I'd come to do, convinced them to back off temporarily and I was able to enter the code Jamey had given me, shutting the door behind my back with a sigh of relief.

Jamey's building was a pleasant, homely brownstone – oak staircase, slightly worn plasterwork on the ceiling, a row of old postboxes in the hallway. I took the stairs two at a time up to the second floor and rang on her bell. Heather must have been waiting right behind the door because it opened before the echo had even died away.

At first glance, the resemblance was striking. Same blonde hair, same facial structure. You could almost take her for Jamey, until you got to the eyes. Wide open, like a young child's. Eyes that could not lie, or even understand

200

what a lie was. But they could certainly cry, I realized, looking at the traces of salt upon her smooth cheeks.

'Hello, Heather – my name is Nick. I'm a friend.' I introduced myself softly, perching forward to kiss her cheek as I'd been instructed to do.

Heather returned the kiss a little too emphatically, leaving a moist lip-print on my cheek, and announced happily, 'I know. We're going to see Jamey now.'

'That's right,' I smiled. 'She's downstairs in a car. Shall we look if we can see her out the window?'

She nodded excitedly and I entered the apartment. It was important that Heather understand where she had to go for my plan to work smoothly. She had to make her way straight to the car once she came out of the building, taking advantage of the distraction I would provide as I let the posse below crowd around me with their questions.

If she didn't, if she got confused or panicked when the moment came, then my one chance of making a diversion for her would be lost and so would any hope of getting her safely away from here. Since there was no way Jamey would leave without her, even if she had to step out of the car and get her sister herself, failure would entail losing my whole control of the exclusivity. It would become a free-for-all.

I could hear the muffled ringing of a telephone and saw, as we entered the living room, that Heather had placed it in the drawer of a bureau, having been instructed by her sister not to answer it any more. She followed close behind me as I went over to the bay window, letting me turn her to look down the street below.

'Do you see that yellow car with the sign on top?' I asked. 'That's where Jamey is waiting for you, OK? She's hiding because she doesn't want all those people down there to see her.'

201

Looking down at the bustle of journalists, I noticed my good-looking rookie had graduated into the centre of the pack, encircled by older reporters who were no doubt haggling with him for information about me.

'Now listen carefully, Heather,' I continued, placing an arm on her shoulder as I pointed down below. 'I'm going to go out of the building first, and I'm going to walk the *other* way so that all those men have their backs turned to you when you come out, OK?'

She nodded uncertainly, shuffling her feet with anxiety. Her hands were sliding over one another as though she were soaping them, and I saw that she wore a bright plastic watch on her wrist.

'Do you know how long a minute is on that?' I asked, gesturing to it. 'I want you to wait a whole minute before you come out, and then you go *straight* to the yellow car, do you understand? You *don't* wait for me.'

She frowned disapprovingly and shook her head.

'I'm not allowed to do that,' she informed me sternly. 'It's dangerous.'

'What's dangerous?'

'The street,' she said. 'It's dangerous to go outside on my own. I could get run over.'

'That's OK,' I argued. 'Jamey's watching you from the yellow car. You just go straight along the sidewalk to the yellow car and it won't be dangerous.'

'I could get lost,' she continued in the same childishly censorious tone.

I smiled reassuringly at her. It was disturbing to see those familiar features mirrored in her face, but for them to be so unfinished, so impressionable. There were no lines, no contours of muscle in the jaw. She was like a doll of Jamey herself.

'No you couldn't,' I told her softly. 'You can't get lost if you keep your eyes on the yellow car.'

'You must always look where you're going,' she argued. 'Sometimes there's dog poo.'

'Well . . .' I sighed, realizing now where Jamey derived that meticulous precision in her speech that had caused me so much trouble when I interviewed her. 'I think that this one time we won't worry about dog poo.'

Her eyes widened incredulously.

'What if I step on it?' she gasped. 'Dog poo on my shoes!'

'It doesn't matter. We can clean it off later. Today is special and we don't mind about dog poo, OK?'

She frowned, knowing she ought to accept what I said because I was a friend, but deeply sceptical of the whole argument. It went contrary to all that she had learned about the world. I started to worry that my authority on the issue was going to prove insufficient and we would have to phone Jamey just to resolve the dog-poo question.

'Listen, I really think it will be all right, but if anything *does* happen . . .' I insisted '. . . I'll buy you a new pair of shoes.'

She smiled delightfully, like a Christmas tree lighting up. The option of new shoes, apparently, changed all the dynamics of the equation. It wrenched my heart to see such simplicity on that face.

A face that I realized was going to spell disaster if anybody below looked at it – Heather was, at first glance, the very woman all those hacks were after. Before we went downstairs, I did my best to cover it up, insisting she tuck her blonde tresses up inside a woollen hat despite her complaint that she'd get hot and had lovely hair, everyone said. It wasn't exactly a disguise, but I thought she was less likely to catch the corner of someone's eye like that.

We went over what she had to do again and again as we stood by the front door, until I was sure that she had got it straight. I would go outside and then, once the fast hand had gone all the way round her watch, she would come out, quietly pull the door to without shutting it, and walk calmly to the yellow car. It was very clear in her mind.

I knew there would be a rush when I went back outside. So I came out fast, trotting down the steps, and started barging my way through the crowd, trying to pull it with me down the street.

'OK! All right!' I yelled once I was a few yards clear of the stoop and the pack had begun to move down the street with me. I didn't want any of them behind me, facing the doorway when Heather came out, so I wheeled on the guys pulling round the edges of the pack, shouting, 'I won't tell any of you what I know if you keep fucking *crowding* me!'

That did it. The suggestion that I might have something hot to impart convinced them all to remain respectfully in front of me, as if for an impromptu press conference. It was exactly as I wanted – I could see the door and down the street towards the car, and they were all looking the wrong way, if not quite as far down the street as I'd have liked to pull them.

They all started yelling questions at once and I let them, knowing the noise would cover up Heather's exit from the building. Trying not to let my eyes stray too obviously towards the door, I began shouting 'What?' 'Yeah?' and 'I dunno, I can't hear you!' to those nearest me, purposely upping the din and chaos with my garbled replies.

Heather seemed to be taking far longer than a minute to come out, but I guess she might have got it right. I guess it could have been exactly one circle of the fast hand, but it felt like five by the time I saw her finally poke her head through the doorway.

She was scared and I begged her not to freeze, willing her to walk on down the steps – which she did, but at an agonizingly slow pace. Some of the older hacks were getting irritated by the anarchy of the situation, yelling at others to be quiet so that everyone could hear me speak. They seemed to command respect because a sudden hush settled over the posse just as Heather started nervously heading down the sidewalk, her eyes glued to the yellow cab a couple of hundred yards away.

I was trying to keep them occupied, improvising a confused and long-winded account of the last time I'd seen Jamey Gatz – and it was working – when I heard someone shout, 'Hey . . . didn't you work for the *Post*?'

I ignored him, pressing on with my story, but he didn't let it go, bellowing, 'The *Post*! You used to be with the *Post*, right?'

My face flushed, and I knew I was fucked. Heather was about halfway to the cab, still keeping to that slow, shuffling pace, and I thought that if I could only hold them for a little while more it would all be all right . . . but then she stopped. She seemed to wobble on the spot, her arms flapping clumsily out to balance her, and then she looked down.

There was a silence just then as everyone waited for me to respond to the guy's accusation, but my mouth ran suddenly dry of words as I saw her turn cheerfully back my way.

'*New shoes!*' she called excitedly, pulling off her hat and waving it in the air. '*New shoes!*'

They all heard her.

They all turned.

There was a momentary pause as they took in the happy, smiling face, the blonde hair falling down to her shoulders, and then a great roar went up.

It still haunts me, that sound, moving from outrage to triumph in one seamless, guttural yawp. Something like a football crowd seeing a match-winning ball rebound off

205

the post only to hit the goalkeeper and drop, dribbling softly into the net.

What is different about humans is our potential for losing control. It's not that we wage war, or murder in cold blood, because if there is a motive, an advantage to be gained, then it is a natural thing to do – other animals will do the same in their own ways. But only humans lose control. Of course, the journalists did not know that this was Jamey's *sister* I had been trying to slip past them, nor that she had the mind of a child, but I do not believe even that knowledge could have stopped them at that moment. Somebody would still have run towards her, impulse overwhelming reason, and the others would have followed.

And though I shouted for them to stop, there was nothing I could have said or done that would have silenced that roar or broken their charge.

Nothing in the whole world.

Poor Heather's own instincts were too sharp and simple to encompass more than one possible danger. She saw the mob hurtling towards her down the sidewalk, brandishing mikes and dictaphones, the smile on her face turned to panic and her arms flapped uselessly as she looked for a place of shelter. What she could not see behind her did not exist – the sidewalk she could run down, the yellow cab waiting. There was only the horde of men charging at her, the wall to her right, and the open road to her left . . .

It was inevitable which way she would turn.

I stood paralysed, solitary, watching with the hideous luxury of seeing the tableau come together in a handful of heartbeats – Heather hesitating and lunging towards the road, Jamey bursting out of the cab with a scream of warning, the posse bearing unstoppably down the sidewalk, the black car racing to meet her . . . exactly the

206

same impression I had watching Jordan Baker commit suicide.

Time stops for death.

It's no illusion. Quite the reverse. It is the end of the illusion that fools everyone under the sun – that seconds, minutes and hours are the currency of our lives. There's something else, though I don't know what. Another form of tender in another dimension – and when death is close, the whole illusory economy of time collapses to be replaced by that something. Awful because it is absolute, yet kinder in its way. I can believe there's more than enough space to live your whole life again in that instant, as they say you do, even if you could not find time for a single kiss.

Your mind can perceive the car in every detail down to every scratch, the driver so clearly that you can look into his heart and feel pity for him as he fails to stop himself from killing you, the hands on his wristwatch . . . but your body cannot take a single step in that dimension, your body has not the time even to make one jump out of death's path.

Or perhaps Heather never even knew. Perhaps even then her mind moved too slowly to comprehend the real danger before the hurtling metal punched the life from her.

But we all did. Every single person there stopped, frozen by the inevitability of the impact. We saw her fly crazily up into the air, her blonde hair floating gracefully with the spin and twist of her body, and watched her fall.

Time returned unevenly, like a spirit walking through the crowd, touching our shoulders and returning movement to our bodies. I ran to join the pack of journalists who were just beginning to turn to one another, the horror of what they'd done written large on their faces, and saw that there was only one who remained frozen, untouched by time. Jamey stood, her face as still and single-minded as a statue.

They never seemed more alike, the sisters, than in that instant.

Entropolis Law Courts,
Eight Forty a.m.

'Presuming we don't just spend the rest of our lives stuck in this bus, Nick,' Wolsheim says softly, 'there isn't a judge in town who wouldn't grant us a postponement in these conditions.'

I sit up, having been lying across the seats for the last ten minutes or more. Lately the mob outside has settled down to a kind of moronic solidarity, chanting 'CARR-A-WAY . . . TIME TO PAY! . . . CARR-A-WAY . . . TIME TO PAY!' over and over and over, banging the bus and stamping their feet in time. Wolsheim's looking a little frayed, his eyes wide with tension. It's the first time I've ever seen him appear anything other than completely confident in himself.

'I thought you wanted this,' I answer. 'Surely it's part of your strategy?'

'It is . . .' He shrugs. 'But I'd understand if you didn't feel up to it.'

'What about *you*?' I ask, looking closely at those harrowed eyes. 'It doesn't really matter what I feel, does it?'

209

He doesn't answer straight away. It's not a long pause, but in Wolsheim's case it amounts to an admission of self-doubt.

'I'm fine. Once we're in court . . . it won't matter to me what's going on out here.'

There's a kind of longing in the way he says 'court', like most people would talk about being home. I think that's exactly what it is for him – I think he's like some highly specialized creature that has adapted to life in an environment too inhospitable for other species, living in the deepest recesses of the ocean or in the sulphur on the edge of a volcano. I can suddenly imagine him as the kind of boy who never fitted in at school, who was highly intelligent but lacked the mundane qualities that would have won him friends and a sense of belonging. So he evolved differently, choosing to make his home in precisely the place where everyone else least wanted to find themselves – on the defendant's bench in a court-room, the place where they are no longer part of society, their right to freedom suspended pending judgement. And there he ruled, better at living in that precise place than anyone else.

That's what life comes down to, I suppose. We like to think it's about who we are, but it's not. It's about how we fit in, about adapting ourselves to a niche and marking out a terrain like any other animal. It has to be that way if there is to be order. And there has to be order.

Jamey's tragedy is that she didn't accept that. Which is something that all these people outside claim they loved her for, not admitting, even now, that it was they who tore her to shreds.

'Don't worry about me,' I finally reply, thinking of the promises I have made to myself. And to Jamey, wherever she is. 'I don't want a postponement. It's time for this to end.'

210

The chant around the bus grows scrappier by the second and gives way to a new bedlam of shouts and curses. Then the bus stops shaking, the hammering of fists petering out, and the pitch of the crowd alters . . . something has changed, something is going on. We turn around but can see nothing through the splattered windows, and my stomach lurches with uncertainty.

There's a loud rap on the door and a voice yells, '*Police! Open up!*'

The driver hesitates momentarily, looking towards Bergman and the other guard for confirmation, then releases the hydraulics. The door sucks open and an anonymous figure jumps up, wearing full riot gear. His face is hidden by the helmet and visor, his body armoured. In his right hand he brandishes a long baton, in his left a clear plastic shield.

'Let's go!' he announces, pointing the baton at me and Wolsheim.

I don't need to see his face to be able to tell he's enjoying himself, pumped up with adrenalin and fear. He doesn't give a damn what this is about, or whether I am the villain or the victim here, he's having a ball. Outside the shouting reaches new pitches of fury.

'Right now!' he insists.

Wolsheim and I look at each other, both scared shitless, and get up. I feel a large hand close on my shoulder and Bergman mutters in my ear, 'It's all right – I'll go first.'

He steps past me and nods to the riot cop, signalling that we're ready to go. We start moving towards the door and there's no time for me to say anything to him, to thank him for all the small kindnesses he has shown me this morning, for his courage. I don't know quite what I would say anyway.

I don't really know anything about Bergman, if the truth be told. Maybe he's gay, maybe not. But whatever

211

he is, I hope someone other than his mother loves him. I hope some person out there realizes what a good man he is. It would genuinely make me happy to know that, but I suspect it's not so. Something about him tells me he's on his own. One of the tragedies of life is that those who deserve most to be loved so often aren't. Tragic – I've used that word so much as a journalist that I'm not even sure what it really means any more, but that's what it *should* mean: the waste of a good person. I seem to have seen so much of that lately. A whole succession of tragedies that have led me here today.

But not mine. I am on the other team.

And whatever happens to the rest of us is just comedy.

We move towards the door. A posse of riot cops are waiting out there, their shields raised to clear a space for us to exit. Bergman braces himself, turning to check that we're ready to follow.

'Can we keep my client's suit clean, please?' Wolsheim says to the cop, gesturing at the filth and grease stuck to the windows.

'The faster you move, the harder the target,' the cop suggests, tapping Bergman's arm. 'Go!'

And then we're clattering down the steps – first Bergman, then me, and Wolsheim pressing close behind. The roaring redoubles in intensity and a group of riot cops close ranks around us, pushing us forward along the corridor they have cut through the crowd.

Bergman takes me by the hand, and we run.

I cannot see anything beyond the wall of armour closed about me, hearing objects whistling by overhead, striking the shields raised all around. I run unquestioningly, placing my faith in Bergman's hand and hoping to god I don't fall over. Within seconds we reach the courthouse steps, racing up them as the crowd howls its fury now that I am visible. A man behind me is saying 'Go-go-go-go!' all the way – it may even be Wolsheim, for all I can tell.

And then the light suddenly dims and we're scattering over the marble interior, the pack instantly breaking apart as the huge doors boom shut behind us, echoing throughout the vast entry hall.

I grin with relief as I get my breath back, laughing nervously when I catch sight of Wolsheim's pale and hunted expression. There is a moment of exhilaration, a sense of victory rushing over me as though all my trials are over, and then my throat tightens as I remember that the trial, the *real* trial, has not even begun.

This is it. This is the moment.

All the rest was just foreplay.

Jamey

The impression I have, when I think back to that day, is of everything being hollow. As though the ground beneath my feet was not solid, but just a skin stretched over a drum on which my heels boomed as I paced the hospital corridor. Like there remained little of Jamey beyond her outer shell, kept full for now by the instinct to breathe but as delicate as a balloon, a pinprick from collapsing. She lay motionless upon the blanketless bed, still in the position that the two medics had placed her in when they eased her back onto it. The promised therapist eventually arrived some time in the early afternoon, a woman called Miriam Dowse. I suppose she was a doctor, but she insisted on being called Miriam, apparently thinking this gave her the right to call me Nick in return.

A lot. I mean there was a 'Nick' in practically every sentence. Miriam really knew how to make a connection with somebody. Well Nick, yes Nick, no Nick, eye contact, eye contact, smile smile smile. It didn't take a lot of staring back at that face before I wanted to connect a fist with it.

She talked to me before trying to engage Jamey in conversation, asking me questions that I do not remember beyond the fact that they struck me as impertinent. Her whole manner radiated an ersatz empathy, the kind of professional hypocrisy whereby everyone is different and special yet nevertheless can be categorized in the space of a few minutes' observation. I remember looking at her, with her pudding-bowl haircut and dry, thin body, and wanting to ask, 'What gives you the idea you can understand people? What have you lived, what passions have you ever felt that give *you* such wisdom . . . *Miriam*?'

I suppose I judged her cruelly because, above all, I felt that hollowness in my own breast. A pit had opened up in there, a fault-line cracked apart by Heather's death, and everything I tried to think about, all the attempts to order my thoughts or distract myself, just seemed to fall over the edge and never touch the bottom, ripping to shreds from the force of the drop.

Miriam announced that Jamey was in shock – something only a professional could have seen, of course. She said that the best thing for her right now was to rest, but recommended that she not be left alone. Being the closest thing there to a next of kin, I decided to take her back to the Cadogan. Miriam arranged for an ambulance to drive us there, which had the advantage of letting us slip by the journalists hanging around outside, and we walked her into the lobby with me on one arm and a medic on the other. Jamey was still saying nothing, but she had at least started nodding agreement to our instructions.

When we reached the elevator, she suddenly broke her arms free from our grasp and pressed the button herself, whispering, 'I'm OK.'

She didn't look at either of us as she said it, and she clearly wasn't, but it seemed best not to demur. She stepped normally into the elevator with us, turning around to face the door, and we rode upstairs in silence. Once in the Family Suite, she went straight to her

215

bedroom and closed the door without a word. The medic and I spoke quietly in the lounge, he saying that her reaction was quite normal and a good sign. Then he gave me a small bottle of sedatives before leaving, in case she had trouble sleeping.

It was late afternoon by now and neither of us had eaten all day. My guilt at feeling hungry at a time like this held me back for an hour or so, but eventually I opened Jamey's door a crack and eased my head in to ask if she wanted anything.

The curtains were drawn and I could barely make her out in the darkness – huddled in a ball under the covers, her head turned away from the door. Her clothes lay strewn upon the floor. I must have stood there for a full minute before I dared to whisper her name.

'Yes,' she replied in a tone as flat as a judge delivering a sentence.

'Can I get you anything?'

For a while it seemed as though she wasn't even going to reply, lying motionless in the darkness. Then she slowly rolled over, turning her face to the door. The light from behind me reflected dimly on her eyes.

'Thank you,' she whispered. 'You've done enough for one day.'

It was delivered in the same neutral tone, and yet I could not help but take it as an accusation. I nodded softly and pulled the door to, keenly aware that my presence was not welcome.

Later, the fact that I calmly ordered a meal from Room Service came to be seen as somehow incriminating. A sign of my callousness. Above all, however, it was the whisky bottle I told them to bring up that looked bad. It's true that I felt like getting drunk at the time, but in reality I hardly touched the damn stuff, finding I had no stomach for it – my glass sat on the table, the ice cubes slowly

216

diluting into the alcohol, and I remained quite sober. For a long while after eating I simply stared into space, then I flicked through the TV channels for an hour or two, and finally worked up the heart to check the messages on my mobile. The voicemail had become saturated around midday, so heaven knows how many dozens of other calls were turned away, but of the twenty or so that were on there, only two were of interest.

One was from a man called Sal Bulo. How he'd tracked down my number was a mystery, but he said that he was Jamey's agent. She had got the part in the Tom Harris movie.

And then McQueen had called. In person. He invited me to visit him at his home at nine the following morning, giving me the address and his personal number should that time not be convenient. Even under the circumstances I could not help feeling a rush at what that call represented: McQueen himself on my voicemail, politely requesting my presence.

The whole damn machine had stopped for me, Nick Carraway.

I kidded myself that I was debating the issue for the rest of the evening, that I was still undecided when midnight rolled around and I finally started preparing to turn in, but the truth was that I always knew I would be there the next morning. I told myself that now more than ever she needed me to take control, to protect her from the horde by making this deal, that I was thinking of her best interests . . . It's amazing how you can convince yourself of something that you need to believe, isn't it?

I was so far gone with my fantasy that everything would somehow be all right in the morning, that Jamey would be willing to go along with the programme, that I confess to even feeling a momentary twinge of irritation when I heard her scream.

I was in the bathroom, having just dried myself from the shower. It was a sharp scream that repeated itself in short, panicked bursts – not the single yelp of someone waking from a nightmare. I hurriedly pulled on my shorts and burst out of the bathroom, slamming the door.

Had I taken time to think about it, I would have turned on the light as I entered Jamey's bedroom, but her scream was so urgent that I could not stop to search for the switch. I crashed into the room, and rushed straight across to the thrashing figure I could make out in the illumination from the open doorway. The bedsheet was billowing as if alive, like some great white invertebrate trying to digest her whole, and my natural reaction was to sit down on her bed, placing my hands upon her writhing body and chanting, 'It's OK . . . it's OK . . . it's OK . . .'

Jamey's eyes snapped open, seeing only a silhouette looming over her, and her reaction was instantaneous: her right arm broke free from the sheet, striking out with all its force at my head.

I saw a flash of light as her elbow connected with my eye socket, and the bed disappeared from under me, the carpet rising up to knock me on the cheek. I gasped in pain, slapping my hands to my eye, and just had time to curse loudly before Jamey arrived on top of me in a flurry of fists, kneeing me in the pelvis as she landed.

I tried to protect my face, but her fists were pounding at my head from all directions, pummelling down on my hands and ears like someone running on the spot. I tried to speak but the words were punched apart into meaningless grunts, and it was only when she broke off with her fists and took hold of my neck to begin thrashing my head against the floor that I could fight back, clutching her wrists with all my force and trying to prise her fingers off, all the while gasping, 'It's Nick! Nick! Nick! . . .'

On the spur of the moment, Jamey recalled no Nick.

The voice may have been familiar and the first glimmerings of a memory of where she was were probably beginning to take shape in her mind, but her body chose to continue thrashing.

I couldn't get her hands off my neck, no matter how hard I pushed her wrists upwards.

'*Daily Post* . . .' I rasped, hunting desperately for items that might mean something to her. '*Hotel* . . .'

Suddenly the back of my head stopped beating the carpet. The hands briefly maintained their grip on my neck and then relaxed.

'. . . fuck,' she softly whispered.

The two of us remained locked – Jamey still holding my neck as she sat astride my prone body, my hands still gripping her arms – and then she broke off, her palms beginning to travel urgently over my face, softly feeling for damage.

'Oh god . . .' she muttered. 'Are you OK? Are you?'

'I think . . .' I groaned. 'Just about . . .'

I was blinking furiously, my eyelashes trying to wipe the tears from my eyes like windscreen wipers in the rain, and I blurrily made out Jamey putting her hands to her cheeks in horror.

'I'm so sorry,' she apologized. 'I don't know what . . . I was on the subway . . . and then you . . .'

Her chest heaved with emotion and exertion, her bare skin tanned by darkness in the half-light from the doorway. She was kneeling astride me, resting her weight on my hips, and I felt her shiver through my groin as a tear cut a path between her hands, hovered briefly on her lip and dropped to her breast.

It glittered upon the night-dusted skin, scuttling meanderingly down like a tiny wet crab on a beach to the castle of her nipple, hiding in its shadow. I sensed her trying to control herself, her breath catching in her throat as the

219

terror turned to tears like melting ice. Unstoppable, they streaked her cheeks and sprinkled her breasts until they were marbled with rivulets of reflected light flowing down over her ribs into the basin of her slim belly.

'I'm sorry . . .' she repeated hoarsely, leaving me unsure whether she was apologizing for the attack or her tears.

My own pain ebbing away, I wanted to comfort her, but I could find no words and hardly dared touch the raw beauty of that tear-streaked body. My hands hesitated in mid-air, fearing any caress would be misinterpreted, and I watched uselessly as the furthest streams were forced by the ridges of her hips to flow into the blonde delta between her legs.

Suddenly, as though losing an inner battle, she fell forward, her hands dropping from her cheeks to the floor on either side of my head. Hair and tears rained simultaneously upon my face, short blasts of choked breaths warming my cheeks, and I reached up to wipe the beads from her chin.

'It's all right now,' I offered quietly, hoping I sounded more convinced than I felt. 'It's over.'

She sniffed wetly, shaking her head as her stomach shuddered with misery.

'No it isn't,' she growled in a low, almost angry voice. 'It won't ever be *all right*.'

I gave up my ineffectual efforts to wipe the tears, letting them pour freely over my cheeks and lips.

'It was a nightmare,' I soothed her. 'It won't always be like this.'

'He's not going away!' she gasped incredulously. 'The fucker is *never* going away!'

At first I was lost, but from the hint of terror behind her voice I realized this was not the first time she had dreamed of Walcott. I clasped my palms on her quivering shoulders, saying, 'He's dead, Jamey! You're alive.'

Jamey briefly ceased her sobbing, looking down at me with an air of sadness and unwanted wisdom.

'You think it's that fucking . . . *simple*!' she groaned.

Suddenly her arms grew weak, her weight shifting to my hands upon her shoulders. She let herself sink into their grasp, her palms sliding forward across the carpet as I lowered her gently down upon myself until her chin came to rest in the crook of my neck and her breasts pressed down upon my chest. My hands slipped out from underneath her and travelled around her back, holding her tight.

Jamey seemed overcome by exhaustion, unable to stop her whole body deflating as her knees slid out to the sides and she slowly unrolled herself onto me from the shoulders down. I felt the soft warmth of her belly upon mine, the press of her hips, and the springs of hair compressing on the cotton of my pants.

She sounded too tired to cry, her breath shallow and her chin trembling against my neck. There was no fight left in her, and once she let the tears have their way they were perhaps not so unwelcome – each small convulsion of her muscles seemed to relax her further, releasing the pressure inside as though she were losing blood, not water.

Her body felt hot, and firm, and smooth.

I held her as the minutes slid by, not knowing what else to do, and tried to ignore the way each tearful spasm made her groin twitch softly upon mine. But the very act of denying it only concentrated my senses, the barrier of my shorts becoming less and less effective as my blood began to swell to her involuntary call until it produced an unmistakable stir.

In the silence of that moment, I felt her tense upon me, suddenly alert to my body. I searched fruitlessly for something to say, closing my eyes and biting my lip. Clearly

221

there was nothing I could offer by way of excuse, and I cursed myself inwardly, dreading her reaction. Then both my eyes and my mouth snapped open in surprise as I felt a small but quite definite press upon my loins.

Just one, as if to check.

I lay trapped, feeling my face flush hot against hers, and assumed that in a second she would snatch back from me in fury.

But she didn't. She lay still, her pelvis pressed down upon me, the tears tapping a slow Morse code from her body into mine. She was not angry, I realized.

And then she began to move.

I was lost. Even as she continued to cry, the muscles of her thighs and behind began to tense rhythmically – a soft, almost lazy rhythm, like some small animal nudging its way out of a winter nest, still too drowsy and weak to push with all its might. I felt her breath tremble on my tear-soaked neck, an edge of expectancy cutting through the sorrow, and realized my own breathing had fallen into step with hers.

The blood began to hum like a beehive between my legs, a deep buzz sounding outwards throughout my body. Under my palms I felt the muscles of her shoulders ripple softly, pulling her minutely back and forth like the bow upon a violin string in some very quiet, delicate passage of a symphony, and I fought the desire to let my hands travel down the stretching skin to the origin of the pulse, sensing that she did not want me to turn this into something mutual. It was not me she wanted, I was simply there.

At the same time, as the little rhythm she was playing upon my body kept mounting in intensity, a note of anxiety entered my thoughts. This was wrong, and, as much as I wanted it to continue, I felt it was my duty to say so. I should stop it. But her body kept stretching and contracting, her fingers scraping through the carpet behind me, and I could not quite find the will to interrupt her.

The hum began to creep up the back of my neck, my skin tingling deliciously to the sound of her stuttering breath, until I knew that whatever hope I still had of resisting – of doing the right thing, if that is what it was – would soon be lost.

'Jamey . . .' I whispered as my mind began to cloud over. 'Are you sure about this . . .'

She grunted with frustration, quickening the stroke of her pelvis, and I gasped in surrender. My arms tightened instinctively around her back as my whole skull began to hum and then I finally let my hands slide down to her behind. She lifted her head from my neck, resting her weight on her elbows, and gasped into my ear, 'Are you sorry for everything you've done now?'

I heard her but was little inclined to answer, my eyes shut and my head trembling as the note crept to its peak.

'Are you?' she demanded, suddenly lifting her pelvis away and pushing up with her hands to kneel above me.

I caught my breath at the interruption, the sudden dissonance in the harmony of our bodies almost physically painful to bear. My eyes snapped open and I saw her, her chest panting, glaring down at me in the half-light, her whole face sparkling with tears. For some reason I could not speak.

Her eyes fixed on mine, an almost cruel smile beginning to hover over her mouth, she lowered herself to stroke me, barely letting the soft, damp flesh between her legs touch my stretched skin.

My lips worked silently, the words refusing to come despite my desperate wish to speak, and her eyes narrowed as her hand reached beneath her legs to hold me up against the entry into her body, letting me just begin to part her flesh.

'Are you?' she whispered.

'Yes . . .' I exhaled tightly. 'I am sorry.'

Closing her eyes in satisfaction, she lowered herself onto me. We breathed in sharply, she frowning momentarily as she took me inside, and then her eyes opened softly to fix me again. She dropped forward onto her hands, her hair falling in a curtain around me, and began to move her hips about me.

'Don't stop saying it . . .' she invited gently.

And I didn't. I said it over and over again, meaning it more every time.

COURT ONE,
EIGHT FIFTY-FIVE A.M.

Amazingly, it looks as though we are going to start on time. It's actually going to happen. I realize now how I was deluding myself in the bus outside, secretly thinking that the trial would have to be postponed. But it's not going to be, it's going to start in five minutes.

Everyone is here but the judge and jury. A team of five male lawyers – clean-shaven, clear-eyed, sharp-suited – sit across from us, muttering softly amongst themselves with the odd glance our way. They are creepily perfect – strong-jawed, tall and sure of themselves. Such credits to their backgrounds. Wolsheim ignores them, calmly laying out his papers on the table. He's a different man again – all trace of his recent terror vanished, he seems relaxed and focused. He catches me watching him and looks my way with a small smile.

He winks.

The benches and gallery are packed. There was a momentary rush of exclamations when we entered the court, but now it has settled back down to a quiet, expectant hum of whispers.

And there are cameras. Wolsheim told me the judge, a

225

woman named Myrtle Wilson, had more or less left it to him to say whether or not he objected to their presence, given how much of a stink he'd been kicking up about media bias in the case. Wolsheim's response was to say that, considering how far things had already gone, he felt the media *should* be there so that they and their viewers could hear what he had to say about their treatment of me. He said that Judge Wilson's reaction was simply to laugh and wave the issue aside – apparently she's no fool and knows damn well what his game is, but considers it fair tactics.

So there are cameras. And they are all pointing straight at me.

I try to keep my face neutral, like he told me. Dignified. Head up. I want to look at them, I want to stare right at those lenses, right at the men behind and all the people watching out there in the world beyond, and let them know with my eyes that I am not their plaything, not just some character in their fucking soap opera, but I can't because that is exactly what I will become if I acknowledge their existence.

My only way of victory is to ignore them.

To give them nothing.

To bore them.

No story.

Let them watch *freshkill* if they want action.

I think of McQueen. I wonder if he is watching. I hope so. I hope he knows what is on my mind, and is smiling quietly to himself . . . knowing he wins either way. I don't hate him.

He never lied to me.

McQueen

I suppose that I had half-expected his penthouse to be like some movie vision of an evil mastermind's lair, which is why I was shocked by its conventionality. It was large, of course – the reception room I was shown into by the maid seemed big enough for a game of tennis – but there was nothing ostentatious about the interior. The off-white walls were hung with paintings, none of which I recognized although the styles of a few artists were familiar, and the room was furnished with an almost eclectic array of antique chairs and department-store couches. The far wall was all window, with a view down over the park, and the morning sunshine bathed the room with a cheerful warmth.

Clearly it was not a space in which McQueen truly lived – there was no clutter, none of those objects falling between the permanent and the disposable that colonize any real room – but if his position required him to hold receptions and entertain the players of Atlantian society, it was as close as one could get to homely on that scale. Almost reluctant in its grandeur. It made our suite at the Cadogan seem both cramped and pretentious.

The thought of the hotel brought Jamey to my mind,

pictured as I had last seen her – sleeping peacefully at last, spreadeagled under the sheet with half a breast uncovered. I had not shared her bed that night. We had talked in the living room, bathrobes wrapped carelessly around our nakedness, at one point laughing as we examined the bruises our tussle had left on both of us. I had a fat lip, one of my eyes was slightly swollen, and both her wrists bore the traces of my grip. It had been quite a fight.

We eventually retired to our separate rooms. By then I had gently convinced her of my argument that we needed this deal with InfoCorps – that even now, after what had happened, she would not be left alone to make the arrangements for Heather's funeral, which was all she cared about. The deal would at least shelter her from the kind of anarchy that had caused the accident, and allow her some peace in which to mourn.

I had not told her about the call from her agent, though. I would do, in time, but I figured it would only confuse matters right then.

She had said little, her red eyes observing me with a disquieting air of perception, as though she could read my thoughts, but had finally nodded her acceptance, sighing, 'I don't suppose I really have any choice then, do I?'

I'd asked her whether she wanted company that night, but she had shaken her head softly, saying that she needed to be alone. I was a little hurt by the immediacy of the rejection, confused by the fact that she could make love to me and yet have no desire to take comfort in my presence, but I tried not to show it. As we stood up I went to give her a hug even so, which she accepted stiffly, her own arms not leaving her sides. I was left feeling awkward and troubled after she said goodnight, no longer knowing where I stood with her, but this morning I felt more hopeful. She needed time. And I would be there when she wanted someone to turn to.

McQueen entered the room after I had been waiting less than a minute, appearing briskly from the hallway. He had aged in the two years since I'd first seen him in the flesh – his hair a little thinner, the jawline softer – but the overall impression, the thing that had struck me most about him, was still there: he didn't look the part. How could this plain, average-looking man be the infamous McQueen everyone so feared and despised? Apart from the fact that he was strikingly tall, nothing else about him seemed capable of casting such a long shadow upon the world. He smiled, striding across the carpet with his hand half-raised to shake mine.

'Good to see you again, Nick,' he announced warmly, not that I was fooled into thinking that he recalled me from that day he came to visit the *Post*.

'Kevin reminded you that we've met, did he?' I suggested, taking his hand. I didn't say it aggressively, but figured it was important not to let him make the running. I was here as a free agent, in no way beholden to him, and behind his show of familiarity was a subtle reminder that he had been my employer.

He stopped short, raising his eyebrows in surprise. His hand released mine and briefly tapped his brow as he frowned in concentration.

'You were wearing . . .' he announced slowly '. . . a black leather jacket and a faded lime polo shirt. Your desk was a complete shambles . . . but that's no indication of a poor mind. Indeed, I rather liked the fact that yours was one of the few waste baskets that was not stuffed full of hurriedly dumped papers in a half-arsed attempt to impress me.'

If he had a similar aim, his own attempt was in no way half-arsed. I was momentarily speechless, and it no doubt showed.

'Useful talent for someone in my position,' he smiled.

'But you're looking quite the businessman today. One that has apparently . . . been in a fight?'

I touched my lip, laughing.

'I fell. The bathroom floor was wet.'

'Well, not to worry – it gives you a rather rugged air. I shall be all the more cautious in our negotiations! Now, Julia is bringing us coffee in here, but I suspect you'll consider that overly casual. On second thoughts, we should go to my office, like real businessmen.'

He led me down the corridor to a door, holding it open and telling me to make myself comfortable while he went to inform the maid of the change in plan. I nodded dumbly, suddenly afraid that I'd choke if I tried to say something. I'm not sure what it was, but he had somehow disarmed me. He'd done nothing that was not frank and natural – his power, his wealth and influence had played no part in the effortless establishment of superiority. His very modesty was a weapon, wielded with hypnotic seductiveness. Within that lanky, almost cumbersome body lurked something with the grace of a tiger.

His office was a pleasant room, also looking out on the park. It contained a large leather-covered desk and a round mahogany table that could seat a dozen people. Three of the walls were given over to bookcases – he was a collector rather than a reader, to judge by the neat shelves of leather-bound volumes, arranged by size rather than author or subject.

There was little on the desk barring a computer, a pile of the morning papers, his telephone, and a photo frame. Wary of the door reopening, I leaned over to look at the picture it contained – a photograph of his wife and three children. Just like any ordinary man might have. I found it hard to imagine McQueen, the great predator of the media, playing the devoted husband and father, but their smiles were undoubtedly genuine. I even felt sure that he had taken the picture himself.

My eye was caught by a movement on the computer screen, and I looked across to see something that was a still greater surprise. A window was open in one corner of the screen, and what it contained was instantly familiar to me.

freshkill.

Even McQueen had the *freshkill* bug.

'I find night the most engrossing time to watch, don't you?'

I wheeled round to see him smiling beside me, holding the coffee tray. How he entered the room so silently, I do not know – perhaps he was aiming to catch me out exactly as he had done – but I tried not to show my embarrassment.

'I'm amazed you have the time.'

'Most valuable thing you can have,' he answered, placing the tray upon his desk. 'And the only one you can't buy.'

He was still smiling, but there was a tinge of melancholy there that I hadn't noticed at first.

'I've just bought that, by the way,' he added, gesturing towards the computer. 'What do you think of it?'

'The computer?' I answered. 'It's . . . nice.'

'Not the computer!' He laughed. '*freshkill.com*!'

'Ah . . .' I exclaimed, suddenly feeling very small. 'I see.'

The man who had just picked up the hot web site of the moment, no doubt paying hundreds of millions for it, busied himself with pouring the coffee and asking how I took it. It felt surreal. Surely a guy like that doesn't stir the sugar for you?

'People will say I've paid too much for it, no doubt,' he confided, passing me the cup. 'They think it's a fad. But they're wrong – it'll be worth ten times the price I got it

231

for in a few years. News in its purest form is what it is –
live and uncut, twenty-four hours a day.'

'Only . . .' I frowned, smiling doubtfully '. . . it's just a
bunch of animals.'

'So?' he shrugged, looking genuinely perplexed by my
reaction.

'News is about people.'

'Oh . . . I don't think so,' he announced, settling down
behind the desk and inviting me to take the seat opposite.
'Not really. I'd say that until now it's just so happened
that people have been the best vehicle for what news is
about, but all of this technology changes that.'

'Drama?' I hazarded, not wanting to seem too slow.

McQueen smiled again, reaching across to close the
window with a click. That same melancholy humour.

'Sacrifice,' he answered softly. 'News is about sacrifice,
Nick.'

He looked questioningly at me, one eyebrow raised and
just a hint of a smile playing over his lips, waiting to see
how I reacted. Later, I would realize that I had been
wrong about McQueen – what seemed strangely banal
about him, that feeling he gave of being too ordinary in
the flesh for the position he occupied in the world, was
not ordinariness at all. The man is calm – extraordinarily
calm. That is his secret. While the rest of us swirl about,
nervously eyeing each other and desperately trying to
keep up with the pace of life, he simply remains still. And
it gives him, on first glance, an air of banality, yet it is
anything but that. I suppose it's actually a form of genius.

'It's funny how people are always surprised when I
suggest that,' he continued, seeing that no response was
forthcoming. 'I'm sure I'm right, though. Every day we
make a sacrifice. Why is that not obvious? Perhaps we're
so accustomed to turning a blind eye to it that it has
become almost invisible. It's like a ritual . . . well, it *is* a

232

ritual, isn't it? It's something sacred – a thing not to be questioned, and if you go long enough without questioning a thing, then you eventually cease to see it's even there. Like streetlamps.'

I felt myself, with a rising sense of panic, getting left behind. He was talking to me, trying to have a discussion, and yet I was so slow to follow that he was replying for me. I suppose almost all conversations are like that for him, that he rarely meets people equal to his intellect, and so this has become his customary way of talking. To himself.

'Streetlamps,' I repeated, trying to catch up.

'Exactly!' he laughed. 'When do you notice a streetlamp? When you pass one whose bulb has blown! We don't even see the rest of them, even though without them we can't see!'

I laughed politely along with him, wondering where this was going and how I would ever be able to negotiate a deal with a man whose thought process seemed to contain a gear or two more than my own.

The irony is that people despise McQueen precisely because they hold him responsible for dumbing down everything he touches. But maybe, it has occurred to me since, he hasn't dumbed down the news at all – maybe he has simply clarified what news has always really been about. Something of that notion came to me then, and I felt a lurch of nausea at the possibility that I had spent my entire life unaware of what I truly did for a living.

'I'd hate to think nobody reads newspapers for serious information,' I announced, rebelling against the thought I'd just had.

'Oh, but *of course* they do!' McQueen agreed, his face still lit up from the laughter of a second ago. 'But I don't think many of us would bother to buy a newspaper *just* for the information, would we? It's so . . . boring.

233

Anything that matters we find out eventually anyway – taxes and inflation and all those tiresome things we're supposed to care about. We pay our *money* for the stories though, don't we? All those tales that make us thankful, because they're not about us!'

He reached into the pile of newspapers for this morning's edition of the *Post*, its front page given over to a shot of Jamey cradling Heather's head in her arms. Variations of the same picture had opened every one of the papers that morning – Agony of the Subway Heroine. The question of the media's own part in causing the accident buried under a great outwash of sympathy.

'Case in point,' he announced, glancing briefly at it before dropping it back on the pile.

He sighed and took a sip of coffee, shaking his head as he placed the cup gently back upon the saucer.

'I feel very sorry for that girl,' he reflected softly. 'But, unfortunately, that just makes her an even better story, doesn't it? I have to say that I sometimes loathe our profession . . .'

He fixed me with his eyes, a certain steel entering his gaze as he asked, 'Don't you sometimes hate it, Nick?'

'I don't know . . . I mean . . .' I floundered, unsettled by the sudden change of tack. 'I don't think of it that way. People need the news – I just report it.'

'Oh, quite – people need the news,' he agreed, folding his hands upon his lap. 'There's no denying that. They need it more and more. I'm not suggesting we're to *blame* for it! We fill an important function in modern society.'

He looked down at his hands, carefully placing the fingertips together to form a steeple and pressing them against each other.

'It used to be – and still is, in some small pockets of the world – that people gave thanks for the things they had each day,' he mused, watching as he brought his palms together. 'We would thank our ancestors. We would thank the animal that had died so that we could eat. But we have lost that sense of connection to the world, for some reason we no longer acknowledge our debts as individuals . . . I suppose that we have become so accustomed to thinking of ourselves just as members of a society that we expect *society* to shoulder the responsibility for our lives, as if it were something separate from ourselves. There's no ritual of giving thanks any more, is there?'

I shook my head, unsure whether he was really even addressing me or simply thinking aloud. Suddenly his head snapped up, his eyes narrowing as though pained by my failure to catch the ball he had thrown up in the air between us.

'Which is why certain sacrificial duties are now fulfilled by a media *industry* that every day places a small number of individuals on the altar to play that role for the whole of society,' he insisted, eyes alight. 'It's a pageant, Nick – we don't have celebrities so that we can *admire* them! We don't give them all these riches and glory out of the kindness of our hearts, but so that we can see them suffer for it! And if they do not suffer, if they appear to have taken it all and be giving nothing in return, then we will *make* them suffer . . . we will say things about them that are untrue, just to make them bleed a little – because they must not be envied. Above all, they must not be envied. They are there so that the rest of us can give thanks for our own humble lives.'

McQueen stared intently at me, and I couldn't escape the impression that he was trying, in some roundabout way, to give me a personal message. That he was telling me this for my own benefit. It was all too emphatic, too heartfelt, to be merely conversation made over a cup of coffee.

'Why do it then?' I asked, finally throwing the ball back his way. 'If you think it's wrong . . .'

'Because for some reason I've always been very good at it! And it's not *wrong*! It *has* to happen, Nick, because it is an essential part of how we hold society together. And as our society expands, as the differences between nations weaken and the world settles into a global culture, we will need it more and more, don't you see? We're going to need stories that can straddle the borders. That's why *freshkill* is so important – it can fill part of that role, and no-one need be hurt. But we will still require people too, global celebrities whose triumphs and tragedies will be familiar to everyone. If people think that we live in a celebrity culture *today*, then they have no idea what the future holds in store! As a spectacle, it will put gladiator contests to shame! Do you understand what I'm trying to say here? I am saying the world needs beautiful martyrs . . .'

He was trying to warn me, and the truth is that I did not hear then what he was saying. I did not listen. Looking back, I can see that his concern was more for Jamey than me, but I was the one who was there in her place. He had been quite genuine when he expressed his pity for her, of that I have no doubt, and yet, for all his power and influence, he apparently did not believe that it was *he* who could help her. That's where that air of melancholy came from, I believe – it's as though he felt there were things he could not allow himself to do, his responsibility being to InfoCorps and InfoCorps alone, like a king bound to apply the law even if it meant punishing those he loved.

InfoCorps.

The great machine, the dragon of my boyhood years, was still rumbling through the night – invisible to the naked eye now in that it had evolved into something too large to fit into any one building, spreading its tentacles into television sets and supermarket magazines and advertising billboards – and McQueen was possibly one of the only people who knew its shape and could see it, at least in his head. He knew how it worked. And that had made him rich beyond most people's ability to comprehend figures. But in the final resort he was its servant, I think, not its master. Whatever he felt as an ordinary man, he was bound to do what was best for InfoCorps.

He could see Jamey entering the dragon's lair, and knew that her last chance of escape was almost gone already. I think he hoped that I might somehow stop it from happening, stop *him* in effect, and that was what he was trying to help me see, a little like a serial killer purposely leaving clues behind him.

But I am not that man.

I'm a coward, no knight in shining armour.

I told myself I had done the right thing, of course. It was a victory, I argued, for both Jamey and me. I had named our price, and he had accepted it, this man who was supposed to be such a shark in business matters. And yet, shortly after leaving his apartment, I realized that I had no sense of catharsis. No sooner had I achieved what I had set out to do than the achievement began to pale. The moment was past already, and I found myself longing to go back and stand on its threshold again.

I suppose that was inevitable. That's why the people who achieve the most, the people like McQueen, seem unable to stop – why they always want more money, even if they could not possibly spend all they already have. Our requirements for satisfaction simply expand to fill the limits of what is conceivable: the man who once liked to go fishing finds he can now afford a boat to go with the fishing rod, and then an island to go with the boat, and then a helicopter to take him to the island, and all for the same fish. The truth of life is that we all want more, and yet we are all nostalgic for the days when we were content with less.

McQueen, I believe, was advising me not to want more. Not to become trapped like he was.

But it was done now, and Jamey was no longer my responsibility. I had settled for a smaller cut of a bigger pie, and was already missing the moment I had waited for her outside the club, before all this started.

Sure, I arrived back at the Cadogan in style – an InfoCorps limo with the obligatory tinted windows. A PR guy rode in it with me, ready to take control of the details once we picked up Jamey, and two bodyguards, there to cut a path for us through the crowd of journalists that had apparently gathered outside the hotel this morning, word having leaked of our location. Security companies, someone in prison told me, rent out their employees by the pound. I guess McQueen had supplied me and Jamey with about 450 pounds of protection, not including the PR guy.

The last time I rode in a limousine, I could stand on the floor to look out through the tinted glass. My mother forbade me to play with the electric windows because the draught messed up her hair, and the city was a silent movie that rolled past my hazy screen. The world smelled of perfume and tobacco.

McQueen's car was no doubt bigger, and had gadgetry that made those electric windows seem as primitive a form of toy as marbles, but of course it seemed smaller and less luxurious to me now. It was just a big car, and the sidewalks were no longer exotic, and the air was not sweet with my mother's scent.

And I was requested not to smoke, same as everywhere else.

The limo stopped just short of the crowd outside the

238

hotel, and one of the bodyguards turned to me as he reached for the door handle, saying, 'Don't stop. Don't say anything. Don't meet anyone's eye.'

I could tell he loved his job.

The flashes burst stroboscopically into life the instant he flung the door open and stepped out, the journalists beginning to record the event before they even knew what the event was to be. I climbed out third, a suited wall either side of me, the PR guy stepping out behind.

I prepared myself for what I knew was coming next – the barrage of garbled questions, the arms reaching in from all sides with their microphones, the blur of faces. I was ready for it, but thankful for the screen of muscle around me – these men were professionals, and cutting a path through a heaving pack of journalists was their speciality.

But I wasn't ready for silence.

The bodyguards began moving, and nobody blocked their passage. The crowd parted, staring sullenly, and all I could hear was a quiet muttering. I looked either side of me and people either looked away or met my gaze with unblinking eyes and set faces.

They didn't want me. It wasn't that they didn't know who I was, or who these men with me worked for . . . they just didn't want to bother themselves with me. I was beneath them.

That was worse.

We walked through them in silence, nobody saying a word, and my skin pricked with discomfort, with the force of those stares. I barely seemed able to breathe until I felt the soft carpet of the hotel lobby beneath my feet and the protein-packed cocoon fell away from around me . . . leaving me staring at the alarmed face of the hotel manager, who was waiting for me.

239

'Mr . . . O'Neil,' he announced nervously. 'Welcome back.'

'So much for the Cadogan's famed discretion,' I accused him haughtily. 'One of your people has been selling tips.'

He was looking at me with an odd expression, mixing fear and condescension, but made no attempt to defend his establishment, merely asking, 'Checkout time was at midday, sir. Will you be staying another night?'

'I think not under the circumstances, don't you?'

'Quite,' he answered, producing a bill in a dark leather booklet. 'I have the bill prepared if you'd like to settle up now.'

My eyebrows rose in surprise, but I figured that he must be so rattled by the mob outside his hotel that he was losing sight of normal etiquette. I nodded, turning to the PR guy and inviting him to take care of it. He paid, and the two of us took the lift, leaving the meat down in the lobby to await Jamey's arrival. Getting back out was going to be a different matter, I imagined, with the two of them now having to protect the person the journalists were really here for.

The elevator reached the top and I took a few deep breaths before knocking on the door of the suite, calling, 'It's Nick, Jamey.'

The door opened and my smile drained away as I found myself faced with a stranger. He was tall, heavily built, and his eyes did not look as though they had often beheld beauty. I frowned, glancing past him for Jamey, but she was not in sight.

'Nicholas Carraway?' he growled. 'Detective Phil Wagner.'

Phil Wagner. Why did I know that name?

'Where's Jamey?' I demanded, immediately fearing that she'd done something stupid in her grief.

'She's resting,' he replied, stepping aside and inviting me into the room.

Once I got through the door, my eyes settled on another man, sitting in one of the armchairs. A man I knew. He was putting last night's whisky bottle into a clear plastic bag. Only the bottle was now almost empty.

'What is this?' I snapped, the panic now filling my whole body. 'What are you doing here?'

'Waiting for you,' Frank Bosch grunted. 'Miss Gatz called me. Told me what you did. You're a real fucking piece of work, aren't you?'

The dreadful knowledge dawned on me that I was in trouble. I hadn't a clue what kind of trouble it could be, but there was no escaping the implication in his voice.

'I don't understand . . .' I frowned, looking from one of them to the other. 'What have I done, Frank? Why are you waiting for me?'

'To arrest you, of course.' Bosch sighed.

My mouth opened but no sound came out. Only my eyes could speak, urgently demanding to know what on earth it was I could have done to earn this. I threw up my hands, still trying to formulate some kind of appeal in my breathless mouth. Bosch narrowed his gaze, clearly unimpressed by my show of amazement.

'For rape,' he smiled coldly. 'I always said you were a cunt.'

COURT ONE,
NINE A.M.

We all rise.

The middle-aged lady in the black gown takes her seat at the front of the court. She is neither ambitiously lean, like so many of this city's high-achieving females, nor hard-faced. She is black. She looks like a mother, her once pretty face fleshed out a little and her black hair beginning to grey – a kindly-looking woman with intelligent, humorous eyes and a soft mouth. She invites the jury and the rest of us to sit down.

The court is in session, Judge Myrtle Wilson presiding.

She looks calmly around the room – nodding a small greeting at the prosecutors and Wolsheim, a minuscule smile fraying the edges of her lips as her eyes settle briefly on me, so fleeting that it is possibly a product of my imagination. Then she lets her gaze travel across the benches, sizing up the crowd who have come to watch the day's proceedings, raising her eyes to the gallery and sweeping from one side to the other until it seems that she has looked, however briefly, at every single person in the room. And her circuit finishes with the TV cameras, giving them a long, imperturbable stare as if to establish that they have no authority over her, no more significance than any other member of the public on her benches.

It does not take her long, this relaxed scrutiny of the scene before her, but its effect is immediate and undeniable. We are in a court of law. Her court. And nothing else, not the months of speculation and expectation in the media, nor the hysterical crowd outside, nor what any person here thinks may be the case, will have the slightest bearing on her whatsoever.

I cannot help but smile. She knows, this woman, that she herself is now a target for criticism and comment. She knows her handling of these proceedings will be the stuff of trailer-park TV dinners and tabloids read in supermarket checkout lines for the duration of this trial. Self-professed experts will dissect her performance and look for signs of bias, for evidence of playing to the gallery, for any damn thing they can accuse her of to spice up the cocktail even further. And she's not having it.

She's not going to let the children pull any of their shit in here.

Whatever happens, however long it takes, she is making it clear that my trial will be no different from any other one in her eyes, and that the verdict reached will be truth.

Satisfied, she signals to the court officer who stands up to read the details of the case, The State versus Nicholas Carraway. I am asked to stand. I rise to my feet, looking straight at him, and the charges against me are enumerated – rape, breaking the terms of bail, violation of a restraining order, the murder of Jamey Gatz . . .

I am asked how I plead to these charges.

It's an impressive array of accusations, but in the end it comes down to one thing. The same thing. A simple question.

Did I, or did I not, murder Jamey Gatz?

THE OTHER UNIVERSE

I suppose that freedom, by its very nature, means something different to every person. If they ever bother to think about it, which most of them probably don't. When I think about freedom, what comes to my mind is the day Jamey died. I think of being in my car – a rusting, bronchitic vehicle that I virtually never got out of the garage – on my way to Otterway. A long drive, a day's journey from Entropolis out to the hills far upstate, with Jamey waiting at the other end.

I think of being on a road, not knowing exactly where I was or what was going to happen. I think of being fidgety with anticipation and uncertainty, afraid that all my hopes would turn out to be dashed. That's what freedom is to me – not something comfortable, not a matter of having limitless choices or being allowed to fulfil all my dreams.

Freedom, *my* idea of freedom, is embracing a fear.

And I was afraid, all that day, but it felt like the best day of my life, and still does. That's exactly where I would go if I was granted one day of my past – right back to the day that put me in this courtroom.

Of course I had already learned about courtrooms by

244

then, and was already the villain in the Jamey Gatz story because of the rape charge. The phenomenon I had helped to create now turned on me, and I became the next chapter of the story. It was an ideal development – the heroine abused by the very man in whom she had placed her trust. The minute I was led in handcuffs from that hotel to the car waiting outside, the minute my name and face were fed into the machine, accused of rape, my former life was effectively over. It was finished. That Nick Carraway was dead – his contacts were no longer good, his reputation destroyed, and even those who knew him best could no longer accept his word on trust. In his place there was Nick Carraway, Rapist of Heroines, like that was what I did in life. Her face rarely appeared without mine somewhere lower down the page, always a picture of myself being led away in chains, head bowed, or the one shot in a hundred where the photographer had caught me staring wild-eyed or pulling a face. Erstwhile colleagues, some of them supposedly friends, wrote pompous columns about the dangers of our profession, and how it was perhaps inevitable, in a climate of spiralling media aggression, that somebody would step over the last line of intrusion and abuse their subject in the flesh as well as in spirit. Mine was a lesson they should all heed, some suggested.

I became a non-person, a pariah, an animal. Someone whom people shouted abuse at in the street, whom they spat upon. Ordinary people, decent people who no doubt raised their children to say please and thank you and not talk when others were talking. They spat at me, refused to serve me, threatened me. At least I had enough money to live on, and there were some people who would accept it with no remark or suggestion on their face that they knew who I was although they surely did, or else I truly believe I could have simply starved.

I had never imagined just how much anger and hatred lay beneath the surface of society, needing only a target, a reason to reveal itself.

Jamey was no fool. She knew how best to destroy me, to avenge all she believed I had done to her and Heather, though there is no way she could have known just how effective Frank Bosch would be in carrying out that vengeance on her behalf once he got me down to the precinct. He really enjoyed himself.

My first lawyer had got me bail at the arraignment – set at an absurdly high level by the judge, who clearly felt that he had to treat my case in terms of its media profile rather than the threat I posed to society. I actually burst into laughter when he announced the figure I was supposed to put down. Carraway Laughs at Rape Indictment. When they led me back to jail I had been resigned to the fact that I would not be leaving it again until the case came to court, but, to my amazement, the very next day I was free. The *Post* offered to post my bail in return for the exclusivity on my story. For a while there I could have kissed Kevin O'Neil – only, of course, the *Post* was owned by McQueen and he had his investment in Jamey to protect, so the exclusivity deal was really about preventing me from talking to anyone else.

So I was fucked. Bound and gagged. And I watched in awe as Jamey became the woman of the moment, her face suddenly everywhere I turned. McQueen's team knew exactly what they were doing, knew how to leave people always hungry for more of this woman – this *real* woman who had nothing to sell, who was not a model or a movie star, whose opinions were the opinions of someone with a normal life, and yet who was so extraordinary and so desirable.

And Jamey seemed to be so at ease with it all. She was fresh, dazzlingly full of life. They turned her into an instant icon, a symbol of courage and strength as attractive to women as men. She had integrity, her fictional past as a stripper giving her a streetwise sassiness, while the Randall Walcott episode, and the death of her sister, and her own rape all gave her a gravitas that movie stars and models could only dream of attaining. Compared to them, she was untainted by vanity or ambition – as gorgeous as they, but not so desperate to be admired. And the public couldn't get enough of her – any magazine with her on its cover was guaranteed a sales boost, even if she was there week after week, doping their performance like a journalistic steroid.

I wanted to hate her for what she did to me, but I couldn't quite manage it. There were moments over that year – a year I spent leaving my apartment as little as possible, watching my money haemorrhage away as the lawyers fought over where and when the trial could be held in a climate that would be fair and unbiased – when I managed, briefly, to despise her, but it never lasted long. I'd think of something real – the moment we had arrived at the Cadogan, she pretending to be my wife, or the sight of her curled up on the couch in her dressing gown – and I could not hate that person. I could not wish her ill.

She did something wrong, she accused me of raping her when I had not, but the rest was not her. It was the story. We were both caught up in the story, our lives no longer ours to control.

I wanted to speak to her more than anything else. I rehearsed a hundred speeches, wonderful scenes of confrontation and reconciliation in which I would forgive her for what she had done to me and ask her forgiveness in return, and we would fall into each other's arms again . . . but it was pure fantasy, of course. I was not allowed, by court order, to approach her or even to try contacting her.

So I watched her from a distance, from the other side of the flashbulb. Watched her hair changing styles. Watched her wear the spring collections, then summer, then autumn, then winter . . . seemingly growing more beautiful and glamorous all the time. And I read everything I could about her, just to be close, like some sad, obsessed little fan. I kept up with the gossip surrounding the Tom Harris movie – they were having an affair, they hated each other's guts, he was jealous of her celebrity, she thought he was arrogant and vain, they were having to use doubles to shoot all the love scenes, they had actually *made* love during the love scenes . . . I knew it was all utter bullshit, but I read it anyway. Hungry for her.

But then, as the movie neared release, the studio rushing to capitalize on all the publicity, I started to feel nervous on her behalf. I sensed something bad coming, my instincts still finely tuned to subtle changes in the media climate. The main trouble was that people didn't believe she had got the part on her own merits. Jamey, Harris, and the studio kept insisting that she had been cast *before* Randall Walcott happened, but nobody was convinced.

I was still good at my job, even if I could not practise it, and I felt a subtle undercurrent growing within all that gossip and seeming adulation, seeing it before anybody had said a harsh word outright. My ex-colleagues, I sensed, did not like the fact that Jamey Gatz – this fabulous, *real* woman they all desired and admired – was going to *act* a role.

It was like they were the boyfriend and the movie was the friend from work whose name was cropping up a little too often for comfort. They were jealous. Plus there was the fact that the actual *critics* were a different bunch of journalists altogether – they had played no part in the Jamey Gatz phenomenon, and her arrival on their territory, already famous and adored, probably piqued their wild sense of their own importance. And there may have been other reasons – perhaps the Jamey worship had gone as far as it could by then, and it was simply time for the pendulum to swing back. Or it could have been that other thing about society, the underside of fame and its unseen roots reaching down into the darkness . . . the thing McQueen had warned me about.

I knew, before it even happened, before anyone had seen the movie, that they were going to tear her apart.

My heart bled for her as I saw what they did. Even though I'd suspected that they were going to ambush the movie, nothing prepared me for how savage they were about it. They were merciless, seeming driven to punish and humiliate her.

And I may have been the guy she and everyone else despised in all of this, but I was also the only one who knew how important acting was to her. How all this time she had been refusing to compromise because she wanted to do it seriously, to earn respect as an actress rather than just take any part that would put her on a screen. I knew how devastated she would be.

They put an end to all of that. They made it unthinkable that she should ever become an actress – not because she or the movie were in any way bad, but because they were jealous and did not want her to escape their control. So they tore her dream away from her.

They did not rest in their ridicule until she eventually announced, during the course of a rare sympathetic interview, that she had decided to renounce the ambition of being an actress.

Then, for what seemed a long time, everything went quiet. There were no more pictures of Jamey in the magazines. No appearances on TV. That I expected as well – they were letting the dust settle now. There would be a time for digestion, a pause of two or three months. Then

249

they would resurrect her again, on their terms this time. They were waiting for the trial to begin, for the great Jamey Gatz show to get back on track. All would be forgiven – she'd be the heroine and victim again, the painful details of her rape splashed across the front page.

Only she called me first.

Under the terms of my bail, I was not supposed to leave Entropolis, but she asked me to come and nothing could have stopped me. I didn't even think about it – she called me first thing that morning, and within the hour I had got the car out of the garage and was on my way out of town. I rarely dared use it because it had developed a number of health problems from lack of exercise. Keeping it taxed and insured and parked was a stupid waste of money, really, but at least if it didn't leave the garage there was no need to pay for a mechanic to fix it up. It started on the fourth or fifth attempt, billowing a large cloud of blue smoke out the back as I cleared its pipes with some ruthless revving, and I prayed, as I ventured out into the city traffic, that none of its various coughs and judders signified a serious problem.

It seemed to settle down once I got out of Entropolis and began heading east to the hills, the late winter rain washing some of the grime from the bodywork. I drove all day, stopping only for fuel. I figured I should reach Otterway by late afternoon, but that just shows how much I knew about hill country.

The land around me was still a winter scape, but there were signs of spring coming – the streams were thrashing down meltwater, the late winter flowers were out, and the leafless trees were beginning to put out new shoots. It was a good time to be out of the city – the hills were empty but for the locals, and the land didn't seem so tame and trodden as it does once the weekenders in their RVs arrive. I was enjoying myself – it was a beautiful journey, and Jamey was waiting for me at the far end. She hadn't explained what was on her mind when she called, simply saying that we needed to talk, and I was no more inclined to get into discussing it all over the phone than she was. I just wanted to see her.

By around four o'clock, the road had stopped being a thing that was intended to take you from one place to another, and become a thing whose main purpose was to prevent you falling off the damn hill. My estimate of when I would arrive was pushed further and further back as I crawled my way painfully upwards, weaving back and forth through the snowbound woods with the patience of a seamstress. Time seemed to have slowed almost to a halt, the thrum of the car swallowed by the snow, and the endless succession of bends making for a fine approximation of limbo for a city boy such as myself, born into a godless world of speed and efficiency. Then, inevitably, the light began to fade and I was forced to go still slower.

I noticed my headlights seemed dim before the battery warning light flickered on, but by then I was already too concerned by the needle on my petrol gauge to care. It had been miles since the road had last forked, and without the help of a signpost I had no firm idea of how far I had travelled since or how close Otterway now was. I could not believe it would be far ahead, but every bend in the road brought a new disappointment as the hoped-for village failed to appear.

In the end, the battery ran out first. Coming up through a bend, the engine gave a despondent moan when I pressed the accelerator – I pumped the pedal desperately, flooring it in a vain attempt to slap it out of its self-pity, but the car just gave up. It died with a miserable sigh a few yards ahead, the feeble headlights dropping to a dim yellow glow.

I got out, kicking the vehicle for its treachery and shouting incoherent obscenities at its corpse. When I was done, and there seemed to be no more insults left in my vocabulary, I paused to assess the situation. It was a choice between spending the night in the dead car, or trying to cover the remaining distance to Otterway on foot, because it was foolish to hope that another vehicle might be coming by. There was no moon, yet the night was so dense with stars that I could make out two-dimensional trees around me, and the road leading on ahead like a dark tear in the white landscape. I'd never seen such a sky. The Milky Way was as distinct as a caterpillar on a leaf, and there were colours – the reds and blues of distant nebulae that I had only ever seen in photographs. It was like an endless city hanging overhead. The night wasn't too cold, so I took my coat and left the car behind with the hazard lights leaking out the last of the battery juice in a dim throb of a warning over the red trees.

Strangely enough, once I began walking I found that I did not mind about the car any more. I found myself thinking that there was a sense of rebirth about this journey, a shedding of my past. The meandering road was not steep in itself, and I advanced at a healthy pace. It was exhilarating to be alone in the woods, the sounds of my footsteps, my breathing, the rustle and swish of my clothes the only noises that existed in the still forest. I wasn't scared because it was unimaginable that any danger could be lurking in that silence – nothing could be so quiet that it could move without breaking the perfect calm of the night. Whatever dangers existed in the world lay far below me.

I walked for almost an hour before I reached the top and the road began to drop down the other side of the hill. Suddenly it became much harder to see where I was going, because the snow disappeared and the road and the

252

woods were almost indiscernible in the starlight. Now there were sounds in the darkness – without the white blanket that smothered them on the northern face of the hill, the trees rustled and wheezed in the breeze. I could hear the trickle of water somewhere, and there was movement in the forest, although my sensory disorientation was such that I could not say for sure if it was the size of a bird or a bear. I quickened my pace down the hill despite the darkness, concentrating on the feel of the tarmac beneath my shoes to keep me on the road, my heart and limbs freezing whenever I felt the ground become soft. The desire not to tarry and the difficulty I had in seeing where I was going formed a mutually beneficial circle of anxiety, and I began to panic at the thought that I might have passed an unseen fork in the road and now be heading in quite the wrong direction. I cursed myself for not having waited till light in the car, for thinking that finding a village on a country road, even in the darkness, would be no great challenge to someone who was used to navigating the maze of Entropolis's streets. I had even begun to convince myself that the best thing would be to turn back when suddenly, through a break in the trees, I saw a light.

No sooner had it appeared than it was gone, and I took a step back up the hill, looking for it again. There it was – a point of light just a few hundred yards away, only visible in the gap between two unseen trunks. I carried on slowly downwards, keeping my eye fixed on the spot where I'd seen it, and sure enough it reappeared after a few paces, before once again winking out. Reassured, I pressed on, praying that Jamey waited somewhere near that tantalizing bulb, and not far ahead the road began to turn, and the trees suddenly thinned, and I saw it was the first light of a village, a streetlamp placed a little way before the randomly spaced houses.

The road continued sharply downhill, far clearer now that I was out of the woods, and I had to resist the temptation to break into a trot. This had to be Otterway – there was no other village for miles around, and even if it wasn't, even if it was some smaller destination that had not been marked on my map, there would be someone there who could help me with a telephone or a ride back through the woods to the place I had been searching for.

As I neared the lone streetlamp, I saw a large long-haired dog sniffing around its base, cocking a leg to pee on a signpost there. He barked once and trotted towards me, adopting a warily defensive posture in the road. Despite his size, he didn't look like he was really up for a fight and I dropped to my haunches, softly invited him over with a crooning tone that was soon rewarded with a wag of his tail and a coy mooch over my way. I scratched him behind his ears and he nuzzled up to me, so nearly knocking me over with his instant affection that I got rapidly to my feet, patting his back and inviting him along with me. He bounded ahead as we entered Otterway, pausing to sniff his own pee on the signpost.

The time was shortly before ten o'clock and the best part of Otterway seemed to be in bed already, to judge by the number of darkened houses. I saw a house ahead that seemed to be located in the right place according to the directions Jamey had given me, and there was a light on downstairs. It was a simple two-floored house clad in whitewashed planks, little different from any of the others in town although no two were exactly the same in shape or size. None of them, one sensed, had been built with the help of an architect or even a plan.

I was so keen to reach it that I almost didn't notice the sight that lay just beyond, where the road ended. But when I did see it, it was enough to stop me in my tracks, even with my destination so near at hand.

At first I didn't understand – the earth seemed to end abruptly just beyond the houses, with nothing after them but the void. The horizon dropped away as though Otterway was perched on a huge cliff, with stars visible both above and below. I stood there speechless, sure that my eyes were deceiving me, until I remembered what she had told me about the lake in the place where she had grown up, and how the ice mirrored the sky in winter. This was it. It was extraordinary – the reflection was so perfect, so crystal dark that even when you knew what it really was, you felt as though you were looking through a hole in the earth to the space beyond. Only by staring long and hard was I able to pick out a horizon on the far side of the lake – a thin dark line, visible only by the absence of stars, marking the boundary between the true sky and its mirror image.

The sight was so eerily beautiful that I stood contemplating it, quite forgetting what had brought me here. I walked slowly forward, gripped by a childlike desire to crouch down and touch the stars at the frozen lake's edge, and it was only when I was so close to Jamey's house that my face was lit by the light from her living-room window that I snapped out of my reverie and turned off the street onto her lawn.

I saw her ensconced in a big armchair, her legs drawn up under her just as she had sat on the couch that first night we spent in the Cadogan Hotel. She was reading a book, absent-mindedly twisting a lock of her hair around a finger until her hand came level with her mouth and she could stroke her lips with the little brush formed by the spraying blonde tips. Then she let go, unwinding the coil so as to free her hand to turn the page, and began the process again as soon as her eyes had touched the top line. She was very near the end of her book, and her expression suggested a kind of fidgety patience – on the one hand needing to know how the story ended, on the other not wanting it to be over too soon.

I smiled out in the darkness, pleased that Jamey did not seem to have changed one bit in the months since I had last seen her. Not that I expected her to have aged, but I was pleased to see that the year of cover-shoots and paparazzi pandemonium, of being constantly scrutinized by everyone around her and expected to put on a show every time she stepped out of doors, seemed to have left no trace. Her beauty was still of that same unpretentious nature that had first struck me, and all the stylists and make-up artists who had pored over her in the intervening months hadn't sapped the tomboy sincerity from her face. Once the glamour dropped away, the radiance was left undimmed.

I approached the front door and knocked softly. As a shadow moved across the living-room window, I took a deep breath and braced myself to face her again. Her silhouette paused in the frosted glass before she opened the door, as though she were preparing herself in the same way, and then she was in front of me. Her expression was hard to interpret – quite neutral as she paused to look at me, and then she announced softly, 'I didn't think you were going to make it tonight. I was about to go to bed.'

'I made it,' I replied obviously.

There was an uncomfortable pause, each hoping the other would say something first. She began to step back to let me in, and then stopped, blowing out her cheeks as she looked around the hallway.

'Do you want to go for a walk?' she asked. 'I feel about thirteen years old standing here.'

She took one of the many big, sensible jackets off the hooks in the hallway and slipped on a pair of rubber boots. I don't think she'd ever been so attractive to me as she was at that moment when she straightened up, bundled in the most unflattering gear I'd ever seen on her. I guess that's my definition of true beauty – something that shines brighter the more you try to dim it.

We stepped back out into the night. Jamey set off towards the lake, her boots crunching on the crisp grass of the lawn, and I kept pace with her in silence, sensing that she was working herself up to say something. I didn't mind the silence as it felt extraordinary just to be there at all, walking with her under that glistening sky – none of my problems mattered a damn to me while I was beside her, my whole body tingling with her proximity. When we reached the lake she began to stroll along the dirt track that followed its perimeter, her eyes barely glancing down the slope to the ice below us with its reflected universe.

'I'm sorry,' she announced at last, wheeling to face me. 'I don't expect you to forgive me, but I just wanted to—'

'I do,' I cut in without hesitation. 'And I'm sorry too.'

That was it. We stood looking at one another for a few seconds, waiting to see if either was going to go on, but it was said. Over. She broke into a smile and then, as if on cue, both of us began to laugh.

'So what's the plan now?' I asked a few minutes later as we sat on the edge of the lake. Close up, you could just make out the silvery sheen of ice, like a thin layer of dust between you and the universe, but your focus was inexorably drawn past it, deeper into the reflection.

'Well, I'll just tell them that I'm dropping the charges and that will be that.'

'No, I mean you. What do *you* want to do?'

'Oh . . . that,' she sighed. 'I don't know what I want.'

I sensed it was best not to press her on the point, and we sat in silence again, staring out into the clear night.

'Do you know what I used to do when I was a kid?' she asked, changing the subject.

'Go walking on the clouds?'

'Oh . . . that predictable, huh?'

'You already told me,' I explained.

'My god – *and* I repeat myself . . .' She laughed.

I laughed too, feeling that this was more like the Jamey I knew.

I would have liked to kiss her at that moment. I turned to look at her suddenly, the desire to kiss her surging over me, but cowardice held me back when she turned to meet my regard. I should have done it. It didn't matter how – just as a friend, damn it – but I should have taken her head in my hands there and then, ignored the consequences, and kissed her. But I froze.

God knows how much time I have spent in that split second since, cursing myself for not having trusted my instincts. The moment was there, waiting to be taken. I don't know how she would have reacted – perhaps she would have kissed me back, perhaps she would have jerked away in shock, but the end result would have been the same. If I had kissed her, Jamey would not be dead now.

'What?' she frowned, seeing a question in my expression.

'Nothing,' I lied.

'No . . .' she insisted. 'You were going to ask me something.'

It was too late now. I had blown it. But then, panicked into avoiding the truth, I asked the question that sealed our fates.

'No . . . I just . . . Did you ever walk on it at night?'

She cocked her head and raised her eyebrows, a mischievous smile playing over her lips as she replied, 'Never dared.'

I hadn't intended it as a suggestion, but that was what it instantly became. I could see that Jamey was in no

258

doubt whatsoever that I was challenging her to accompany me onto the night ice, and pleased to discover a hitherto unexpected taste for adventure in me. She took the spark in my eyes for excitement, not desire. And because of that desire, I couldn't tell her she had misunderstood.

'So?' she grinned. 'I'm up for it if you are.'

'Are you sure?' I bluffed, desperately hoping she would have second thoughts. 'You know best – it's not exactly midwinter, after all, is it?'

'I used to walk on it at this time of year,' she shrugged, setting off down the short slope to the lake's edge. 'Spring comes late up here.'

Reaching the bottom in a few strides, she knelt down to feel for a pebble in the dark and flicked it out onto the ice. It bounced and skidded with a loud metallic twang, like someone tapping and scraping on a taut steel cable. Satisfied, she turned my way.

'Who's going first?' she asked.

I stared at the pitch-black void beneath me, my stomach knotting at the thought of walking out onto it. Nothing would have got me out there under any other circumstances. But I couldn't not do it, because of Jamey. I took a deep breath as I made my way down the slope to her side.

'Neither,' I whispered on arrival. 'I say we go together – hand in hand.'

She didn't answer, but slipped her hand in mine, our fingers brushing until they matched and intertwined with a squeeze. We glanced once at each other for encouragement, neither wanting to think too hard before doing it, and stepped onto the void.

When I think of what it means to be human, what it is to be this creature as opposed to any other, I think of that moment. What sets us apart, what is both best and worst about us, is not that we are *aware* of ourselves – I don't know why people even say that, because it's so ridiculous to think other animals aren't aware – but we are aware of a particular thing about life, about the world and ultimately the universe, and this is something that we may be alone in sensing.

A kind of terrifying beauty.

Such as Jamey and I saw, standing on that frozen lake in the night, the silver ice reflecting the universe below our feet. Terrifying and beautiful, the one inseparable from the other.

That's what is in the fruit on the tree in the story. The thing we should have been shielded from. Our problem, contrary to our own propaganda, is not that we don't comprehend life. We do. We always have. But we *prefer* to pretend we don't. We have always been able to sense the terrible beauty of existence, and all our supposed 'spiritual quests' have been about searching for some *other* truth that will override it. Or, failing that, a damn good lie. Which is why we tell stories. Why we made up God. For what exact purpose does God serve, what is his role in the story?

He takes the terror out of the beauty. He tames the universe and turns the tiger into a pet. He's a ringmaster.

But whether or not we choose to believe, we all end up doing the same thing – we're all trying to tame the beauty. That's the mad mission we've set ourselves – impossible, misguided, and ultimately cowardly. Absolute denial, a refusal to face the truth.

Maybe I'm wrong.

Maybe there is solid ground under the ice, not a cold, deep lake.

*　　*　　*

Jamey and I didn't have any such faith. We just had each other's hand to hold as we stepped out onto that dark mirror, our eyes bright and wide with terrifying beauty. How can I describe how beautiful it was? I can express something of the terror – of the way the ice wheezed and sighed in the silence, of feeling a racing pulse in my palm and not knowing if it was hers or mine, but I can't find words to explain the rapture that stopped us turning back. The universe was our carpet. All those suns, all those faraway galaxies – so many points of light that it was like walking on incandescent grass – beckoned us forward. We edged onwards, staring down to see our toes winking out tracts of cosmos as our feet slid cautiously forward.

Now, with my feet on the ground, on a floor in a building, it seems incomprehensibly foolish. But it was that very foolishness of what we were doing together that was so bewitching – it felt like the wildest kind of romance. It felt like taking the intoxication of the very moment when two people first discover each other, and turning that sensation into a landscape that you could walk upon. It was like being in love. I don't say it was real – I don't know how one knows what reality is when it comes to love – and maybe, had the sun suddenly come up and the stars evaporated from the ice around us, I would have lost her again. But at that moment she had to love me as I loved her or neither of us could have continued. We knew each other's mind, and had no choice but to keep moving forward until – again by that same unspoken consensus – we both suddenly came to a stop.

Why there, I can't say. I cannot explain how we both decided the same thing at the same moment. Maybe there was some subtle configuration to the stars that gave that spot a certain intensity. Maybe they formed a pattern, like a clearing in a wood, that made it a natural place to stop, but we both halted at the same moment, and turned to face one another.

One of us was going to say something, or reach across to the other. I can't say what, but I know something was going to happen.

Except then the gunshot cracked.

That's exactly what it sounded like – the deafeningly loud, echoing crack of a rifle in the silent mountain air. Only I knew it wasn't a gun because I felt an accompanying pulse run up my legs. From the soles of my feet. Instinctively, we reached for each other, clutching tight.

'Don't move!' she snapped in a whisper, as if to speak louder would increase the danger.

We stood, so deathly still that we barely breathed, and listened to the ice. My heart was pounding so fast that I could hear it behind my eardrums, an alarm bell furiously hammering in my brain. The ice was silent, like a hunting jungle cat that freezes after treading on a dry twig.

'Where was it?' I asked softly, knowing we had to move away, but unsure which direction to take.

'The way we came?' Jamey hazarded, sounding no more certain of the sound's origin than I was.

We looked pointlessly around us, as though there were any way of seeing the crack in the darkness. A star sliced in two, perhaps.

'I think it was the other way,' I whispered, convincing myself that I had felt the pulse in my right foot fractionally before my left.

All about us, the universe was calm and silent. Still beyond the capacity for stillness of anything that can be seen by daylight. So permanent. So impassive.

'It may have been nothing,' Jamey suggested reassuringly. 'The ice does that when it expands . . . it's pushing against itself. It made noises like that sometimes when I was little . . . but it never cracked – not at this time of year.'

'But you *were* little . . .' I pointed out. 'You've grown, and there are two of us.'

She decided to ignore my pessimism, determined not to let the noise scare her into paralysis, and announced, 'I say we head back the way we came – it's the shortest distance. But maybe we should keep further apart, just to be safe.'

I had to agree, because of course it made sense for us to spread our weight, but the idea of walking back alone over the lake petrified me. I didn't want to let go of her. I'd rather have stayed there, holding onto Jamey for dear life, until the sun rose and we could see what we were walking upon. But I couldn't say that. I have wished a thousand times that I had played the coward and insisted we stay where we were until the sun came to save us.

'OK . . .' I whispered, barely able to get the word out of my dry throat.

She kissed me – a fast, emphatic embrace that caught me by surprise and gave me no chance to respond – and then she slipped out of my arms and began stepping cautiously backwards, saying, 'About fifteen yards apart, all right?'

At fifteen yards away, I couldn't even see her. There was a shadow moving across the stars, no more than that. I think she was as scared as I was by finding herself alone, because she kept up a stream of conversation as we moved slowly back the way we had come – her voice momentarily catching whenever the ice wheezed around us, only to return louder and more stridently relaxed than before.

'What would you do in my position?' she asked loudly, although a whisper would have been sufficient to carry

263

her words over the ice. 'How would you get your life back?'

To be honest, I couldn't even begin to think about it. I just wanted to be back on land. But so did she – she was just trying to keep us both calm – and I owed it to her to play along.

'Is it so bad?' I asked hoarsely. 'Being famous?'

'I'm not,' she barked as the invisible ice sighed somewhere ahead. 'It's someone else. A woman everyone would like me to be.'

'It's still you,' I answered, trying to sound as composed as her, even though it was almost more than my panicked brain could handle to make conversation. 'Seen a certain way.'

'Bullshit,' she growled. 'You know that's bullshit. I'm a character in a story, that's all. And I'm not allowed to step out of the boundaries that have been set for me. I know that now. I'm never going to be able to do the things I wanted to do, because this fairy-tale Jamey Gatz will always be in the way. And who seriously wants to live like that? What normal person would want to be some fucking icon?'

'Quite a lot of them, actually,' I replied softly.

It was helping – so long as we kept talking, it felt as though we must be going to be all right. We would just keep talking until we reached the shore again.

'What is the point of everyone knowing your name if it only isolates you? All I know is that I want a real life again, Nick, no matter what it consists of or how far it may be from the life I used to imagine for myself. Better to be a nobody than a fake somebody.'

I was about to reply when the rifle cracked again, louder than before. I froze, staring intently into the darkness where she should be, and could just make out a hole in the stars that was her body.

'Come this way, Jamey,' I commanded, convinced the noise had come from her direction.

She was silent and still. The ice groaned and hammered twice like an iron knocker on an oak door.

'Fuck,' she whispered.

'Come over here!' I repeated urgently.

'It's OK . . .' She laughed, her voice ringing with panic. 'It's not going to break. Just keep talking.'

'*Jamey, please!*' I begged her, wishing I could take hold of her and pull her away from that spot, but certain that adding my weight was the worst possible thing I could do.

We stood, each invisible to the other, hardly daring to breathe as we listened to the ice. There was another heavy knock on the door that seemed to echo downwards into the lake.

'*Jamey!*' I shouted, sensing that she was paralysed by fear.

'*It's just expanding! It's OK!*' she snapped back.

I was giddy with horror. I was sure that she was wrong, but it was as though the terror I felt was having the opposite effect on her, bringing out that same stubborn refusal to give in to her fears that had brought us together in the first place.

'If it's safe then walk over here!' I argued, trying to keep my voice calm and persuasive. I waited for a reply, each beating second seeming to me like a countdown to disaster, until I could take it no more and shouted, '*For fuck's sake, Jamey – please!*'

I heard her breathing, shallow and rapid, and the sound of a foot scraping on the ice – then it knocked again and she screamed, '*I can't! I can't see where I'm going!*'

Jamey's admission of fear had the effect of calming me, forcing me to take charge. Perhaps she was right, I reasoned – perhaps the ice was just compacting in on itself as it froze thicker, and I could walk over, take her by the

265

hand, and lead her back to the shore. Either way, I could not stay where I was, leaving her alone with her terror.

'Stay there,' I commanded softly. 'I'm coming.'

I forced my feet to slide forward against their will, my every muscle tensed to flee, and held out my hand although we were still far apart. It was hard to keep sight of her silhouette against the stars, and I told her to keep talking, to guide me towards her voice.

'I was thinking of travelling for a while,' she said in a voice that was teetering on the edge of tears. 'Money isn't a problem. I can get by for . . . a few years, maybe. What do you think?'

'Sounds good,' I answered, not really thinking about it, just talking for the sake of talking. I could see her now, see the terror on her beautiful face, and I smiled encouragingly. 'I'm envious.'

'Do you want to come?'

I don't know if she was serious, because right after she said it there came a rapid thrash of knocks, of slamming doors, that shook the silence and broke our conversation right there. Through the soles of my shoes I could feel the sounds vibrating through the ice, almost like placing my hand on a speaker and letting the bass play through my skin. We were standing on a vast drum.

I waited for the beating to stop before I risked moving closer, barely daring to breathe. Keeping my gaze locked on Jamey, I saw a small star trickle down her cheek and realized that she was crying.

'I still see him, you know,' she whispered in a voice that seemed very far away. 'He still comes when I sleep.'

I didn't like what I heard in that voice. There was a hint of resignation there, as though she didn't believe there was a way out for her. A slow creak sounded between us, echoing across the ice like an old hinge on a great thick door.

'Can you see me, Jamey?' I spoke softly, urgently. 'I don't think I can come any closer. You have to walk towards me now. Take my hand.'

She sniffed, her breathing shallow and rapid, and I saw a dark hand rise in the darkness to brush a tear from her cheek. I was standing, legs flexed and tense, holding out my hand towards her.

'Take my hand,' I repeated sternly, trying to impose my will upon her fear.

She took a deep breath and let it out slowly, the air stuttering as it escaped her lips. Her fingers stretched out to mine and she began to edge towards me in tiny, almost imperceptible movements.

The ice was silent as the stars.

'Take my hand, Jamey,' I said again, watching the distance between our fingers begin to close and praying that she didn't stop.

She edged closer until the gap between us was no more than could be filled by one person stretching out their arms, and announced, almost laughing, 'I don't believe this . . .'

It was the last thing she said.

When the final door slammed, it did so with a force that shook me almost from my feet. Instinctively, I jumped backwards, hurling myself away from the noise. I slipped, landing on my back and cursing myself as I scrambled to my knees to reach out, screaming her name over the sudden howling of the ice.

I saw her frozen in place, her arm still reaching for me.

And then the stars broke free.

They flew up on either side of her as two sheets of ice broke loose like great wings rising to beat. They rose and rose with a sucking roar, their reflections streaming up across the ice until the last of them slid over the edge and, for a single heartbeat, the only thing that caught the night's dim light was Jamey, her legs trying to straddle the darkness and her arms reaching out to nothing on either side.

Her mouth was opening in a silent scream and her eyes held onto mine as if a look could throw a lifeline . . . and then she dropped. Her feet slid from the ice on either side, and the darkness seemed to erase her before my eyes as she plunged into the water. The stars splashed up again and dropped, the surface of the water reflecting a rippling, unstable universe, and I lunged forward, waiting for her head to tear a hole back through to this dimension.

But then the edges of those great black wings became visible again, tinged with stars, and they began their slow, heavy beat.

They inexorably swallowed up the darkness, sucking the universe back into place behind them, and I watched helplessly as the tear in reality closed from either side until it shut with a thunderous clap that pounded me with a wet, ice-cold wave.

And by the time I had wiped my eyes and blinked, coughing water from my lungs, the universe before me was again still, and seamless, and silent.

Right Now, Right Here

'Not . . .' I answer hoarsely, my mouth too dry to speak '. . . not . . . guilty.'

There is a low murmur around the courtroom, almost a snigger.

Judge Wilson's head snaps angrily towards the benches, her hand raising the hammer to slam it down and call for order . . . and the sniggering stops. She turns back to me, her face stern but her eyes not unkind.

'Mr Carraway . . .' she sighs, 'for the record, I'm going to have to ask you to be more precise with your words. Are you pleading "Not guilty", or did you say "*Not* not guilty"?'

She glances back at the spectators, warning them not to make a sound. I am thankful to her for it, sensing that she is on my side, determined not to let my trial become a circus act for the greater amusement of anyone here or beyond this courtroom.

But her efforts will be in vain, I know.

The curtain has risen, betting shops are offering odds on my sentence, and there is nothing she can do to stop this whole court case becoming entertainment. Nothing. All she can do is play her part well.

And even when it is over, it will not be over. I have faith in Wolsheim, but even if he gets me out of this, the greater judgement still awaits me outside this room, a sentence imposed in the living rooms of the land. And the point is not just that they all believe me to be guilty – which they do, given that I was there, breaking my bail terms and the restriction order upon me, and that I had an obvious motive for wanting Jamey Gatz dead – but that they all *want* me to be guilty. Because it makes for a better story, and if I am clearly guilty, then no-one else need be involved. None of them had any part in what happened.

So it never ends.

'Mr Carraway . . . ?' she urges me gently. 'Can we begin?'

I look at her, and nod softly. Of course. The show must go on.

My mouth goes to speak and then I stop, turning to look at the cameras that are waiting so hungrily for my next two words. I look at them, and all the millions of people hiding behind them, and raise my eyebrows, letting them know that I, Nick Carraway, am aware that they are all there, watching me. And I am not a character in their story because I do have a choice – two words, or one word.

I think of Jamey, and smile.

She would understand if, with one word, I chose to end this story.

Right now, right here.

THE END

ACKNOWLEDGEMENTS

My thanks again to Ganesh,
although I remain reluctant to believe in a god,
especially one with the head of an elephant,
and the great Mr Fitzgerald,
who I hope is not spinning in his grave.